Farmed and Dangerous

Books by Edith Maxwell

A TINE TO LIVE, A TINE TO DIE

'TIL DIRT DO US PART

FARMED AND DANGEROUS

Published by Kensington Publishing Corporation

Farmed and Dangerous

EDITH MAXWELL

KENSINGTON BOOKS
www.kensingtonbooks.com

KENSINGTON BOOKS are published by

Kensington Publishing Corp.
119 West 40th Street
New York, NY 10018

Library of Congress Card Catalogue Number: 2015934122

ISBN-13: 978-0-7582-8467-9
ISBN-10: 0-7582-8467-5
First Kensington Hardcover Edition: June 2015

eISBN-13: 978-0-7582-8469-3
eISBN-10: 0-7582-8469-1
First Kensington Electronic Edition: June 2015

10 9 8 7 6 5 4 3 2 1

Printed in the United States of America

*For Susan Bond, a graceful, funny friend, my partner in anchovies,
her dear John's dance partner, who lived life fully and left it too young,
and who inspired Cam to think a little more deeply about death.*

Acknowledgments

Once again I am grateful to so many for helping me get this book into the hands of readers. My Wicked Cozy partners in crime—Jessie Crockett (aka Jessica Estevao), Sherry Harris, Julie Hennrikus (aka Julianne Holmes), Liz Mugavero (aka Cate Conte), and Barb Ross—you are the best support group and role models ever. My agent, John Talbot; my editor at Kensington, John Scognamiglio; copyeditor Rosemary Silva; and the entire Kensington staff who make it happen: thank you. The awesome writers in the Monday Night Salem Writers' Group heard every word of this book and much improved it with their spot-on critiques: Rae Francouer, Doug Hall, Margaret Press, Elaine Ricci, Patricia Shepherd, and Sam Sherman. Sherry Harris also expertly edited the manuscript before I turned it in.

A childhood friend and fellow Camellia Festival princess, Debbie Becnel-Bush, came up with the fabulous title. My son John David, Lisa Forbush-Umholtz, Darryl Ray, and the hens at New Harmony Farm taught me all I know about chickens. Ruffles the rooster is a blatant copy of Greg and Heide's rooster at Toddy Pond Farm in Maine. I also borrowed their cool solar power setup. Heron Pond Farm, where I held a winter share while writing this book, kindly let me visit the winter greenhouses. Dan Kittredge, with his expertise on bionutrient-dense feeding, plays a bit part, as does Jessie Crockett's maple syrup farmer Dani Greene. Sheila Connolly (and her character, Meg Corey) helped with apple information. John David's commitment to the theory and practice of permaculture also appears in these pages, as does his experience with vermiculture.

My son Allan provided inspiration about technological invention, as well as loving support, as always. Cam's canvas OtisRein bag is a real product, featuring hand-painted crows, made by my friends Giselle Rein and Susan Otis. D. P. Lyle's *Forensics for Dummies* provided valuable information on poisons. I borrowed Kai Fujita's last name, Eugene Papa's opera expertise, and our local cheese shop's proprietor, Luca.

A special thanks to Detective Kevin Donovan of the Amesbury Police Department for patiently answering all my questions ever since I graduated from the Citizens' Police Academy.

Two people generously contributed to worthy causes in order to win character-naming rights: Ann Jaroncyk for her friend Lou Dispenza (I threw Ann in, too), and Pat Cook. I hope you like who you became! The Merrimack River Feline Rescue Society and the Save the Screening Room fund—thank you, too.

Sisters in Crime both locally and nationally, the Guppies, the New England chapter of Mystery Writers of America, I embrace you. I wouldn't be here but for what I have learned from you. Locavores, farmers, and faithful readers everywhere: a bow, a wave, and a thanks. And if you like the story, posting a positive review somewhere is a great way to help authors.

I have broken one cardinal rule of fiction in this book. I included a real person. My smart, talented, caring mother, Marilyn Flaherty Maxwell Muller, didn't live quite long enough to read any of my books, so I thought I'd put her in one. Great-uncle Albert's new sweetie is Mommy cut from full cloth, except she would never have had a glass of wine and never really caught on to anything digital. Whether she's smiling down on this book from somewhere or not, I don't know, but it makes me smile to write about her.

Finally, my dear Hugh soldiers on with home renovations, even as I sit in my upstairs office, not helping, and instead typing away with the door closed. I thank him for not minding that I left my day job to live my dream, and for being there for my crazy, glorious journey.

Chapter 1

Cameron Flaherty sidestepped in surprise as a tall man with gleaming skin the color of dark-roasted coffee beans stormed into the institutional kitchen at Moran Manor Assisted Living, his deep brown eyes flashing.

"I'm going to kill that woman." He carried a tray holding the remnants of someone's lunch and slammed it onto the counter. A dark spot stained the front of his green caregiver's polo shirt. "Nothing I do satisfies her."

Cam had seen him in the halls of the residence, but he wasn't one of the caregivers who tended to her great-uncle, Albert St. Pierre. The man glanced around the kitchen, which was empty except for the two of them.

"Where's Rosemary?" he snapped.

"The cook?" Cam asked. If Rosemary was who he wanted to kill, this could get dicey. Cam took a couple of steps back, until she neared the doorway.

He nodded as if he doubted Cam's intelligence.

"I don't know. I'm looking for her, too." Cam would have thought the cook would be hard at work in mid-afternoon, prepping Saturday night dinner for a hundred-odd residents. A huge pot bubbled on the back of the stove, and the room carried the aroma of sautéed onions with an undertone of cleaning solution. Cam had arranged to provide her own organic vegetables for an upcoming dinner and needed to make the final arrangements with the chef, who seemed to be missing in action. "You have a problem with Rosemary?"

The door next to Cam swung open, nearly whacking her. She stuck out her hand at the last minute. "Whoa."

Ellie Kosloski sauntered into the room, her red Moran Manor polo shirt tucked into skinny jeans. "Oh, hey, Cam. Sorry about that." The slender ninth grader hadn't gained any weight since Cam met her last June, when Ellie had shown up to volunteer on Cam's farm, but her legs seemed to get longer every time Cam saw her.

"No problem," Cam said.

"Oscar, what's up?" Ellie said, catching sight of the man. "You don't look very happy."

He slapped his hand on the stainless-steel island. "She's been here only a month, and she's driving me nuts. It's no Happy New Year for me so far." He threw his large hands into the air.

Ellie frowned at the clatter but didn't recoil. "Mrs. Montgomery?"

Cam raised her eyebrows. *Uh-oh.* So Bev Montgomery was making trouble again.

He nodded. "I wish she'd never come here."

"What's she doing now?" Ellie asked.

"Well, for one thing, she's some kind of ethnophobe." He clenched and unclenched huge fists. "Telling me because I'm Eritrean, I can't do my job right."

"She has a history with that kind of opinion," Cam offered, staying safely near the exit. Bev, an old friend of Cam's great-uncle and late great-aunt, had been involved in an anti-immigrant militia group.

"Who are you?" The man frowned in her direction.

"Cameron Flaherty. I'm a local farmer. I'm supposed to be finalizing arrangements with Rosemary to provide some of my produce for tomorrow night's dinner."

"Cam's great-uncle is Mr. St. Pierre," Ellie said. "Cam, this is Oscar Zerezghi. He's a caregiver, and he helps the cook, too."

"Nice to meet you," Cam said, not sure if it was. He hadn't extended a hand, so she didn't, either, instead crossing her arms, her shoulder resting on a cool stainless-steel wall.

"Mr. St. Pierre seems like a decent guy. Unlike some of our residents." He turned on his heel and stalked out.

"Oscar's having a tough time." Ellie stuck her hands in her back pockets and leaned against the island.

"He's a professional. He should be used to it. Speaking of professionals, have you seen the cook? I need to talk to her." Cam eyed the boiling pot. Its aromas made her stomach growl. Where was the woman?

"No. Actually, that's why I came in here. The director was looking for Rosemary, too." Ellie pushed pale hair away from her face and resecured her ponytail. "Maybe she's off with her boyfriend somewhere. My friend Ray said she saw them outside kissing one time." She rolled her eyes after the manner of teens.

"That doesn't help me at all."

"So what's the dinner?" Ellie asked.

"I'm donating produce for the meal. It's kind of a trial balloon. If they like it, I hope to get a contract to supply the residence regularly next summer." Cam moved back into the room and tapped the counter, frowning. "Sounds like Bev giving up her farm and moving here haven't improved her attitude."

3

"She's still saying bad stuff about you, too."

"Me?" Cam sighed.

"The whole business about you, like, stealing her hens. You know, with the rescue chickens last fall."

"I thought we'd put all that behind us. Although she was sure upset at the time, when my volunteers rescued her neglected hens. But the health department was about to put them down." The birds were now healthy and were living in a new coop at Cam's farm tucked in the woods of Westbury, a semirural town north of Boston.

"I guess she's still mad," Ellie said.

"What are you doing here today, Ellie? I thought you worked as a server in the dining room only on weeknights."

"On Saturdays I, like, come in to take reading material around to the rooms and deliver meals. And I play cards with the residents. I'm the activities director's helper. It gives me more hours and doesn't interfere with school."

"That's cool."

"Some of the people are totally interesting. Even the ones in the Neighborhood, you know, the residents with dementia and Alzheimer's." Ellie glanced at the big clock on the wall. "It's almost three o'clock. I have to get over to the community room to help out with the anagram game."

When Cam turned to go in search of the elusive Rosemary, she bumped her hip on the corner of the counter. *Ouch. Such a klutz.*

"You should have heard this guy Oscar, Uncle Albert." Cam stretched her legs out from her chair a few minutes later in Albert St. Pierre's homey room on the second floor. She hadn't been able to locate the cook and had finally given up. She cupped a mug in both hands, inhaling the peppermint tea he'd fixed her in his kitchenette.

4

"He is Beverly's care provider." Albert sat, as usual, in his recliner, with a red plaid lap blanket covering his own legs, or rather, his one complete leg and the other missing its foot. He'd offered Attic Hill Farm to Cam over a year ago, when the amputation forced his retirement from farming. "Oscar tends to get a little carried away in his reactions, I have heard. But I also know Beverly has been loudly unreasonable since she moved here." He grabbed a stack of books off the table at his elbow and dumped them on the floor. "You can set your tea here."

"It sounds like Bev might be going off the rails. She said he couldn't do his job right, because he's from Eritrea."

"I believe she is developing dementia." Albert raised his abundant snowy-white eyebrows. "And she's in the angry phase, as it starts out for so many."

"Maybe she simply misses her friends in the Patriotic Militia." Bev's involvement in the shadowy group last spring had caused headaches for several immigrants in the area.

"Perhaps. You know that I volunteer in the Neighborhood downstairs. I'm a little overfamiliar with the stages of dementia these days." He sighed. "Beverly is so angry, she doesn't even take her meals in the dining room with everyone else. She apparently complained about the other residents—didn't want to share a table with any of them—and they complained right back about her."

"So nothing has changed."

"No. Now, enough about that. It's January in Massachusetts. Tell me how winter farming is treating you."

Cam shrugged. "It's a struggle. You know how cold it's been, but so far the crops in the hoop house are surviving. I spread a floating row cover over them every night and uncover them in the morning. The cover raises the temperature a couple of degrees. And I have the air layer insulating the house, too."

"What's that?"

"The house is covered with two layers of plastic, and an electric fan blows air between them. If we get a big snow, though . . . Well, I hope the pipes and plastic won't collapse. I'd be out of business until April."

"I never tried to extend the season all the way through the winter, you know. You're brave to try, honey."

"Or stupid." Cam tapped her mug. "Did I tell you that I'm providing the produce for dinner here tomorrow night?"

"Excellent. Is the dinner a tryout for a summer contract?"

She nodded. "You're my marketing genius. You suggested doing exactly this last summer."

"I wasn't much of a genius when I ran the farm, but now I have time to come up with new ideas, don't you know?"

"I couldn't find the cook just now to arrange final details. I think we're all set, though."

"I'm sure it will be a success." Albert's pale blue eyes crinkled. He reached out and patted her hand.

"Can we get back to Bev for just a minute? I heard that Richard Broadhurst is going to buy her farm. Is that true? It'd be a great addition to his own farm since they abut. And I know he wanted to expand his orchard."

"I read about it in the paper. Don't believe the sale's been completed yet. And that daughter of hers, Ginger . . . Somebody heard her trying to cut a deal to develop the land into housing."

"Oh? Is that what Bev wants?" Cam asked.

"You'd have to ask her," Albert said. He took a sip of his own tea and gazed out the window. Outside, fat snowflakes floated down like errant cotton puffs. He brought his gaze back to Cam. "Ginger Montgomery tried the same trick with my farm when she nosed out the news that I had plans to quit, you know, with my foot and all."

6

"What? She wanted to buy the land and build housing on it?"

He nodded. "Some fancy town house plan. I said I wasn't interested, but she pushed pretty hard. And when I heard you lost your programmer job in Cambridge, why, that's when I offered the farm to you."

"I'm glad you did. I think. Farming isn't easy, but I'd hate to see luxury condos on such a pretty piece of the hill."

"Happening all over town. Fertile farmland and woods disappearing into fancy kitchens and three-car garages for bankers and lawyers who work down to Boston. Ginger comes around here to play guitar on weekends. Acts like she's some kind of do-gooder." He shook his head, with a sorrowful look. "She's playing this afternoon, as a matter of fact."

They sat in silence for a moment. Cam gazed at his desk in the corner of the room. She snapped her fingers.

"I just remembered. While I'm here, I wanted to show you something on the farm's Web site, see how you like it."

"Computer's all fired up," Albert said. He reached for his crutches and transferred himself to the office chair at the desk. "That class they gave here last year really got me going on this computer stuff. And I should show you some pictures that I scanned in, of my dear Marie before we were married. Nineteen forty-nine, it was."

Cam pulled her chair to his side. She checked the time in the lower corner of the screen. She might be able to catch Ginger Montgomery's guitar gig downstairs when they were done here.

A teenage girl with bouncy black hair pushed a man in a wheelchair ahead of Cam in the main hallway of the residence twenty minutes later. A short woman with a long gray braid, hanging down over a turquoise quilted jacket, walked next to them.

"Felicity?" Cam called out. Felicity Slavin, one of the most avid locavores who subscribed to Cam's farm-share program, volunteered frequently on the farm.

Felicity turned with a smile. "Cam." She patted the polo-shirted arm of the young caregiver, signaling her to stop, and waited for Cam to catch up. "Have you met my father? He lives in the Neighborhood here."

"No, but I'd love to."

"Dad, this is Albert St. Pierre's great-niece, Cam Flaherty. She's the farmer I've been telling you about."

The man, in red suspenders over a striped shirt, smiled up at Cam. His smile extended to his watery blue eyes under a tweed Irish cap. He extended a quavering hand.

"I'm pleased to meet you, sir." Cam shook his hand with care. His skin felt like parchment, but he gripped her hand more firmly than she'd expected.

"Nicholas. I'm Nicholas, dear."

Strains of guitar chords drifted their way. Nicholas tapped his foot and beat his hand on his knee.

Felicity introduced the girl as Ray. "She helps out on weekends." Felicity nodded at the girl.

After Cam introduced herself, Ray said, "Mr. St. Pierre's niece? He's really nice."

"Are you going to the music?" Felicity asked Cam.

"I thought I'd check it out before I go home. Although I shouldn't stay long. Did you see that it started to snow?"

"Sure. It's January, Cam." Felicity smiled.

Cam lowered her voice. "How's Wes doing?"

Felicity let a breath out. "He's under house arrest, awaiting trial. How did such a smart man and such a sweet husband do something so stupid?" She lifted her chin and squared her petite shoulders, but Cam could still see bewilderment in her eyes. Wes, a tall, aging hippie who doted on his tiny wife, had

indeed done something stupid last October and was now paying the price.

They arrived at the wide side doorway of the common room
that opened off the front lobby of the residence. A slender
woman perched on a stool at the front, one leg extended in
front of her, one foot hooked on the stool's rung. Her outfit,
green leather ankle boots, a calf-length suede skirt, and a
green sweater, could have come straight out of a Talbots cata-
log. She strummed the guitar and encouraged the residents to
sing along to "Oh My Darling, Clementine."

Felicity pushed her father to the end of the front row of
chairs, while Cam stood near the doorway. Residents filled the
row, mostly women, many white-haired and several with careful dye jobs. Most sang along and clapped. One woman, with a
short cap of hair more dark than silver, took tiny stitches in a
piece of cloth stretched over a ring, listening and tapping a
sneaker-clad foot. A row of wheelchairs formed the second
row. In two of them, a man and a woman sat side by side, holding hands. Next to them a man slumped over, his head listing
to the side. Cam was glad to see he had a wheelchair seat belt
strapped around him.

"Great singing, ladies and gentlemen." Ginger smiled and
tossed her artfully tousled blond hair. "Now, how about 'The
Yellow Rose of Texas' to brighten up this winter day?"

"What's with all the old-fogy songs?"

Cam glanced around for the source of the voice. Just as
she'd thought. Bev Montgomery stood at the rear of the room.
She leaned against a table, with her arms folded tightly across
her chest. She didn't smile. Cam had never seen the former
farmer in anything but work pants and a faded plaid flannel
shirt. Now she wore new jeans and a fresh-looking plaid flannel shirt. The bangs and ends of her straight slate-gray hair appeared recently trimmed.

"You can't play anything newer than from nineteen thirty?" Bev continued in a snarl.

Ginger strained to complete her smile, and her eyes did not participate.

"What's wrong with 'The Yellow Rose of Texas'?" the woman doing the needlework chimed in. A few others nodded.

"I like that song," Nicholas added.

"We'll do 'Yellow Rose,' and then how about 'Charlie on the MTA'?" Ginger surveyed the room.

Bev rolled her eyes and pursed her lips but stayed where she stood. When her daughter began to play, Bev did not sing along.

Cam mustered her inner social being, never an easy task for her, and slid along the edges of the room to Bev's side. Cam greeted her in a low voice.

"How are you settling in?" She smiled with what she hoped was a welcoming look. She and Bev had had several conflicts in the past year, and Cam hoped they would cease now that Bev no longer needed to see Cam as the new competition on the block.

Bev snorted. "What do you care?"

"I thought you might like it here. Albert certainly does." Cam gestured around the room. "You know, find it an easier life. We both know how hard farming is."

"Well, I don't like living in a fishbowl with a bunch of old folks." Her voice rose. "And you're the one who put me out of business. Stole my customers and my hens, too. Don't go all friendly on me, Cameron Flaherty."

A man in a necktie, whom Albert had once introduced to Cam as Jim Cooper, the director of the facility, stood nearby. He frowned at them, and the woman with the needlework turned around and said, "Ssh."

"I'm sorry," Cam whispered. She grimaced and made her way back to the wide doorway.

Ginger didn't stop playing and singing, but she didn't look particularly happy about the outburst. She finished "The Yellow Rose of Texas" and launched into the MTA song. Nearly every resident joined in on the chorus of the famous tune. Some likely had lived in Boston during the time the song described. And then also after that, when the Scollay Square mentioned in the lyrics was bulldozed to make room for the Stalinesque Government Center, with its ugly concrete buildings and windswept wasteland of a plaza. Even Bev seemed to scowl less than usual during the popular tune.

When the song ended, Jim Cooper stepped, clapping, to the front of the room. He thanked Ginger for entertaining the residents. "And let's welcome her mother, Beverly Montgomery, our newest member here at Moran Manor. I know you'll all do what you can to make her feel at home in our cozy community."

Several of the residents clapped for a few seconds, but the applause didn't exactly deliver a roaring embrace, probably as a result of what Albert had mentioned about the dining room complaints.

"Do you play Scrabble, Beverly?" The needlepoint woman twisted in her chair to glance at Bev. "I could use another good opponent."

"Maybe." Bev lifted her chin and directed her next comment at the director. "I don't know why you let *her* entertain here." She gestured at Ginger. "She's trying to steal my land, you know. Her and her brothers. None of them would farm with me, but they'd grab the land to build houses on. If they could."

The director gaped. The residents stared at Bev. A melliflu-

11

ous voice sang out from the far end of the lobby, which led to the wide doorway. Heads now turned in that direction.

A man let the outer door swing shut behind him. He strolled in, singing an aria, one hand on his chest, one arm extended. A full head of salt-and-pepper hair swept off his wide forehead and nearly reached his shoulders. His barn jacket fell open to reveal a brilliant turquoise vest over a white collarless shirt. The stains on the legs of his faded jeans, on the other hand, made it look like he'd been shoveling compost in the jeans. Which he probably had.

Cam smiled at the sight of her fellow farmer Richard Broadhurst. Opera singer turned farmer, that is. A master organic grower, he'd been focusing more on tree fruits than vegetables in the past few years. She'd visited his farm several times during her first season and had appreciated the open way in which he shared information with her. She gave him a little wave, which he returned, even while belting out the operatic tune.

At the sight of Richard, Ginger closed her eyes for a moment and took a deep breath. She opened them, thanked the residents for participating, then grabbed her guitar and headed for her mother.

Cam couldn't hear their conversation over the noise of chairs sliding and caregivers taking the wheelchair bound out of the room. But she watched for a moment. Ginger and Bev's interaction didn't appear to be a calm and affectionate conversation between mother and daughter by any means. Stealing her land was a strong accusation. Bev kept her arms folded and her chin up. Ginger seemed to be pleading with her.

Richard paused at the reception desk and sang directly to the woman sitting there, who blushed and applauded. He caught sight of Cam and strolled toward her.

"Cam." He leaned in for an air kiss. "How's the winter CSA going?"

"It's not easy, but so far, so good. The hoop house hasn't collapsed, and I'm still harvesting greens. I'm providing the raw ingredients for a dinner here tomorrow. It'd be nice to get a regular contract with this place."

"Is that so? Good luck with it." He glanced toward Bev and Ginger. "Catch you later."

He turned into the room and approached Bev, kissing her on the cheek.

"Beverly, my dear," he boomed. "This must be your lovely daughter."

"Thanks for coming by again," Bev said, eking out a smile. "This is Ginger."

Ginger's gaze met Richard's. Cam couldn't exactly interpret the look, but it appeared that they already knew each other, or at least had met before.

"Are you ready?" Richard asked Bev.

"Where are you going, Mom?" Ginger looked confused.

"Richard's taking me out for a decent meal." She pulled her mouth down and blinked. "Come with me while I grab my coat," she said to Richard, who nodded.

Cam turned to go. She probably ought to look for Rosemary one more time, but she'd had enough hustle and bustle for one day. Time to head back to the farm. She signed out and donned her down jacket at the coatrack. She glanced behind her before pulling open the heavy outside door. Richard followed Bev up the wide central staircase. Ginger stood with one hand on her hip, watching them.

Chapter 2

Cam's truck crunched over fresh snow when she pulled into the driveway next to her antique saltbox farmhouse. She sat for a moment, watching the flakes fall in the headlights. A gust of wind stirred them into a dance, and then they settled to a straight free fall again. She'd have to shovel in the morning, but so far the snow fell light and dry, not heavy with moisture, as it did when spring approached. She pulled into the barn and turned off the engine, then tugged her wool cap down around her ears. Time to put the chickens to bed.

She fetched a big flashlight, then headed around the rear of the barn. The A-frame coop sat on a trailer, with an attached fenced-in area around the entrance. During the summer she planned to rotate the ensemble around the farm to weed and fertilize various areas for a couple of weeks at a time. At this time of year, though, she kept the few dozen hens and their home close to the barn.

Cam shone the light around their yard. Most of them hunkered inside when the temperature dropped like this. She kept an incandescent bulb burning in the coop to add a bit of extra warmth. One silly bird had such a tiny brain, she liked to stand outside in any kind of weather, though. Sure enough, TopKnot sat on the ramp going up to the coop door. Cam had named the black-and-white Silver Laced Polish that because of the way her feathers formed a poufy crown on the top of her head.

"Go on in, you goofy bird." Cam shooed her with her hands.

TopKnot only cocked her head, staring. Cam picked up the bird and set her in with the others. She made sure they had enough feed and water, switched off the light inside, and latched the door.

Keeping hens had its down side. Once she'd nursed these rescue birds back to health with organic feed, fresh water, and clean bedding, they'd begun to lay. Customers loved being able to buy a dozen organic eggs when they picked up their shares. But in the cold, dark weather of winter, the hens were down to laying only one egg each twice a week, even with the extra light Cam provided. She had to make sure she latched them in every day before dark. Foxes and coyotes prowled the woods that bordered the far boundary of her fields. Plus, hens were smelly and, well, birdbrained, although the several Speckled Sussex seemed a little smarter than the rest. But she had them now, and her avid volunteers Alexandra and DJ, who'd spearheaded the rescue and the coop building, often stopped by to help out with the job of parenting the flock.

The snow seemed to be tapering off as Cam shuffled her way through two inches of white powder to the hoop house. Tired, cold, and hungry, she struggled to draw the floating row cover over the long beds to keep them a little warmer overnight. A helper right now would make her life a lot easier, but she had no partner, no spouse, and she ran the farm alone. At least for now. She had to keep walking back and forth, pulling the cover that stretched the length of the hoop house over the mini hoops that bent over the individual beds. When she finished, she made sure she pulled the door tightly shut, and headed for the house.

Preston sat patiently on the top step in front of her back door. With his double layer of fur, the Norwegian Forest cat went outdoors every day of the year. Even in a rainstorm she would see him sitting Sphinxlike at the base of the big maple that grew in the middle of the yard.

"Come on in for dinner, Mr. P."

He mewed his tiny but enthusiastic agreement. For a big, fluffy cat, he had the littlest feline voice she'd ever heard.

As she unlocked the door, he reared up. He rubbed his head and his arched body along her knee, as was his habit with his favorite humans. She let him in, locking the door carefully once she arrived indoors. She'd never locked the door when she moved over a year ago to this centuries-old farm. But after being threatened first by the murderer of her farmhand last June and then by the killer of one of her customers in October, she'd installed not only a motion-triggered outdoor light but also a new lock set and dead bolt. She secured the door even when she was inside the house or out in the fields. Living alone, it seemed only prudent. Although with any luck, she wouldn't be involved with any more murders in her life, ever.

She spooned Preston's portion of wet food into his bowl. He turned his head and asked with his eyes for her to pet him while he ate, as was his habit. She obliged for a moment, then heated a dish of leftover stew in the microwave for her own dinner.

Last night she'd tried out the recipe that she planned to provide to Moran Manor for the dinner. Local eating in a New England winter featured lots and lots of stored root crops, a few greens from the hoop house, and vegetables frozen and canned from the summer. So this particular stew included parsnips, carrots, cabbage, and potatoes from the root cellar. Kale, pesto, and one Scotch bonnet pepper from the freezer. Garlic and onions from the basket in the closet. A jar of her own canned tomato sauce. Rosemary and sage from the covered herb bed near the back door. And a ham bone simmered in stock with cut-up ham from Tendercrop Farm over in neighboring Newbury, which raised all its own meat animals.

A glass of a hearty Cabernet Sauvignon and a hunk of sourdough bread rounded out the meal. She settled at the wide, worn table where farmers had been eating for decades. Where she herself had eaten all her meals during her childhood summers, alone with Great-Aunt Marie and Great-Uncle Albert while her own academic parents had been off at far-flung research sites. She'd had her older relatives' full and kindly attention and had learned about farming and self-sufficiency without even trying.

The stew tasted even better the second day. Cam hadn't committed to being a locavore, unlike many of the subscribers to the Attic Hill Farm CSA, her farm-share program. But growing and selling food locally so they could feed their enthusiasm for local foods? No-brainer. By the end of March, though, even the locavores would be craving fresh, crunchy produce, a hard find in an environment where the ground consisted of either frozen soil or mud.

Eating the stew, she perused the local newspaper. An article about a proposed farming restriction caught her eye. She picked out the names Montgomery and Broadhurst. She sipped her wine and read on. The article said Richard Broadhurst, a local apple farmer, had made an offer to buy the Montgomery farm. He'd proposed adding an agricultural preservation restriction so that it would always stay farmland. He was seeking approval from the town. Bev didn't want the land to be developed, and the restriction would give the owner a payment up to the difference between the fair market value and the current agricultural use value.

But both Albert and Bev had said Ginger had proposed to develop the land. Did she not know what her mother's wishes were? Maybe the look Ginger and Richard had exchanged involved the plan to develop.

Cam finished reading the paper, amused by several of the items in the small town paper's police blotter column: "Saturday, 2:00 p.m. Lost identity investigated on Maple Street." "Monday, 9:00 a.m. Suspicious person reported walking on Main Street." She imagined an old lady gazing out her window and calling in about a pedestrian who might have appeared a little bit out of place.

She carried her wine over to her desk and fired up the laptop. She always had farm business to deal with, but that could wait for tomorrow. Tonight she wanted to prowl the Internet for information on Ginger Montgomery and on Oscar, as well. His temper didn't seem to mesh well with taking care of elderly residents. It didn't take long to discover that Ginger, in fact, sold and developed real estate and owned an apartment complex in Boston. But she'd also developed a property in the nearby small city of Newburyport, building a condo complex at the edge of town, on a piece of land that had been a dairy farm. Cam dug a little deeper, until she ran across a letter to the editor complaining bitterly about the shoddy construction of the Montgomery condos and about the absence of a response from the developer to disgruntled owners. *Interesting.* How had Ginger gone from growing up on a farm to building poorly constructed housing on farmland?

Cam couldn't recall if Ginger sported a wedding band. Perhaps she was married to someone unscrupulous. She headed over to Facebook and examined Ginger's page. Even though they weren't Facebook friends, Ginger hadn't set many pri-

vacy settings, Cam could see her whole profile. It didn't indi-
cate her relationship status, but lots of people would just as
soon keep that optional field private, anyway.

Now for Oscar Zerezghi. Cam had just typed his name in
the search text box when she heard the *zoot-zoot* of her cell
phone vibrating. She'd turned the sound off at Moran Manor.
She strode to her bag, which was hanging on the back of a
chair, and managed to extract the device at the moment the
call disconnected. Checking the caller ID, she smiled. Pete
had called. She pressed SEND to return the call.

"Is this the famous detective Pappas?"

Pete chuckled. "Famous or infamous, it is I. How's my favorite farmer?"

"Not bad. Having an exciting Saturday night home alone."
Cam scrunched up her face for a moment. She'd never get the
hang of small talk.

"I'm on call tonight, or I'd ask myself over to remedy that
situation. But how about you come over here for a home-
cooked Greek dinner tomorrow night instead?"

"Let me check my social calendar." A split second later, she
continued. "Why, I do happen to be free. What time do you
want me?"

Pete let a beat go by. When he spoke, his husky voice sent a
zing through her. "I want you right now, Cameron Flaherty."

Cam didn't respond for a moment. All of a sudden her legs
were made of Jell-O. Sinking into a chair, she cleared her
throat. "It's entirely mutual," she murmured.

A rattle of static came through from Pete's end. He swore.
"Hang on," he said in a terse tone.

The line went quiet. Cam waited. She mused on how her
life had changed since summer. She'd ended her budding romance with Jake Ericsson, the chef at The Market restaurant.
His constant jealousy and fits of temper had proved too unset-

tling for her. And then he'd traveled back to Sweden to wait until his undocumented immigration status cleared. Meanwhile, an attraction between Cam and state police detective Pete Pappas had blossomed. Cam had helped him with information about the murder that took place after her farm-to-table dinner. They hadn't acted on their feelings, though, until the investigation was finished. Pete came back on the line. "Sorry, Cam. Have to go. See you at five tomorrow."

Cam was about to agree when the call was disconnected. She sighed. Did she really want a romantic relationship with a law enforcement officer? Well, she'd jumped in with both feet and with her eyes open for now.

Cam retrieved her sunglasses from the truck the next morning. The eight o'clock sun lit up every crystal in the fresh snow, and the sky was a perfect blue. She tromped out in her cross-country ski boots to the chickens, stamping the snow flat in their yard before opening the door. She scattered a couple of handfuls of cracked corn on the flattened snow. They hated to tread on loose snow. She didn't blame them, with those skinny feet and legs.

"Come on out, girls. You need the fresh air." She made the clicking noise she'd learned from DJ, who seemed to be able to communicate directly with these fowl.

TopKnot popped out, followed by Hillary, the hen that tended to boss the others around. Their funny, gargling voices delighted Cam, as always. The others hopped down the ramp and pecked at the corn.

She uncovered the low tunnels inside the hoop house so the greens underneath wouldn't burn up from too much heat, and returned to the barn to grab her ten-year-old skis and poles. A fresh snow on a clear, sunny day shouldn't be wasted. She needed to get all the food ready for the dinner, but she had time for an hour's ski. She'd already created a trail in the woods behind the farm. The skiing should be easy with a few new inches of snow in the ruts to glide on. She clicked the toes of her boots into the bindings of the long, narrow skis, adjusted her mittened hands in the loops at the tops of the poles, and set out along the open field on the left side of the property. Taking long gliding strides, her arms swinging with the poles, she filled her lungs with the clean air, which tasted almost metallic from the cold.

The fields and beds of her farm looked like a giant hand had tucked them into pristine white blankets. The fence posts supporting her new grapevine stuck up out of the snow, as did the knobby stalks of the remaining Brussels sprouts plants, which she'd never gotten around to harvesting. A few wizened brown apples still clung to the bare branches of the two antique-variety apple trees that had been there forever. A hawk caught an updraft in a kettle of warm air and spiraled lazily.

She skied off her land into the woods along a wide path that connected with the back of an adjacent farm. Here no wind stirred the tall firs, and quiet reigned, except for the crunch of skis on snow. She thought about what she'd read on the Internet the night before. She'd awoken feeling uneasy about the caregiver Oscar. It worried her that someone with a temper like his was working with the sometimes fragile elderly. He had blemishes in his past, she'd discovered after searching for his name. From a police log column and a court report entry she'd learned he had been arrested for assault once, but the charges had been dismissed. On the other hand, he seemed to be active in the Eritrean immigrant community. He served on a committee that sponsored English classes for new arrivals and on an advisory board at what had to be his children's elementary school in Lynn, a somewhat beleaguered city on the coast north of Boston. It was a bit of a drive up here to Westbury, but he probably couldn't afford to live in this increasingly affluent community. And consequently, maybe Moran paid more than similar places in Lynn.

She shook off the thought of Oscar's temper. Surely a business dealing in the care of the old wouldn't hire someone who would be a danger to them. Would they?

As she navigated down a gentle slope, an odd shape on a bare branch high above her head caught her eye. She slowed to glance up. An owl perched on the branch. A big owl. She smiled to herself. She'd heard the *hoo-hoohoohoo-hoo-OO-hoo* of the great horned owl at twilight. She felt privileged to see—

Cam cried out at a crunching sound. The crust of snow broke through into the icy water of a small stream that wound through the woods. Cam's right ski caught and twisted sideways. She fell onto her right hip, landing on a stump that stuck up out of the snow. Her other ski jutted off at an odd angle, twisting her left knee into a configuration God hadn't designed it for. With the new snow, she must have missed the path where it curved over the stream on a wide fallen log.

She swore. Her right foot and her entire right ski sat in the water. Maneuvering her pole to click the boot out of the binding, she kept missing the right position and leverage. Having extra-long legs didn't help in this predicament, and neither did the lack of automatic-release bindings on cross-country skis. She aimed the pole at the left binding and succeeded in freeing that boot, which let her straighten her knee. It throbbed, and she hoped she hadn't seriously damaged it. She poked at the right binding again until it gave way, then grabbed a branch and dragged herself to standing on the slope next to the stream.

Her cell phone rang in her pocket. *Sheesh.* Cam bit her right mitten and dragged it off her hand. She glanced at the caller ID. *Jake?* She connected the call.

"Jake? Where are you?"

"At home in Uppsala. I miss you."

Cam squeezed her eyes shut for a second. She reopened them. "I hope you're well. But I can't talk right now."

"I suppose you're busy with your cop." His voice sounded sad even from thousands of miles away.

"No, I'm actually out skiing in the woods. By myself. But I just fell into a stream. And my foot is cold, so I have to go. I'll call you another time."

"Take care, Cam. Go get warm." He disconnected.

Cam sighed. She glanced at the time before she stuck the phone in her pocket and pulled her mitten back on. Jake had been sweet to her much of the time. He excelled as a chef. They had a strong attraction to each other. But a volatile temper and unpredictable reactions were not what she wanted from a partner. She hoped he could get over her.

But right now, if she didn't return to the farm and get changed, she'd never get all the food together and delivered to Moran Manor in time. She used a pole to lift the ski out of the water. She lined both up on the path toward home and clicked her boot into the left binding. She put the toe of her right boot into the binding, her toes numbing in the ice water that had seeped inside, but the boot wouldn't click in. First the ski slipped on the snow. Then she realized stream water had frozen inside the binding. She scraped it out with the pole's tip and tried again. The boot would not attach.

She swore again. What a time for her old bindings to give way. She had to get back home. She clicked the left binding open, releasing her boot, and hoisted the skis and poles on her shoulder. Heading for home, she tramped along the trail, in the tracks, her right foot barely sensate, her feet sinking into the path with each step. Which ruined the ski tracks, but it couldn't be helped. The snow next to the path was so deep, it would mean even more exertion.

When she cleared the woods, she paused to catch her breath. A nearly silent whoosh sounded above her, and she caught a shadow moving on the snow. She darted her gaze to the sky. The great horned owl flew along the border of the trees, its powerful wings beating slowly, quietly. A mouse struggled, the last movements of its life, in the predator's powerful talons.

Chapter 3

Cam glanced at the clock on her kitchen wall when she made it back to the house. Eleven o'clock. She pressed Lucinda DaSilva's number. "If you could come over right away to help me, I'll owe you big-time." She disconnected after Lucinda said she would be over. Less than three hours to harvest several of the ingredients, pull together the rest from storage, and deliver it all to the cook at Moran Manor.

She pulled off her pants and socks, despite still feeling sweaty from the exertion of the hike home. Her foot was red from the ice water, so she rubbed it with bare hands until it regained feeling. At least it didn't show the yellow-white color of frostbite. Her knee ached a bit, and her hip would have a big bruise on it tomorrow, but overall the health inventory was positive. She donned dry pants, thick wool socks, and her snow boots, then downed a glass of water and grabbed a muffin. The combination of the exercise and the fresh, cold air had worked its usual magic. She felt calm and energized, like she could meet whatever the world brought, even falling into a creek and breaking a binding.

As she headed for the barn, an old blue Civic pulled into

the drive. Lucinda climbed out, wearing a yellow down jacket, jeans, and sturdy boots.

"Fazendeira," Lucinda called out, using the Portuguese word for *farmer,* her nickname for Cam. "I'm here."

"Thanks for coming." Cam set her hands on her hips and smiled at the Brazilian, her friend and favorite volunteer. "You're rescuing me."

Lucinda waved a hand encased in a rainbow-striped glove. "Now that I got a job as a librarian, I miss working on the farm."

"I'm glad you're not cleaning houses anymore, but I miss working with you, too. How's the job going?"

"Those private school teenagers think they're a little bit entitled. But they're smart, mostly, and the headmaster likes what I'm doing. So far." She pulled a multicolored knit hat a little farther down on her mass of black curls. "What's the chore list for today? I can give you two hours, until I have to go in and work Sunday study hall."

Cam explained the Moran Manor dinner. "Help me cut greens in the hoop house, and we can talk while we work."

"Lead the way."

The two women grabbed scissors and baskets in the barn and trudged to the hoop house. Cam carefully shut the door behind them. The three-foot-wide beds of greens stretched in front of them the full length of the structure. Bright green baby arugula, reddish-green kale, dark green mâche, each row with knee-high mini hoops placed every couple of feet. The bunched-up white row cover ran down the middle. The small electric motor that blew air between the layers of plastic over-head hummed. The air smelled damp and earthy, and Cam welcomed the warmer temperature now that her sweat was drying and chilling her.

As they stooped to cut, Cam told Lucinda about falling into the stream. "That frigid water about did me in."

"This skiing thing? I don't get it. Where I come from, we like to be real warm. We don't have any snow in Brazil, except on the high plateaus way in the south."

"Well, I love it. You can't beat it for exercise, and the woods are quiet and beautiful, covered in snow."

"Until the ice gives way under it, you mean." Lucinda held a finger up. "Hey, I saw a news article about an herbicide last week. I've been doing a bit of research in the library when it's not busy."

"The one about G-Phos? I heard a bit on the news but never got around to reading the paper that day."

Lucinda nodded. "Conventional farms use it to kill weeds." She straightened and stretched. "The main chemical is glyphosate. There's studies that show it causes Alzheimer's disease and other old-people problems. It looks like it's responsible for killing all those honeybees lately, too."

"That's the reason I farm organically. I have lots of reasons, actually, but that's one of them." Cam worked in silence for a moment. "Can you imagine? You work trying to grow food for people, and instead you're poisoning them. And yourself."

"That's why I eat local food. I can see what the farmer's putting on it. I can buy something labeled organic from California, but I have no idea how it was grown."

Cam frowned and stopped cutting.

"What?" Lucinda asked.

"Mr. Slavin. You know, Felicity's father. He has Alzheimer's. And he had a career as a landscaper. I bet he sprayed a ton of that stuff in his lifetime."

"Bad news." Lucinda shook her head. "The study said they have a blood test for it."

"I wonder if Felicity knows. I'd much rather have a few weeds than add that kind of chemical to my soil and body."

"You know what they say. Weeds are only a plant you don't want."

It took an hour to cut the greens in the hoop house, even with Lucinda's help. They had to bend over and cut carefully, and Cam's back ached before they were done. They moved on to the leeks. Even though she'd loosened them in their beds and mulched them heavily before the ground froze, they were difficult to get out intact. When they got to the rosemary, half of it was frozen, despite the mini hoop house she'd erected over the perennial herb bed so she could continue to cut during the cold months.

Two hours later *calm* and *energized* no longer described Cam. She'd worked too hard, too fast, on top of the skiing and slogging through the snow on foot. Her head pounded, and her hands ached from the cold. Lots of farm tasks didn't mesh well with wearing gloves, like using scissors to cut greens. She'd cut the tips off of a pair of gloves, but it meant the ends of her fingers stayed chilled. A lot rode on this dinner going well, and she worried the amount of food she'd gathered wouldn't be sufficient for Moran Manor. She hadn't stored as many squash in the root cellar as she had thought, but what she had would have to suffice.

She loaded everything into the rear of the truck. Getting that used cap to cover the bed of the old Ford had turned out to be a brilliant business decision. No snow clogged the bed of the truck, and whatever she hauled didn't blow around when she drove.

She headed to the house. She didn't have time for a shower, but she could at least wash up and swap these work clothes for a fresh set. First, she checked her list for the dinner. As a former geek, she was grateful for possessing the organization gene. Root crops: check. Greens: check. Herbs: check. Onions and garlic: check. *Oh. The frozen goods.* She headed for the chest freezer in the basement and brought up a cooler packed with bags of frozen kale, a pint of her own pesto, and a bag holding two bright orange habanero peppers. She loaded it into the truck, then dashed into the house to change. She'd barely get there in time.

Chapter 4

"**A**bout time."

Cam glanced up as she set a carton of acorn squash on the counter of the Moran Manor kitchen.

The cook folded her arms. "I'm Rosemary. We spoke on the phone." A white chef's uniform encased her robust figure, and a floppy white toque mostly tamed her blond hair.

"Nice to meet you in person." Cam smiled, trying to squash the butterflies in her stomach. What if the chef didn't approve of the quality of the vegetables? Or didn't deem the stew recipe appropriate?

Rosemary watched Cam set out the produce on the stainless-steel island. Besides the squash, which Rosemary planned to stuff and bake, Cam lifted a bag of leeks. She added a box of parsnips, carrots, and potatoes for the hearty stew. The onions and garlic went next to them, along with several big bags of cold-hardy salad greens. Cam left the basket of apples from a neighboring farm on the floor.

"How does it look?" Cam stroked the round ridges on one of the nearly black squashes. "The frozen stuff is in this cooler." She pointed.

"Should be all right. Though they won't like those dark green greens. Old people are kind of particular about their salads." She pulled her mouth and raised one eyebrow.

"That's the easiest kind to grow in the winter."

"I expect half of those'll come right back, untouched. But, hey, we compost here."

"You do?"

"Your great-uncle pushed it through. I didn't much like it at first, but now, well, it's a better use than throwing food in the trash. Saves the facility money, as well."

Cam nodded. "Here's the stew recipe I proposed." She extracted a couple of sheets of paper from her bag and slid them across the island to Rosemary. "And the one for the apple-almond cake."

The cook pulled reading glasses out of a pocket in her apron. She perused the recipes. "Pesto?"

"I brought a pint. It adds nice flavor and also thickens the stew a bit."

"We'll see."

"That cake recipe is delicious." Cam checked the cloth bag at her feet. "Oh, I almost forgot the herbs." She extracted rubber-banded bunches of rosemary and sage and laid them on the island. She frowned at the rosemary. Freezing hadn't treated it well. She hoped it retained its flavor.

Rosemary scrubbed her hands at a deep stainless-steel sink and then pulled on a pair of thin gloves of the type medical personnel used. Without turning, she said, "I'll let you know how it goes."

"Thanks." Clearly dismissed, Cam grabbed her bag and left the kitchen. She stood in the open hallway for a moment, glad to be done with that encounter. Adding a contract with the Manor for the summer would increase her workload, but it would also be a guaranteed income. If this dinner succeeded, she could expect more financial stability, always a benefit for a small farmer. But then she'd need to hire someone to help her.

The reception desk in the lobby was to her left; the stairway up to Albert's room, to her right. Cam couldn't decide if she should pop up for a visit or just go home and collapse. Ellie came bounding down the stairs.

Cam greeted the girl. "Working again?"

"Yeah. Hey, I saw your great-uncle in the common room a little while ago. He's about to start a game."

Cam entered the big, sunny space to see the woman who had been doing needlepoint the day before sitting across a table from Albert, with a Scrabble board in the middle.

"Cameron, join us in a game," Albert called. "Have you met Marilyn Muller?" He introduced Cam to the woman.

"It's nice to meet you, Marilyn." Cam shook Marilyn's hand, which was knobby with arthritis.

"I'm happy to meet a relative of Albert's. Will you play?" Marilyn gestured at the board, one of the deluxe models that sat on a turntable and had little ridges around the squares so the tiles didn't slip out of place.

Cam checked the big analog wall clock. "Sure. I'd love to." She sat.

"What brings you over again so soon?" Albert asked. He rearranged the tiles on his rack.

"For the dinner I'm supplying the produce for, remember? But I kind of fell into a stream while I skied in the woods this morning, and then my binding broke. I had to really hustle to get everything picked and assembled."

"Marilyn, Cameron here took over my farm, and she grew all the vegetables for tonight's dinner. I'm sure it will be fine, my dear," he said to Cam.

"I certainly hope so."

"You look like you might benefit from an adult beverage. Since it's Sunday afternoon, they set out the happy hour supplies early." He pointed to the sideboard, where bottles of red and white wines stood ready to be poured. A tray of wineglasses sat near a jug of cider, and snack-sized bags of chips and nuts nestled in a big bowl. "Help yourself, and also bring over a glass of white for me."

"Marilyn, would you like one?" Cam glanced at the woman.

"Oh, no, not at all. I'll take a glass of the apple cider, though, if it's not too much trouble."

"I'll get that for you." Cam noticed a red walker standing behind Marilyn's chair. She delivered the cider and the white wine to the table, and returned to pour a glass of red for herself. She grabbed a few bags of snacks, too. The little touches, like early happy hour and real glasses instead of plastic cups, set Moran Manor apart from some other facilities.

They played and chatted for two hours. Cam refilled their drinks once and munched on the snacks, since she'd missed lunch.

Marilyn tried a couple of bluffs on them.

"Blimpy." She smiled, with a twinkle in her eyes. "You know, when you feel kind of bloated, you feel blimpy." But she also seemed to possess the contents of the entire Scrabble dictionary in her head, using a two-letter word like *jo* and combining it with a "triple word score" space and an existing word to soar ahead on the score sheet.

Albert was no slouch at the game, either. He and Marilyn bantered like old friends, or maybe their interaction had become more than that, Cam realized. *Good for him.* Marie had passed away three years earlier. He deserved a new romance in his life.

Oscar pushed a resident in a wheelchair into the room and

deposited him in front of the television, which played a black-and-white movie at low volume. From the man's closed eyes, it didn't seem like he would care one way or the other. Oscar stopped by the Scrabble game on his way out.

"Nice board."

Albert greeted him. "Do you play?"

"My children's school uses it in the after-school program to help kids with their English reading and spelling skills." He leaned down, pointed to something on Albert's rack, and whispered in his ear.

"Young man, I thank you." Albert winked at him and rubbed his hands together before Oscar strolled away.

This was a different side of Oscar than what Cam had seen in the kitchen. She was losing miserably and didn't care. Her worries about the dinner were melting away, too. The game was down to the last tiles when Cam spied Frank Jackson through the wide doorway. He stood at the reception desk a few yards away, even thinner than the last time Cam had seen him. Frank was the estranged husband of Cam's childhood friend, Ruth Dodge, and the father of their twin daughters. He'd gotten so deep into the activities of the Patriotic Militia that he'd left Ruth and the girls the previous summer. Ruth, an officer in the local police force, hadn't heard from him since, and she'd said nobody had seen him around town. Cam would have to tell her he'd shown up here.

"I need to talk to Bev Montgomery." His voice resonated in the high-ceilinged lobby.

Heads in the common room turned in that direction. Albert raised his eyebrows but kept his gaze on the board. It was his turn to play, and his score hovered only a few points away from beating Marilyn's.

The receptionist said something Cam couldn't make out.

"Just give me her room number."

The receptionist spoke again. She shook her head, then picked up the phone on the desk.

Frank stuck his hands in the pockets of his jeans. He paced back and forth in front of the desk. His straggly ponytail hung over a wool pea coat, and his boots left tracks of snow on the carpet.

The director emerged from his office. *Jim Cooper working on a Sunday?*

"Frank." Jim extended his hand, his hearty greeting extending to where Cam sat. "We love the picture." He waved his other hand at a large sepia-toned photograph behind the receptionist's desk.

Frank pulled his hand out of his pocket and shook with Jim. "Thanks. Doing them keeps me sane." He seemed to calm down in Jim's presence.

"I'd buy one in each season if you can produce them."

"Shouldn't be a problem. You know, I use real film. And a darkroom. Makes me old-fashioned, but I believe it makes a better picture."

Cam hadn't ever taken a close look at the picture and reminded herself to check it out when she left.

Albert nudged Cam's elbow and pointed to the Scrabble board. "Your turn, dear."

Cam was studying her tiles when Ellie sauntered over. She leaned over Cam's shoulder.

"You're in bad shape." Ellie pointed at Cam's tiles.

"Don't I know it." Cam added an *s* to *bottle* for a pitiful score of nine. She glanced up to see Bev stomping down the stairs.

"What are you doing here?" Bev glared at Frank.

"We need to—"

"No, we don't." She turned to go.

Frank reached for her arm. She shook him off, but he leaned toward her. He put his hand between his mouth and her ear and said something. Bev's eyes widened. She cast a quick glance around. When she saw Cam watching, she scowled but returned her gaze to Frank.

"All right. But only for a minute." She headed for the stairs. Frank followed close behind.

"Who's that dude?" Ellie asked in a low voice.

"Frank Jackson. You remember Ruth Dodge, right? It's her husband. Sort of." Seeing Frank with Bev flooded Cam's brain with memories from the preceding spring. Most of them not very nice ones.

"Bingo, and out," Marilyn declared.

Cam looked back at the board. Marilyn had played all seven of her remaining tiles, spelling *braised*.

"That's ten, plus eight, plus fifty for the bingo."

Cam picked up the bag of tiles and jiggled it. Empty. Albert groaned, but the sound held a hint of delight at his friend's triumph.

He took the last sip of his wine. "Congratulations, my dear. How many wins in a row is that?"

"I shouldn't keep track." Her blue eyes smiled under long, curly lashes. "But since you ask, eight since we started playing. You won the first three, don't forget." Marilyn's round cheeks pinkened. Cam would have to ask Albert sometime why she needed the walker.

"You did that like butter, Mrs. Muller." Ellie nodded and gave a thumbs-up gesture to Marilyn.

"Thank you, young lady."

Cam's phone buzzed in her bag. She retrieved it and checked the new text message. "Oh, no."

"What's wrong?" Albert's forehead creased.

Cam pushed her chair back and stood. "I have a dinner date, and I lost track of time. Good thing he asked me to pick up a bottle of wine." She glanced at the time on the phone. "I'll barely have time to get home and put the chickens in for the night."

"Off you go, then."

"This was really fun. I very much enjoyed meeting you, Marilyn." Touching Marilyn's shoulder, Cam leaned down to give Albert a kiss.

"We'll do it again," Marilyn said.

Albert nodded with a smile. He covered Marilyn's hand with his own.

"See you, Ellie," Cam called, walking out of the room.

Should she pop into the kitchen and see how the meal preparation was going? No, she needed to get home and then to Pete's, and she didn't imagine Rosemary would appreciate the visit, anyway. On her way, she paused at the receptionist's desk to sign out and then remembered she'd brought the vegetables in through the back door to the kitchen. She glanced up at the framed picture, a striking photograph of Moran Manor in the fall. Leaves in different shades clung to the trees, and pots of mums lined the walkway. The yellowy-brown sepia tint gave the picture a timeless feel, despite showing the residence's modern ramp railings and double-hung windows. If Frank had created this, he had real talent. Ruth had never mentioned her husband's photography.

She headed for the front door. She was about to reach for the handle when the door began to swing open, so she stepped away.

"Excuse me." Ginger Montgomery sailed in with a rush of cold air, nearly whacking Cam with the door. The beret perched on Ginger's head matched her white quilted jacket. "I'm going up to see my mother," she told the receptionist in an imperious tone and swept up the stairs. The scent she wore trailed behind her.

Cam could only imagine the fireworks that might be shooting out of Bev's room in a minute. She imagined the pyrotechnic combination of Bev, Frank, and Ginger could be downright lethal.

Chapter 5

"You should have seen that silly hen," Cam said to Pete an hour later. She perched on a stool at the island in his kitchen and watched his smooth-skinned hands chop vegetables. "TopKnot just stood there in the cold. The true definition of a pea brain." She'd been only a few minutes late, since the farm lay between Moran Manor and Pete's apartment in nearby Newburyport. She'd raced through a quick shower at home, too, since she hadn't had time earlier.

"I have my mother's recipe for avgolemono. Lemon chicken soup would work just as well with a frozen chicken—"

"Pete Pappas." Cam shook her finger at him. "Don't you even consider cooking poor, stupid TopKnot." She sipped the red wine he'd poured into a wide-bowled glass for her.

"Just saying." He waved the knife he held in the air with a wicked smile.

"What's on the menu for tonight?"

"Nonlocal lamb chops. My special Greek nonlocal eggplant-tomato bake and nonlocal potatoes." He frowned playfully. "Can you manage to eat it?"

"Of course I can. I don't really care if it's local or not. I know several of my customers go a little, shall we say, overboard in wanting to eat only local foods. But, hey, if they want it, I'll grow it. Whatever helps the bottom line."

Pete nodded.

"Speaking of that, the president of the Locavore Club came by to help me today," Cam said.

"Lucinda?"

Cam nodded. "Her new job is great for her, but she misses working on the farm." Pete and Lucinda had had a run-in the previous June, but they'd come to a wary peace since then.

"And how are things over at the Manor? You said you were providing dinner ingredients."

"I did. They should be eating the dinner right now." She filled him in on Bev's adjustment to communal living, or lack of it. "She's still pretty mad at me about the hens and what she describes as me stealing her customers." She took another sip of wine. "And Frank Jackson dropped by to see Bev today. She didn't appear overly happy to see him."

Pete's heavy dark eyebrows went up. "That's very interesting. I wonder where he's living these days."

"No idea. Last time I talked with Ruth, she didn't know, either."

Pete slid a casserole into the oven and set a timer. He picked up his own glass of wine and came around the island. A pink oxford shirt warmed his Mediterranean coloring, and he appeared more relaxed than Cam had ever seen him, the skin around his deep brown eyes not showing the tension it often did.

"Thirty minutes. Come sit on the couch with me." He put his free arm around her and leaned in for a long kiss.

When they came up for air, Cam said, "What did you say about a couch?" She slid off her stool. Her five feet eleven made her two inches taller than Pete. He didn't seem to mind at all, and neither did she. Jake stood half a foot taller than her, and while she'd liked that aspect of their relationship—she rarely found a man she physically looked up to—the rest of her dealings with Jake had been so stormy, she couldn't handle it.

They made their way to the sofa, which faced a bay window. The kitchen and living room occupied a single space in the apartment Pete had moved into last summer, after his marriage had ended. A framed photograph on the wall portrayed a sunny, whitewashed Greek village on a hillside above the sea. The houses wore blue doors and shutters. An herb garden filled one of the yards. Cam could almost taste the olives and the freshly caught fish grilled with rosemary and oregano. Pete sat next to her, and Cam laid her hand on the soft fabric of his faded jeans.

"Guess what?" Pete poked her gently in the ribs with his elbow.

Cam shook her head. "Surprise me."

"I get Dasha for a week, starting tomorrow. Alicia has to go out of town." His smile reflected sadness. "I'm at peace with being divorced—I don't miss being married to Alicia at all. But I miss that dog something awful."

"Remind me what kind of dog it is."

"He's sort of a Siberian mutt. His markings and build are mostly like a husky's. He's smart and clean, but one of his parents must have been another breed, because his coloring isn't typical and he's shorter than most."

"You should have gotten custody of him. I thought you said your ex doesn't even like dogs."

He nodded. "She pulled a power trip. I told you, I didn't want to fight her about anything. That's why she's in our lovely house and I'm in this little rental apartment."

"It's big enough for you, isn't it?" Cam squeezed his hand.

"It's a lovely place." The wide pine floors shone, and early-twentieth-century woodwork lined the doorways and windows. A graceful arched doorway led to a small hall, off of which lay the bathroom and the single bedroom. It was the top half of a ninety-year-old house that sat at the end of a dead-end road in Newburyport, which made for quiet surroundings.

"It's fine for now." He gazed out the window, into the darkness.

The timer dinged. Pete moved to the kitchen. He took the casserole and another dish out of the oven and put something else in, changing the oven setting. He set the small table with blue place mats and napkins and added silverware and plates.

"Let me help."

"Sure. Bring the wine to the table and light the candles. And then sit down." He placed the two dishes from the oven on cork trivets. He removed a broiler pan from the oven and brought over a plate heaped with small lamb chops, then sank into the chair across from her.

"This looks wonderful." Cam inhaled the aromas of the meal. "And it smells like Greece must."

Pete served her a portion of the eggplant casserole, with tomatoes oozing juice and melted feta cheese on the top, along with a heaping spoonful of scalloped potatoes and a lamb chop.

She cut a bite of lamb and savored it. "Oh, my, Detective. What did you do to make this so delicious?"

"Olive oil—the real stuff—plus lemon juice, salt, and oregano. Broiled." He smiled. "The best meat is next to the bone, you know. I get these from the butcher down in Rowley."

"So the meat is local, after all."

He smiled. "Could be. I didn't ask."

"We can save the bones for Dasha. Will he like them?"

"You don't know much about dogs, do you? Bones like that can splinter and kill a dog."

"You're right, I don't." Cam had never had a dog, but any dog so dear to Pete's heart as this one was an animal she might as well get to know. She only hoped Dasha didn't habitually jump up and stick his nose in one's crotch.

They ate and talked for some minutes. The candles bathed the table in a glow as soft as fresh snow. When they'd finished, Cam started to stand to clear the table, but Pete put his hand up.

"I'm doing all the work tonight. You just sit there and look beautiful." He winked at her.

She wasn't sure she quite qualified as beautiful, but she looked as good as she ever had. Fresh air and honest physical work were a much better beauty treatment than sitting in a cubicle all day, every day.

He cleared the dishes and brought out two pieces of baklava. It oozed honey and bits of walnuts from a flaky crust.

"I love this," Cam said.

"Not homemade, but I get it from Iris's Greek bakery in Ashford. It's almost like my mother used to make."

She was biting into her portion when a staticky sound came from the hallway. Pete turned his head sharply.

"The police scanner. I need to check that." He rose and disappeared down the hall. He returned a minute later, carrying a black device that reminded Cam of an old walkie-talkie. A thick antenna stuck out of the top, along with a knob. He set it on the table and fiddled with the knob before sitting.

More static erupted, and then a tinny voice.

"Unattended death, code seventy-nine. Repeat. Unattended death of elderly resident, code seventy-nine."

Pete frowned. He drummed the table with his fingers.

The voice continued. "Location, Forty-four Maple Way, Westbury. Car thirty-two, come in, please. EMT, come in, please."

Cam gazed at Pete. She opened her mouth to speak, but he held up his hand.

He listened to more of the transmission until it returned to static. He turned a knob and reduced the volume.

"This isn't good," he muttered.

"I know it isn't. That address is Moran Manor." Cam's heart thudded in her chest. "What if it's Uncle Albert?"

Pete gazed into Cam's face. "Any idea what a code seventy-nine is?"

"None."

"Unattended deaths must be checked out every time. Code seventy-nine means there is also a report of suspicious behavior."

"You mean murder," she whispered.

Chapter 6

"I need to call Uncle Albert." Cam glanced at the clock. "It's almost seven. He's probably still at dinner. But what if—" Her throat thickened. Tears threatened to fill her eyes. Her emotional ties to her great-uncle were stronger than to her own parents.

"I'm sure it's not him, Cam." Pete put his arms around her for a moment. "But why don't you call, anyway?" He stood and paced to the window and back, his brow furrowed.

Cam picked up her bag and dug out her cell phone. She took a deep breath, wiped her cheeks, pressed Albert's number. His line rang six times and then went to voice mail. "Albert, please call me as soon as you get this message," she said, trying to keep the worry out of her voice. She disconnected and remained standing.

Pete paced some more.

Cam watched him. "If it's murder, you'll be investigating, right?" She clutched the phone.

"I have to wait for them to call me. The Westbury department responds first, but as you know, they're too small to be able to muster sufficient resources."

"To investigate a murder. So they call the state police. I know. I sort of wish I didn't." If someone had been murdered, it would be the third time in a year in the small town. At least this death didn't have anything to do with her farm. Unless . . . the person died from eating her produce. Then it absolutely involved her.

"I need to go to Moran Manor." She slung her bag over her shoulder as she glanced at the door. "Everybody there ate my produce for dinner. What if something was spoiled?"

"You won't be able to do anything there, and they probably wouldn't even let you in. Let's finish our dessert." He reached for her hand and led her to the table.

Cam only picked at hers. "It's delicious. But I'm so worried about Albert, I can't really enjoy it. I'm sorry."

"Cameron, I'm the one who's sorry. I wanted us to have a quiet, intimate night." He covered her hand with his. "But that phone's going to ring any minute now, and when it does, I'm out of here."

When they were done, he fixed small, sweet Greek coffees. They sat on the couch to drink them. Cam laid her phone carefully on the coffee table. She took one sip from her cup and set it down.

"That's fabulous. But I'll never sleep if I finish it."

Pete nodded. "That's sort of my plan. And I'll drink yours, too." His knee jittered up and down.

Cam's stomach roiled. Why hadn't Albert returned her call?

"Maybe the Westbury police decided the behavior wasn't suspicious, after all," she said. "Maybe a ninety-three-year-old simply died in her sleep, unattended."

Her phone rang. She picked it up from the table and fumbled to connect, dropping it in the process. Pete retrieved it for her in one swift scoop. She pressed SEND just in time.

"Cameron?"

She closed her eyes in gratitude. "Uncle Albert. I'm so glad you're all right."

"Of course I am. I was at dinner. I do eat dinner every day, my dear."

"We—" She opened her eyes again at Pete's tapping her arm. He shook his head with a quick move.

"I heard some commotion here tonight, though," Albert said. "An ambulance took someone away. Not certain who. I saw Ruthie Dodge, too. Now, why did you call? Is everything all right with you?"

"I'm fine. I wanted to—" Cam racked her brain. "To say what a good time I had playing Scrabble with you and Marilyn this afternoon. She seems sweet. And smart."

"She's quite the gal, I agree. We've taken to dining together every evening. You'll join us sometime soon, I hope."

"Of course."

"The dinner tasted fine, by the way. Very nice winter stew, excellent stuffed squash. Not many residents partook of the salad, but Marilyn and I very much enjoyed it. The almonds in it were a nice touch. And the apple-almond cake? A perfect ending."

"I forgot to even ask. I'm glad it went well. The cook must have decided to throw in the almonds on the salad. Nonlocal ones, of course."

"I should think the residence will want to buy from you regularly once the season gets under way. But that's not my decision, of course."

"Thanks. Well, good night, Uncle Albert."

He said good night and disconnected.

"Sorry. Rules of conduct." Pete let out a heavy breath. "Don't share scanner news with civilians. Which you are." He drummed his fingers on his knee. "It won't be easy hanging out with me, Cam. You might want to reconsider this, whatever we're doing."

"I quite like this *whatever*." Cam snuggled into his arm. The poor soul at Moran Manor wasn't Albert or, apparently, Marilyn. Cam's jitters were gone. She noticed that Pete's weren't. His work still loomed.

"He didn't know who died, I gather?" he asked.

"No. He said an ambulance had taken someone away. Oh, and that Ruth Dodge is there."

He nodded. "She must be the officer on duty tonight. You're friends with her. Remind me how you know her."

"I spent every summer with Great-Aunt Marie and Great-Uncle Albert. I stayed with them on the farm from the time I was six until I went off to college. Ruth grew up nearby, and we played together all summer long. Playing when we were teenagers involved hanging out at Salisbury Beach and hunting for boys, of course, and getting in various kinds of minor trouble."

"Minor trouble?"

Cam snorted. "I was the foolish geek, and she was the clown, but a sensible clown who kept our trouble to the minor sort."

Pete's phone sat on the coffee table. It vibrated twice, then twice again, then twice again. He gave Cam a baleful glance and sat forward to answer it.

"Pappas." He listened for a moment. "I'll be there in twenty. Thank you, Officer." He disconnected. "The life of a statie is never really his own. I hope you can get used to this." He held out his arms to Cam.

She sank into them. She burrowed her face into his neck and inhaled his scent—a combination of olive oil, aftershave, and man—and murmured, "I have so far."

He kissed her and then untangled the two of them. He tossed down the rest of both coffees.

"I'll clean up in the kitchen," Cam said. "You go on."

"You're a treasure." He squeezed her hand and stood.

"Call me when you can." She also stood. "And stay safe."

"You give me great motivation to do exactly that."

"I know Frank," Cam said to Ruth Dodge over the telephone line. She'd called her the moment she arrived home from Pete's at a little after eight. "I'm not mistaken." She leaned over from where she sat on her couch to stroke Preston as she spoke.

"I haven't seen him or heard from him since last summer. Did you get any idea of where he's been living, or what he's living on, for that matter?"

"No. I didn't talk to him directly. He sort of demanded to see Bev Montgomery."

Ruth didn't respond for a moment. "That's interesting," she said at last.

"I didn't realize he did art photography. He has a real talent for it."

"What?"

"There's a black-and-white photograph of Moran Manor hanging in the lobby there," Cam said. "It's a fall shot, sort of sepia toned. It's really nice, a very artistic shot."

"Huh. He did photography when we first met. He's very creative. He used the darkroom at the community college. He shot a dozen stunning portraits of the girls when they were toddlers. But so far as I know, he hasn't touched it in several years."

"The director over at Moran asked him to do more. The rest of the seasons."

"I'm gobsmacked, as my Australian friend says. I wonder where he is. . . ." Ruth's voice trailed off.

"Albert said that they took someone away from Moran Manor in an ambulance tonight and that you were there. What's going on?"

Cam heard voices in the background.

"Hey, I have to go," Ruth said. "I'm actually at work. Just took a break to answer your call."

"I'll let you know if I see Frank again."

"Thanks. I'd appreciate that. Let's fit in a glass of wine one of these days. It's been a while."

Cam agreed and disconnected. Ruth and Frank had seemed pretty happy when they married—Cam had attended the wedding—and now Ruth didn't even know his address or that he sold high-quality photographs. *What a shame.* Not every marriage was destined for sixty years together, like Albert and Marie's, she supposed. Cam realized Ruth hadn't told her what had happened at the residence, either.

Cam answered her ringing cell phone out of a deep sleep the next morning.

"Beverly Montgomery is dead. At Moran Manor." Pete's voice on the phone sounded terse.

"That's terrible." She glanced at the clock by her bed. Six thirty and still winter dark outside. "Did she have a heart attack or something?"

"I'm not at liberty to say." He cleared his throat.

Someone must be standing nearby. "What about the suspicious behavior?"

"I need a favor from you."

So he didn't want to talk about the death. "What's the favor?"

"I told you I was getting Dasha for the week. I can't be there this morning when Alicia drops him off. Would you, please, go over to my apartment and meet her, and then bring him to the farm? I'll get him sometime later today."

A dog on the farm? How would Preston react? *Yikes.* "Sure. What time? And will she know who I am?"

"I'll tell her. She wanted to hand him off at eight o'clock."

"I've got it. Don't worry." She swallowed. She definitely wasn't a dog person.

"Thank you. I owe you one." He disconnected.

Now she was wide awake. She'd asked him to call, and he had. Bev Montgomery had died. The woman had been unhappy and unpleasant, but she'd been relatively young, in her late sixties, Cam thought. A premature death.

She stretched in her bed in the same room she had stayed in as a child and teenager for all those summers. She'd painted it when she moved in over a year ago. White trim set off walls in a pale shade of rose that picked up one of the colors in the braided rag rug on the wide pine floors. A refinished antique bureau sat against the wall, and Great-Aunt Marie's little white wicker rocking chair occupied a corner. Cam's ancient stuffed lion sat in it, reigning over the room. Her parents had brought the lion back from one of their anthropological sojourns to southern Africa. Cam expected they bought it at the airport before they left the country. Despite the fresh paint and the new bedding, she still inhaled the aroma of the old house: dry wood, a hint of lilac, and memories.

Her copy of Albert and Marie's black-and-white wedding picture sat on the bureau. Marie smiled directly into the camera, slim and lovely in a simple white wedding dress with sleeves and a neck of lace. Albert, in a dark suit and tie and not yet displaying the stocky build of a farmer, beamed at his bride. They'd had a long and happy marriage, and Marie had lived into her eighties before dying from pancreatic cancer.

The diagnosis had come so late that no treatment would have been effective. The illness was short and not overly painful, but it gave Marie time to say good-bye to her loved ones.

Albert had told Cam once that Bev had been incredibly kind and helpful to both of them while Marie lay dying. When Bev wasn't tending to Marie, she cooked meals or helped Albert with the farm chores. He'd seen through Bev's cantankerous attitude to a good heart within. Now Bev was dead, without her own chance to live into her eighties.

Chapter 7

An hour later, dressed and caffeinated, Cam drove toward Pete's house. She'd finished her early morning chores. The chickens were fed and watered and free to go outside. She'd watered the seedlings in the hoop house, grateful that she'd had the water source put deep enough underground that it didn't freeze, although they didn't need much water in the winter, since growth was so slow. Today dawned another one of those clear, cold winter days, but at least with little wind to drive the cold deeper inside. The ten-degree air made her pull her wool scarf closer around her neck under the robin's egg–blue sky.

But now she was about to meet her new boyfriend's difficult ex-wife and bring home a dog she had never met, an even chillier prospect than a morning of shoveling snow. What was she supposed to do with a dog? She'd never owned one, not as a child, not as an adult. Albert and Marie's farm dog, Scout, had been a working dog, kept mostly to ward off foxes and woodchucks. In her view canines were needy animals, always making eye contact and wanting approval.

She pulled on sunglasses when she passed an open field on the left. The sun bounced off the snow cover and into her eyes. She tried to adjust the glasses so she could see better. They'd gotten bent when she sat on them once. Scratches on the lenses also made looking through them resemble peering through a spider web. She supposed she could get new ones at the drugstore. If it ever were a priority for her.

The heater in the old Ford started to warm her feet only minutes before she arrived at Pete's. A shiny SUV sat idling in front of the house, a woman in large square-lensed sunglasses at the wheel. Cam pulled into the driveway and slid out of the cab.

The woman—it had to be Alicia—now stood at the back of the car. Slender and petite in a puffy, pale pink jacket over ironed jeans tucked into snow boots with furry tops, she shoved her shades onto her head and pulled open the rear door. A plastic mat protected the floor of the compartment, and a grate walled the compartment off from the passenger section. A dog crouched with his paws in front of him.

"Come on, Dasha," the woman said in an impatient tone. "I'm already late."

Cam walked toward her. "I'm Cam Flaherty. Pete asked me to pick up his dog."

"*His* dog. Right. I know. He told me." Alicia looked Cam up and down.

Cam glanced down at her own outfit. Dirt stains on the knees of her jeans. Her winter boots that doubled as work boots, now with flecks of chicken manure and sawdust stuck to them. Her navy blue parka with the rip on the front pocket where it had caught on a nail in the attic once. She was suddenly back in high school, ever the over-tall, gawky geek, being checked out by an immaculately put-together cheerleader.

Alicia turned to the car. She reached in and pulled Dasha by his collar until he jumped out onto the shoveled sidewalk.

"Here he is," she said out of pursed lips. "Pete couldn't pick Dasha up himself. Nothing ever changes. His precious work is more important than anything else." She raised the side of her top lip and glanced at Cam, as if she wanted company in bad-mouthing Pete.

Instead, Cam knelt on one knee and extended the back of her hand to Dasha. Ruth had once shown her the correct way to approach a new dog. "Hey, buddy."

Dasha sniffed her and then butted her hand. His eyes were a pale arctic blue. The white mask around his face contrasted with the dark gray markings elsewhere. His pointed ears stood up straight. He would fit right in pulling a sled over the tundra.

"I have a plane to catch. Key West," Alicia said. "I can't wait to get out of this cold." She headed around the front of the car.

Cam stood with her hand on the soft fur on Dasha's head. She was opening her mouth to thank Alicia when she heard the door slam.

"Not a good-bye for you or a thank-you for me. No wonder it didn't work out between her and Pete." Cam patted Dasha on the head and watched the SUV drive away. "Well, we're off to the farm, big guy. You and Preston are both northern animals. You should recognize each other." *So far, so good.* He hadn't pushed his snout into her private parts or started barking without ceasing.

Dasha began to bark and didn't stop. *So much for that.*

"Hey, be quiet, doggy. I'm your babysitter for today. Get used to it." Cam was surprised when he instantly quieted.

She led him to the truck and opened the passenger door.

He placed his front paws on the seat and jumped in like he'd always been there. She smiled. Unlike Pete's wife, she certainly didn't need a plastic sheet to protect the bench. The vehicle had seen plenty of dirt, and even dog hair, in its long life as a farm truck. She shut the door carefully.

She glanced up at Pete's windows. He was out working. And had been all night long. Which could mean only that Bev had been murdered. Cam would call Albert when she got home. He might have gleaned some information about the death through the grapevine. Or maybe Ellie knew something.

A shiver ran through Cam, and not only from the air temperature. If Bev had been killed, that meant her murderer was walking around, free to kill again.

Preston strolled up to the truck after Cam pulled into the barn twenty minutes later. She'd made room in the barn for the Ford before winter descended in earnest. Cleaning snow off a truck after shoveling wasn't her idea of a good time.

"We have company, Preston," she said, climbing out of the cab. She went around to the other side and opened the door for Dasha, Preston at her heels.

Dasha bounded out. Preston took one look at him and split out the door in a blur of motion. Dasha went after him.

"Dasha, come here." Cam used what she imagined a good dog-owner voice would be: a low-pitched, firm tone. She patted the side of her leg.

He gazed at her, looked at the door, and then trotted to her side.

"Good dog." She stroked his head and back. "Now what am I going to do with you? That mom of yours didn't leave me a leash or anything."

Cam found a plastic food container left over from a farm

potluck and rinsed it out. She filled it with water and set it on the floor in the office in a corner of the barn. She'd had her carpenter add the room the summer before, when the barn had to be rebuilt. The room included a small desk and chair, an electric space heater, which she now switched on, and two tables with grow lights hanging above them. She also kept her seeding supplies—flats, seeds, and seed-starting mix—in the office so she could plant seeds in a warm environment and nurture them along until they were ready to go out into the colder hoop house.

The main area of the barn stayed warm enough to work in as long as she kept a coat on, thanks to the radiant heat in the poured slab floor. It was provided by an array of solar panels on the roof and a bank of batteries that stored the solar energy. She once again offered thanks to both the subsidies and the grant she'd received that let her put all that free sunshine to good use.

"Stay here." She pointed to the water. When he went over and lapped some up, she left, closing the door behind her. She had no idea if he would stay on the property if she let him roam around. He might go after the chickens or chase Preston again. She found a couple of old beach towels in the house and brought them back to the barn, favoring her bruised hip from the day before. Folding the towels into a bed, she set it near the water dish.

"I have to work now." She patted the towels. "Come and lie down. Dad will be by sometime to get you. He promised."

Dasha obliged. Then he laid his head on his paws and gazed up at her. Needy but compliant. She could live with that. She stroked his head a few times. "Good boy."

Shrugging off her parka, she checked the harvest list tacked to the wall by the desk. Pickup day didn't fall until Saturday, but she needed to make sure she had enough to supply the twenty CSA customers, avid locavores, every one of them. This winter she'd gone down to an every-other-week pickup schedule, which took a little of the pressure off. The list for this two-week period included kale, beets, radishes, leeks, lettuce, Asian greens, and Swiss chard for crops she needed to cut or dig. She also had storage potatoes and various squashes to offer.

The most urgent task for this morning was seeding more greens so she'd have a crop to harvest in March. Setting two seventy-two-cell flats on the tables beneath the grow lights, she filled the cells with the lightweight seed-starting soil mix and extracted a bag of hardy romaine lettuce seeds from a cupboard. She wished she'd invested in one of the new vacuum-seeding devices. The job would go much faster, and she wouldn't waste as many of the minuscule germs of life. But the price was prohibitive for an operation of her scale, at least in the winter, when her income was lower.

While she worked, trying to drop only one or two tiny lettuce seeds into each one-inch-diameter cell, she thought about Bev's death. She realized she didn't even know how Bev had died.

"Oscar wasn't so happy with her. But kill a cranky resident?" Cam glanced at Dasha, who watched her every move. "I don't think so." She continued dropping seeds into the cells. "Frank didn't seem that pleased with her, either. I wonder what that meant. What's your opinion, Dasha?"

He perked up, gave a little bark, then rested his head on his paws again. Preston rarely attended to what she said. Maybe there was something to this dog business, after all.

"I need a dog translator." Cam smiled at him before she returned her focus to her work. "Bev's death will let Ginger get what she wants, I guess, if she inherits the property. That fertile farmland will turn into chemically treated lawns for McMansions. What a waste."

Dasha declined to comment. Cam finished her task. Most of the cells had gotten more than two seeds, which meant she'd be thinning and throwing away plantlets in a couple of weeks. She sprinkled a little more of the soil mix on top of each cell and then gently pressed it down with her fingers. The seeds were tiny and barely needed to be covered. She filled her watering can at the sink in the main area of the barn and gingerly watered each flat, glad she'd invested in a high-quality can that sprayed the water from a wide disk with tiny holes so the seeds didn't get swamped. She lowered the rectangular light fixtures that hung from chains until they were suspended only a few inches above the flats and switched on the heating pads under them. The pads provided a low, steady warmth and let the seeds sprout sooner rather than later.

She checked the clock above the desk, her stomach rumbling. The clock read 9:15 a.m. Time for breakfast.

"Come on, doggy. I'll show you the house."

Dasha sprang to his feet. He looked ready to run off. She grabbed a length of rope and tied it to his collar to serve as a makeshift leash. She carefully switched off the electric space heater and closed the office door behind her.

As they approached the house, a vintage Saab pulled into the drive. Dasha strained toward the car and barked. Cam almost lost hold of the rope.

"Dad's here." She waved.

As Pete stepped out of the car, Dasha tore loose and bounded toward him, ending in a happy reunion, with much licking on the part of one and much stroking on the part of the other.

"You're just in time for breakfast," Cam called with a smile.

As he straightened from bending over Dasha, Pete's face looked flat, almost like he was avoiding expressing any kind of feeling.

"I'll come in for a minute." He approached her, with Dasha close at his side. The dog kept gazing up at Pete and nudging Pete's knee with his head while they walked.

"What's up?" Cam tilted her head.

"Let's go in." He didn't return her smile.

She gazed at him for a moment before she turned. On the third step her knee felt like it was going to give way. "Ouch."

"What's wrong?" Pete asked from behind her.

"I twisted it a little while I was skiing yesterday. It's okay." She led the way indoors after unlocking the door. She stomped her feet on the mat. "Don't worry about taking your boots off. The floor's a mess, anyway." She walked to the coffee machine, ground a scoop of beans, and started a pot of French roast before turning back to him.

He stood just inside the door. "How has Dasha been?"

"He's a good dog. We've had a fine morning. Better than I expected. I'm not much of a dog person, you know."

"Oh? You didn't tell me that."

"He totally looks like he should be pulling a sled in the Iditarod."

Pete smiled. "He's part Siberian husky and part unknown. He'd never place in a show, but he's stronger for not being a pure bred. Thanks for taking him." His smile disappeared. "We need to talk." The lines in his face spoke of a night without sleep and more. Something more.

"Absolutely," Cam said. "I'm glad to see you. Sit down."

"I can't stay."

"Well, if we need to talk, then let's talk sitting down. My feet are tired, and I had a good night's sleep. You appear totally wiped out." And something more. She pulled out a ladder-back chair and sat at the table.

He sighed, sinking into a chair across from her, but he kept his coat on. Dasha sat on his haunches nearby. Pete absently stroked Dasha's head. He drummed the table with the fingers on his other hand and then stopped. He rubbed his forehead and then folded his arms.

"Tell me what you found at Moran." Cam reached a hand across the table to him. When he kept his arms folded, she pulled hers back, stung.

"She was murdered," he said.

"That's awful. How?"

The expression on his face changed from fatigue to steel. "I'm afraid you've become a person of interest."

"Me? Why me?" Cam frowned. "I didn't have any beef with Bev. She didn't like me much, but I had no reason to kill her."

"There are preliminary indications that someone put a fast-acting poison in her dinner—"

"What? Do you believe I put poison in the food?" She stared at him. "But I provided only the raw ingredients. The cook made the meal, assembled the salad. Somebody delivered dinner to Bev. Anybody could have done it. Do you truly think I could actually kill someone?" She pushed her chair back so hard, it fell over as she stood, and then she strode into the kitchen and back. The coffeepot popped and hissed as the coffee finished brewing. Cam was about to pop and hiss, too. How could he accuse her of murder?

"No." He rapped the table with his fingertips. *Buhdum, buh-dum, buhdum.* "But it's my job. I should probably recuse my-self from the case entirely. I'm not going to, though. We'll clear you, and that will be that."

"*Clear* me? I'm innocent!" She swallowed hard.

"Calm down. I know you didn't do it. But I need to back away from our relationship for now."

"Back away? What are you saying? Not only do you think I killed somebody, but you also don't want to see me anymore. That just stinks."

"I told you this wouldn't be easy."

"Then, you were right." Her face heated up, and her heart pounded in her neck. She rose and poured herself a cup of coffee with a shaky hand. She added a splash of milk, spilling a little, but left the cup on the counter. She faced him, folding her arms. "It's not easy at all."

"I'm sorry." He stood. Dasha jumped to his feet, as well. Pete spread his arms, palms up. "I'm sorry, Cam." He walked toward her, Dasha at his heels, and stopped in front of her.

She tried to avoid meeting his gaze but couldn't. He laid his hand on the side of her face, his palm cool on her hot cheek. She closed her eyes. She opened them when he spoke.

"I've never been in this situation before, Cameron. It's killing me. But I can't see you again romantically until this is resolved."

She nodded. She opened her mouth to speak. And then closed it, mad and hurt all at the same time.

"I want you to be careful. Whoever killed Bev is still out there." He cleared his throat. "And I need you to come down to the Westbury station today to be interviewed. I have to be meticulous where you're concerned." His gaze pleaded with her.

Cam nodded again.

Pete's phone buzzed. He turned, heading for the door, grabbing the phone off his belt and putting it to his ear.

"Pappas. Hold on a second." He lowered the phone and gazed at Cam. "I'll be at the station by noon. Have to take

Dasha home and try to sleep for an hour." He patted his leg. Dasha started to follow him, then trotted back to Cam and barked.

"Bye, buddy. See you around." She stroked his head.

He rubbed his head against her hand before he followed Pete out the door.

Cam locked it behind them. *Nice way to start the week.*

Chapter 8

"Wouldn't someone else have gotten sick, too? That dinner was served to everybody in the residence, as far as I know." Cam tried to keep her voice level, but being asked the same questions over and over was getting old. The metal chair in the Westbury police station's interview room hurt her tailbone. She wondered if she should have called a lawyer, after all. She hadn't thought she needed to. She hadn't poisoned anyone. She glanced at the clock. Quarter past two. She'd been here for forty-five minutes already. The room, painted a mustardy yellow, smelled faintly of stale doughnuts and bad coffee.

Detective Ann Jaroncyk cleared her throat. "Let's talk about how long you'd known the deceased, Beverly Montgomery." Her blond hair stretched into a severe bun, which matched an equally severe blazer and slacks. She tapped something into the iPad on the table between them.

"I met Bev at the Haverhill Farmers' Market last spring. She was the market manager."

"And her son was killed on your farm, correct?"

"He was." Cam decided to keep her answers as short as she could, in hopes of getting out of here before nightfall.

The detective checked her notes. "She threatened you with a gun on your property last June."

"Correct. I managed to take it away from her."

"And in the fall you removed her chickens?"

"The board of health planned to exterminate them. Bev hadn't been taking care of them. We—"

"Who is *we?*"

"Several volunteers. Alexandra and DJ. Anyway, we picked up the hens. The volunteers built a coop. The birds are healthy now on my farm." *So much for short answers.* Cam clasped her sweaty palms together in her hands.

"Mrs. Montgomery didn't like that plan."

"Yes. But those are all reasons Bev might have wanted to get rid of me, not me get rid of her. Right?"

"They are. But we need to ask you. She was also heard accusing you of stealing her customers."

"Right."

The detective waited. Cam waited. The detective remained silent. Cam decided to cave first, in the interest of getting out of there.

"Bev farmed traditionally. She grew the usual crops and didn't mind applying pesticides and herbicides. There are customers who want that. I grow the newer Asian greens and other unusual varieties. My farm is in the three-year process of becoming certified organic. If a few of her customers preferred my vegetables . . . Well, that's the free market."

"Now, about the produce you supplied. How did you handle it after the harvest?"

Cam frowned. "I put it in bins. I brought it over to the Moran Manor kitchen."

"Do you use chemical sprays? Preservatives of any kind?"

"No. I farm organically. Why would I do that?"

"How do you clean what you pick?"

"With water. Well, some of it. Pumpkins, squashes, potatoes don't get washed. It might lead to rot. I don't wash herbs, either. I just dust any dirt off. As I said, it's all organic."

"Where did you go when you left Moran Manor yesterday?"

"I returned to my farm."

"Anyone else there?"

"Nobody you could interview."

The detective raised her eyebrows.

"Sorry. I'm getting punchy. The only other beings on my farm are the hens and my cat, and I've never heard them speak English."

Detective Jaroncyk did not even crack a smile. "Did you stay on your property all evening?"

Uh-oh. Should she say she'd been with Pete? If he hadn't already informed them, this could get him in hot water. The detective watched Cam.

"I ate dinner out. With a friend."

"And the friend's name would be?"

The heck with him. She didn't need to protect him. "Pete Pappas."

"Would that be state police detective Pappas?" The detective glanced over at the uniformed officer sitting in the corner. They exchanged a look.

Cam nodded. Then remembered she'd been instructed to answer verbally for the recording. "It would."

"Did you spend the night at your house?"

"I did." Next, she'd ask if Cam had been alone. That would be easy to tell the truth about. It occurred to her that maybe she could barter information in return.

"So how did you figure out what killed Bev?" Cam asked. "Do you analyze stomach contents or something?"

"I'm asking the questions here." The detective noted something on the iPad. She stood. "That will be all. For now. We'd appreciate it if you stayed in town."

"I'll be here." Cam also stood, her rear end doing a little glory dance to be off the unforgiving chair. "I run a farm. It doesn't exactly allow for road trips or tropical vacations." Babbling again.

The uniformed officer, one Cam hadn't seen before, rose and ushered her to the door. Before she left, she heard the detective formally end the interview for the recording.

Cam hurried down the hall toward the outer door. The walls appeared freshly painted in institutional beige, an improvement from their battered condition last June. She paused at the hallway that led to the cells. Last time she'd visited here, Lucinda had been locked in one of them. Cam hoped she wouldn't be next.

Cam stopped by the Westbury Food Mart after she left the police station to pick up a few items. The warm air smelled delectably of fresh baked goods. She browsed the cracker selection in the small local grocery, searching for her favorite rice-flour-and-seed crisps.

"I told you not to touch." A thin woman slapped her son's hand off a package of cookies at the other end of the aisle. She wore a fashionably styled blue coat and a matching beret on shoulder-length blond hair, but dark patches under her eyes gave her a haunted appearance.

Cam watched the scene. The boy, who seemed about six, burst into tears. A somewhat older girl in a puffy pink coat punched the boy in the arm.

"Yeah, Mom said not to touch," she said in a taunting tone.

"Don't you be hitting him," the mother said. She slapped the girl's arm, hard.

"Well, *you* did." The girl turned her back and grabbed a bag of gingersnaps off the shelf.

"Put those back. Now." The mother raised her hand at the girl, who obeyed but glowered. The mother glanced down the aisle and caught sight of Cam. She lifted her chin and held Cam's gaze for a moment, then hustled the children toward the registers.

The girl had nailed it. Her mother was modeling behavior she told her children not to follow. Cam watched the children jostle each other while their mother paid for her purchases. A sadness dragged on her heart. As a teenager on one of her summer visits, she'd witnessed an even worse scene right here in the Food Mart. A father had rapped his little son's hand so hard, he broke it. Cam had resolved right then never to hit her own children, whenever she had some. Or assault anybody, for that matter. She knew parenting wasn't easy, but physical violence wasn't the solution to anybody's problems. Ellie's friend Vince had had his share of violence at home before he finally got free of his abusive father. He seemed to have overcome that trauma so far, at least according to Ellie.

Cam, watching three of the hens peck in their yard, shivered with her hands deep in her coat pockets. A biting wind sliced at her cheeks. An icy cloud blew over the sun, which already hung low in the sky. She thought about shutting the hens in early for the night. She checked her phone: barely three o'clock. The temperature was dropping fast. She hoped the girls wouldn't freeze inside the coop if the temperature kept dropping, but they seemed to be able to puff out their feathers to insulate themselves. Tiny birds, like chickadees and sparrows, lived outside all winter long, after all. She'd already covered the hoop-house beds, and depending on the temperature tomorrow, she might just leave them covered.

The crunching noise of tires came from the driveway on the other side of the barn. A door slammed, then footsteps approached. Cam's heart raced. She wasn't expecting anyone. She whirled in that direction.

"Wicked cold, isn't it?" a cheery voice called out.

Cam let out a breath. She greeted Alexandra and DJ when they came into view. Alexandra, a recent college graduate living with her parents while she figured out what came next in her life, was a committed locavore, an artist, a whiz at Web design, and lots more. DJ . . . Well, Cam didn't know much about his life. He seemed to be in his mid-twenties and was infinitely talented with animals, carpentry, and good cheer.

Alexandra waved a gloved hand, her flaxen braids trailing out from under a Nordic knit hat with pointed earflaps. Her other hand was linked with DJ's. His scruffy light-brown beard bore ice crystals near his mouth, and his blue eyes looked happy. He held a big bag of chicken feed on his shoulder.

"Thought we'd stop by and see if you need help with the girls." DJ surveyed the yard. "Everybody else inside?"

"The smart ones are," Cam said. "As you can see, it's only our dear, dim TopKnot and a couple of her friends who don't possess the sense to go in. Or the brains."

Alexandra gazed at Cam. "We heard Bev Montgomery died after eating your vegetables. That's bad."

News traveled fast in a small town. "It's bad, all right. But everybody at the residence ate the same dinner, so my produce didn't kill her, obviously. Or I hope it will become obvious to the police. They had me in there for an hour today, grilling me. I arrived home only a little while ago."

"That poor lady. Hey, picked you up another bag of organic

feed." DJ raised his eyebrows. "Dude, that stuff is expensive."

"I know," Cam said. "I'm losing money on the eggs, even charging six-fifty a dozen. I'm not sure offering organic eggs is worth it."

"I'll stick it inside the barn." He detached from Alexandra and carried the bag around the corner of the barn.

"So maybe Bev died from a heart attack." Alexandra frowned. "She was pretty old."

"I wish. And she wasn't that old, you know." Then Cam remembered herself a decade earlier, when she was Alexandra's age. A sixty-five-year-old woman seemed a lot more ancient then than one did now. "Anyway, she didn't have a heart attack. Someone murdered her." *Oops.* She probably shouldn't talk about what Pete had told her. Too late now.

DJ reappeared. "What did you say?"

"Someone apparently poisoned Bev Montgomery. Murdered her."

"Oh, Cam. Not again." Alexandra slung her arm around Cam's shoulder and squeezed. They were nearly the same height. "What's up with you and murderers?"

Cam rolled her eyes. "I'd be happy never to even hear about another murder, let alone one that seems to have a connection to me."

"That's totally bad news," DJ said.

"No kidding." Cam shivered again. "DJ, mind shooing those birdbrains inside? I need to get out of this wind. Can you both join me for a hot toddy in the house?"

They glanced at each other and seemed to exchange a silent message.

"Sure," Alexandra said.

DJ stepped into the enclosure and made clicking noises at the hens. Cam had called him the Chicken Whisperer when she'd first seen him do that in the fall. He seemed to be able to communicate with them in a way she couldn't. He convinced them to go in and latched the door behind them.

"You guys should take home a dozen eggs." Cam stepped into the barn and drew an egg carton out of the refrigerator.

Alexandra followed her. "Totally."

"The production is way down, of course, but I still collect about four dozen eggs a week."

Alexandra, carrying the eggs, and DJ followed Cam to the house. Once they were inside, Cam put on the teakettle and drew honey and cognac out of the cupboard.

"Have a seat," she said, waving at the table.

Alexandra pulled out a chair and sat.

Cam brought over a tin. "Oatmeal chocolate-chip cookies, anybody? They're not local, but I make them with whole-wheat flour, and they're relatively healthy."

DJ shrugged out of his green winter jacket, which sported a six-inch piece of duct tape covering a rip in one sleeve. He helped himself to a cookie and took a bite as he wandered around the room, examining the several pieces of art and the framed pictures decorating the walls. He popped the rest of the cookie in his mouth and picked up the mallets to a small wooden instrument that sat on a bookshelf in the living room. He tapped out a simple melody. The music carried a rich, round tone.

"Nice, isn't it?" Cam said. "My parents brought that from Lesotho."

"Does it have a special name?" Alexandra asked.

"It does, but I don't remember. It's some kind of xylophone."

After the teakettle whistled, Cam fixed three toddies with peppermint tea, honey, and lemon, and brought them to the table. She got the cognac and added it to the collection.

"Add your own poison." She grimaced. "Oh, that didn't sound good, did it?" She poured a couple of glugs of cognac into her mug and set the bottle in the middle of the table. "Anyway, I'm done working for the day." And she'd be alone tonight. Pete had to do the right thing.

DJ joined them at the table. The young man always seemed upbeat and competent and interested in all kinds of things. She could see why Alexandra wanted to spend time with him.

Alexandra poured a bit of cognac into her own mug and offered the bottle to DJ.

"No, thanks." He smiled. "I'm working on staying present these days."

Did that mean Cam wasn't present when she'd had a drink? Likely.

"I've been studying permaculture lately, Cam," DJ said. "You ought to look into it."

"A North Shore Permaculture Group contacted me about their Meetups, but I haven't actually met up with them yet. Give me the two-minute thumbnail on what permaculture is and why I should utilize it." Cam smiled at him.

"It's a design science to take sustainability to the next level. Water management, permanent companion planting, the no-till method developed into an art form." He smiled with an earnest look. "Seriously, we could do design work on your land in the spring if you're interested. I need to accumulate a boatload of hours for my certificate."

"Swales and berms. Berms and swales. That's all he talks about anymore." Alexandra nudged DJ affectionately and then folded her forearms on the table. "So, Cam, who do you think killed Bev?"

"That's the million-dollar question. The only person who would truly benefit would be her daughter, Ginger."

"Because she'd get the farm?" DJ asked.

"I expect so. Although she does have two brothers, come to think of it," Cam said. "She wants to develop the property, build houses, I heard, and Bev didn't want her to. She wanted to keep it farmland."

"Ginger would kill her own mother?" Alexandra widened her eyes.

"Let's hope not. She seems kind of difficult, and I saw her arguing with her mom. She does go over and play guitar for the residents at Moran Manor, which is a nice thing to do. She played for them even before Bev moved there."

DJ sipped his tea. He tapped the side of the mug. "I might be able to do a little snooping. My brother Eddie worked on that housing project over in Newburyport. The one Ginger Montgomery built. He might know something about her. I'll ask him tonight."

"Did you grow up here in town, DJ?"

He nodded.

"Do either of you know anything about Richard Broadhurst? My great-uncle said that he had an interest in acquiring Bev's farm so he could expand his orchard, and that she was negotiating with him about that."

"He's my friend's stepfather. Or was." Alexandra pulled a cell phone out of her pocket and thumbed it with both hands. "There. I texted her. I'll let you know what she says about him."

"Thanks, guys. The sooner the police find out who actually killed her, the sooner they'll stop harassing me about it." And the sooner she could see Pete again. As she sipped her own tea, she thought about whether she even wanted to keep spending time with Pete. He was absolutely right. Hanging out with a state cop wasn't going to be a smooth ride. It still smarted that he'd said he had to distance himself from her during the investigation. With any luck, it would be only another day or two before he tracked down the real murderer.

Her computer scientist brain knew it was logical and appropriate for Pete to disappear from her life in the interim. Her heart had other ideas.

Chapter 9

After Alexandra and DJ left, Cam had called Albert and had made arrangements to pick him up in an hour. Now they sat in a booth in the rear corner of the Westbury House of Pizza, the town's only restaurant. The Formica tables were worn but clean, and the Greeks who ran the place made a thin crust to die for.

"Thanks for springing me, Cameron." Albert sipped his glass of red wine. He waved at a couple who sat across the room.

Cam finished chewing her bite of pizza, with a piece of anchovy sparking a salty taste. "I didn't want to sit in the Moran dining room with you and have everybody stare at me."

"I didn't particularly want to make small talk in the dining room, either. I'm not in the best of spirits, with Beverly dead. May she rest in peace."

"I'm so sorry, Uncle Albert. I know you and she were friends." Cam reached across the table and squeezed his hand.

"I'll admit I've heard talk going around the place about poisoned produce. All hogwash, but still." He helped himself to a second slice from the platter in the middle of the table. "My, this is tasty. Good idea to order anchovies with the mushrooms and artichoke hearts. The usual fare at the Manor is never very interesting, don't you know. And I do love a good pizza."

"I wonder if the goat cheese on it is local?" she said and then laughed. "Listen to me. Those crazy locavores are starting to mess with my head."

"We can ask on our way out."

Cam sipped her wine. She frowned. "I imagine Jim Cooper is going to decide he doesn't want to contract with me for vegetables this summer, after all. But nobody else has gotten sick since the dinner, have they?"

Albert gazed at a nearby poster of the Parthenon for a moment. "I did hear tell of a lady not feeling well this morning, and Doc, my old fishing buddy, complained of stomach pains at lunch today. But you know, we're all a bunch of old farts. Residents are always grousing about one thing or another."

"I hope they'll both be fine. And that their ailments are totally unrelated to my dinner."

A man and four children brought tall soft drink cups to the booth behind Cam and Albert's and sat. Two boys facing Cam huddled over a small digital device, which emitted beeps as they played. A little girl kicked the base of the bench repeatedly, the bench that shared a back with Albert's.

"The police were about this morning. Collecting dishes and whatnot. Asking questions," Albert said. "They took over the library for their interviews. Strung up that yellow tape across the door to Beverly's room, just like on television."

Cam leaned toward Albert. "Did that upset people?" *Thunk. Thunk. Thunk.* The girl kicked with the regularity of a metronome.

Albert smiled. "It's the most excitement we've had there since I moved in. I wheeled by her room this morning. The door stood open, and I saw an officer actually dusting for fingerprints." He turned somber. "Don't mistake me. I am sorry about losing poor Beverly. But she's in a better place now. Her life here had always been tough. Now she's sitting in heaven, playing cards with my Marie, I daresay."

Cam smiled at the image. Then heard the *thunk, thunk, thunk* again. The father seemed oblivious to the noise. Cam wrestled her attention back to what had happened at Moran Manor. "Do you know who the police interviewed?"

"The cook. The director. Her caregiver, Oscar. He didn't like that at all, I can tell you."

The incoming-text tone sounded on Cam's phone. She pulled the phone out of her purse and glanced at it in her lap. The text was from Ellie.

Can u come over? Mom wants to talk. Police interviewd me today. Scary.

Cam glanced across at Albert, who gazed at her with pursed lips.

"You young people can't stay away from those wretched devices for anything. Why, in my day—"

Cam broke in. "It's Ellie." She relayed what the girl had said.

"Ah. Well, then," he said.

"I'm sorry. I shouldn't have interrupted our time together."

"Do you need to leave now?" Albert asked. He reached for her free hand and patted it with his.

She glanced at the wall clock, which read six thirty. "No. Let me tell her I'll be over in an hour." She tapped out the message and pressed SEND. Nearly instantly a K. C U soon popped up. She stashed the phone. The little girl climbed out of the booth, followed by her father. They walked together toward the pizza counter. The cessation of the noise from her snow boot–clad feet was like finally tweezing a splinter out of an inflamed finger.

"Ellie served in the dining room yesterday. I'm sorry she had to be questioned by the authorities, but perhaps she can assist the investigation," Albert said.

"Her mother must be terrified. After our horrible experience last June, I'm surprised she even let Ellie return to the farm. And she probably thought her daughter would be a lot safer with a collection of retirees." If Ellie had, in fact, seen anything significant, she could be in danger. Cam would get over to Ellie's as soon as she returned Albert to Moran Manor. Scary, indeed.

Cam sipped the cup of apple-cinnamon tea Ellie had made for her.

"My mom will be right out. Thanks for coming over, Cam."

Ellie perched, with her knees drawn up in front of her, on the arm of the sofa. Cam sat at the other end. The living room of the house felt light and uncluttered. Accents of turquoise abounded, so even in midwinter it felt like breaking waves and a sea breeze were somewhere nearby. A hardwood floor gleamed. Ellie herself didn't look as well put together. Her fine blond hair lay limp around her shoulders, and she wore a Bruins sweatshirt with frayed cuffs and smudges of paint on the front. Mostly her eyes gave away her worry.

"Are you all right?" Cam had almost never seen the girl when energy and fun didn't sparkle off her.

"I guess." She shook her head. "This afternoon, though, it was, like—"

"Thank you for stopping by." A woman wheeled herself into the room and positioned her wheelchair so that she was facing Cam. She extended a hand. "I'm Myrna."

"So nice to meet you at last." Cam shook Myrna's small hand, which felt remarkably cold to the touch. "You have an awesome daughter." She smiled, gesturing at Ellie.

"Thank you. I have to agree." Myrna returned the smile and wheeled over next to her daughter. She patted Ellie's knee, leaving her hand on it. The streaks of white in Myrna's short dark hair seemed premature, and smudges under her eyes spoke of pain.

"My husband—well, you know David, of course—is out of town," she continued. "When that detective, a Mr. Pappas, wanted to talk to Ellie, I insisted he come here so I could be present." She spoke slowly, forming the words with difficulty.

Ellie had told Cam the previous summer that her mother had multiple sclerosis. Cam had seen Myrna only once before, in their car when Ellie's father picked her up at the farm after one of the girl's volunteer stints. Ellie had been working on her Locavore badge for the Girl Scouts and had helped out with farm chores on a regular basis. Cam caught sight of the purple skin on Myrna's feet, which were clad in slip-on sandals.

"Mommy, that's the law, anyway." Ellie spoke with the exasperation of any teen daughter toward her mother. "He said you had to be present because I'm underage."

"And how did the conversation go?" Cam asked. "Ellie, you said in your message that you were scared."

Ellie nodded. "Sort of. I mean—"

Myrna broke in. "He kept asking Eleanor if she'd seen anyone near the food trays who shouldn't have been there. He meant, did she see the murderer?"

Though she was dying to know what, in fact, Ellie had seen, Cam didn't want to traumatize her by having her answer difficult questions twice in one day. Cam wasn't supposed to be poking her nose into the case, anyway, although she'd already blown that by talking about it with Alexandra and DJ. Except that Ellie had asked for her help. And should she tell them that Pete was actually a sweet person and was only doing his job? She waited instead.

"I just told him what I did. It's what I do every time I serve. I take residents' orders. They don't have to take the daily special. Which yesterday was your meal, Cam. They also get a choice of the regular, like, stuff on the menu. A hamburger, a piece of quiche, a tuna sandwich. Whatever. Then I take the order in to Rosemary and sometimes to another helper, and when it's ready, I bring it out. It's totally not very complicated."

"Did Bev eat in the dining room?"

"No way. She's been taking her meals in her room. She's kind of . . . I mean, she *was* kind of cranky."

"You told the detective the only people in the kitchen were the cook and that caregiver. . . . What was his name, honey?" Myrna glanced at Ellie.

"Oscar was helping out. You met him, Cam, right? And he delivered all the room meals. So it was us three, plus the other two kids who do what I do. Ray and this other kid, Sean."

"Ray?" Myrna asked. "Who is he?"

"It's a she, Mom." Ellie shot a look at the ceiling and then back at her mother. "It's just what we call her. Her real name is Raya, but she hates that. Her parents are subscribers to your CSA, Cam. Or they were last summer."

"They must be Neela and Sunil." Cam nodded. "I met Ray on Saturday. She was pushing Felicity's father in a wheelchair."

"Yeah, that's her. Anyway, Mr. Pappas kept asking me the same questions over and over. Like, did Mrs. Montgomery get the special meal? Who touched her plate? Did I see anybody in the hallway? Did I go to her room?"

"He questioned her relentlessly." Myrna's voice rose.

"They questioned me today, too, except I had to go to the station," Cam said.

"It wasn't that bad, Mommy. But I kept telling him the same answers. The room meals always get the special. Rosemary put the food on the plate, and Oscar put the plate on the tray, and the tray on that big cart. And I had too much to do to bring food to Mrs. Montgomery's room. A lot of residents have guests on Sunday night. It's a super-busy night to serve."

"I hope you didn't think the detective suspected you of poisoning Bev's meal, Ellie," Cam said.

"No. But just knowing that somebody could actually do that—that's the scary part. And what if they, like, thought I saw them do it or something?" She hugged herself.

Myrna stroked Ellie's arm. "You're not going back there until this issue is solved. Until they put the killer behind bars."

"Mom. It's my job."

"Eleanor, you are fourteen."

"I'll be fifteen next month." Ellie stood and stuck her hands in her pockets. "I'm not a baby."

"I spoke to your father about it. He agrees. That place will find someone else to do your work." Myrna lowered her voice. "You're my only child. If something were to happen to you—"

"I have to do my homework. See you, Cam." Ellie stomped out of the room.

"I don't know what's come over her the past few months." Myrna's gaze followed Ellie's departure. "She used to be so sweet."

"That tends to happen with teenagers. I know I got pretty difficult for a few years there."

"I suppose. She's both my eldest and my youngest. It's tough." Myrna cocked her head and gazed at Cam. "All I want to do is keep her safe."

As Cam drove home, she bet that look of Myrna's had referred to the barn fire she and Ellie had barely survived the previous June. Ellie's employment at Moran Manor didn't have anything to do with the murder. Cam wanted the girl to stay safe, too. She thought her parents' prohibition against returning to work until the killer had been apprehended was wise, even if Ellie didn't much like it.

Interesting that Oscar had been working in the kitchen and had delivered the meal. He certainly had the means to add poison to Bev's portion. But why would he?

As she locked the house door behind her, her cell phone rang. She greeted Lucinda on the other end.

"Hey, Cam. I got a great gig for you." Lucinda sounded breathless. "Tomorrow night."

"Slow down a little. What kind of gig?" Cam reached down to pet Preston. He turned his head up, and he headed for his dry food dish, his expression asking, as always, that he be stroked while he ate. She obliged, listening to Lucinda at the same time.

"It's a forum with a guy from the company that makes the herbicide that has glyphosate in it, that G-Phos we were talking about. The event is kind of like a debate. Remember, I told you about it?"

"Sort of."

"A representative from an organic seed company was going to come, but he broke his leg. Can you do it?" Lucinda asked.

"Wait. What?" Cam straightened. "Me? Debate a giant agrochemical company? I'm only a farmer. And a beginner, at that."

"But you're smart. You decided to farm organic because you believe in it, right?"

"Sure, but—"

"It's in the library at my school. Lots of people will be there. You have to do it."

"Aren't there any more experienced organic farmers to ask?"

"I called Zeke up in Londonderry, but his mother is ill and he has to go out of town."

Cam sighed. "I suppose I'll do it. The guy will eat me alive, though."

"Cool. I'll give you each fifteen minutes to do a presentation, and then you can talk with each other. I'm going to moderate. I'll e-mail directions. It starts at seven, so come around six thirty. And bring your farm brochures. Consider it a marketing opportunity."

Cam said good-bye and disconnected. *Sheesh*. She hated public speaking. She disliked having to defend her views. She avoided conflict at all cost. And tomorrow night would involve all of those. She'd better muster her facts tonight. And eight thirty had already come and gone.

She headed for her desk in the corner of the living room, fired up the computer, and opened a browser. Her home page opened to Weather.com, a farmer's best friend. Or worst. She groaned. A Montreal Express would approach the region tonight and tomorrow. That meant arctic air was heading their way straight down from Canada. The old farmhouse was poorly insulated, and frigid air plus wind meant she'd be using a lot of heating oil this month. And getting mighty cold fingers while she worked.

She navigated to the Web site of the Massachusetts chapter of the Northeast Organic Farming Association. NOFA had a good set of links to information about growing organically. When she saw the NOFA Organic Principles and Practices Handbook series, she remembered she'd bought it for her Kindle the previous winter, when she'd set herself to learning as much about organic growing practices as she could. She located the device and opened *Growing Healthy Vegetable Crops*. She'd start there.

She was typing notes into slides for the forum when the old rotary phone rang on the corner of the kitchen counter. She barely reached it by the tenth and last ring. Almost nobody but Albert called her on that number. Sure enough, his voice sounded on the other end.

"Bad news over here." His tone was grim.

"What is it? Are you all right?"

"I am. But another resident has died. A Miss Lacey."

The death couldn't be related to Bev's. "That's terrible."

"Everybody's saying it was poison again." Albert cleared his throat.

"Who's everybody?"

"The residents. Several of the caregivers."

"Not the police?"

"You know the authorities don't tell us what they are thinking. But the lady who died was the one who felt sick earlier in the day, the one I told you about."

"I'm so sorry to hear that." Cam cocked her head. "Did she have any connection with Bev?"

"I don't rightly know. If she didn't and someone murdered her, too, perhaps the killer is someone who doesn't like old folks. We're all getting a little nervous over here, I can tell you."

"Don't worry, Uncle Albert. I'm sure she died of natural causes. And the police are bound to find Bev's killer soon. I'll come over for a visit tomorrow, and we can talk more. All right?"

"I'd like that. Come at eleven. I'll be in my room."

After Cam hung up the phone, she stood and stared at it. No way were these deaths related. Or maybe they were. If so, was it someone targeting senior citizens, as Albert had said? *Yikes.* That would mean he could be in danger, too. No wonder he was nervous.

Or maybe it was somebody trying to frame Cam herself. Again, since the woman had eaten the same dinner Bev had.

Double yikes. She couldn't even imagine who disliked her enough to do that. Pete had better get on the stick and nail this guy before anybody else died.

She checked to make sure the door was locked and bolted. And then checked it again.

Chapter 10

"They ought to change this weather's name from the Montreal Express to the North Pole Express," Cam said out loud, rubbing her gloved hands together. Simply walking from the house to the chicken coop at seven the next morning chilled her through and through. She opened the small door to the chicken coop, but the hens were smart enough to stay puffed up inside. She slid the rubber flap over the opening so they could get outside if they wanted to. The flap, which DJ had rigged up in the fall, resembled a cat door, and it kept much of the warmer inside air inside.

She made her way into the hoop house and latched the door firmly behind her. The wind whipped the plastic covering the high tunnel and whistled through a crack where the door met the jamb. She wished it had a human-sized rubber flap to keep the cold air a little farther at bay. DJ seemed to be able to create anything. She'd have to ask him about making one. In the meantime she could hang a woolen blanket over the entrance.

The thermometer above the worm bins read forty-five. Not too bad, considering that the sun hadn't yet risen. Adding worms was one of the smarter things she'd done after she'd read an article about vermiculture in the fall issue of the *Natural Farmer.* DJ and Alexandra had built the bins, now arrayed along the north side of the hoop house. The busy worms added warmth to the hoop house. They blocked part of the cold from the side that received little direct sunlight. And, of course, all their digesting and excreting created high-quality compost. Last winter the outside compost bins had frozen solid, and whatever farm or kitchen waste she'd added had to wait until spring to start breaking down. Now she was creating organic material to nurture the soil all winter long, with the help of hundreds of her wriggly little friends.

She pulled out her phone and snapped several photographs of the bins. She stuck a small shovel in one bin and stirred, taking a close-up shot quickly while the worms were still on top of the rich black soil. She would add it to her presentation for tonight. And to the farm's Web site.

The air inside the hoop house warmed to fifty on still days, but odds were it wouldn't reach that today. As long as the beds didn't actually freeze, she could cut greens to sell. She walked the length of the hoop house. She groaned when she got to the beds at the far end, where the temperature dropped even more. She knelt and felt the overly crisp leaves of a head of Red Sails. An entire bed of lettuce had frozen, despite the row cover. The bed sat next to the eastern end wall and simply didn't get enough warmth. The forecast had been for temperatures dropping throughout the day again. She would definitely leave the cover on today and hoped she didn't lose any more crops. At least she'd invested in the thicker fabric for the winter temperatures.

As she worked, Albert's words about the second death at the assisted-living residence filled her head. His approach to life was usually even-keeled, but he'd sounded uncharacteristically worried last evening. Cam wished she could talk about the case with Pete. When one of her customers had been killed in the fall, he'd asked her to keep her eyes and ears open in the community. Obviously, he couldn't work with a suspect, even informally. But that he might even entertain the possibility of her being capable of murder made her question who he really was. And if her feelings were no longer to be trusted.

Cam greeted the Moran Manor receptionist and glanced at the clock on the wall behind her. Eleven. She jotted the time next to her name in the sign-in book and added Albert's name as the person she planned to visit. A notice had been posted in a clear holder on the desk, next to the book.

BEVERLY MONTGOMERY MEMORIAL SERVICE. WEDNESDAY, ELEVEN O'CLOCK, ONEONTA CONGREGATIONAL CHURCH. ALL WELCOME.

Cam straightened. "A memorial service and not a funeral?" she asked the woman behind the desk.

"Exactly." She leaned toward Cam and whispered, "The children wanted the service right away, but the police won't release the body yet." She raised her eyebrows and appeared almost delighted at the prospect, likely the stuff of television thrillers for her.

"They need to do their work." Cam turned toward the central stairway. She could give Uncle Albert a ride to the service. A woman leaning on a red walker and a taller one with a cap of blue-tinted white hair stopped in their tracks in front of her.

The woman with the walker grabbed her companion's arm. "That's the murderer right there," she said in a loud whisper. She pointed at Cam.

The tall one said something in her ear. They reversed direction and made their way down the hallway. The tall woman glanced behind her.

No, I won't follow you, lady. What could Cam do? Wear a button that read I AM NOT A MURDERER? She'd stepped onto the first stair when someone called her name.

"Ms. Flaherty? Could I have a word?" Jim Cooper stood in front of his office door. He motioned her toward him.

Cam greeted him when she neared the office.

"Please come in." He held out his arm to usher her into the room, then shut the door behind them.

She looked around. Some kind of award for Moran Manor hung on the wall, next to a framed picture of Jim beaming as he shook hands with their state representative, a Republican from the next town over. The desk held only a computer monitor, a pad of paper with nothing written on it, and a pen lined up neatly next to it. A long leather sofa lined one wall, and two armless chairs faced the desk.

"How did the residents like the dinner I provided?" Cam asked. She stood with her hands in her coat pockets. He hadn't asked her to sit.

"That's what I wanted to talk with you about. We won't be needing you to provide produce for us in the summer." He lifted his chin.

"People didn't like it? My great-uncle said the meal was delicious." Cam frowned.

He cleared his throat. "It's this matter of the deaths. Mrs. Montgomery's and now Miss Lacey's. They both ate your food."

"Do you believe my food killed those women?"

"Well, no, of course not." He pasted a smile on his face and erased it just as quickly. "That is, the police are investigating. It's our residents, you know. They tend to be concerned, and we simply can't have any question of . . . you see—" He trailed off, apparently hoping she would fill in the gaps.

"I don't see. And I'm sorry you were unhappy with what I provided. If you change your mind, please let me know." Cam left the office as fast as it felt safe. It wouldn't be a good idea to lose her temper with Jim. Maybe he'd change his mind once the murder was solved. Or murders.

She grumbled under her breath while she climbed the stairs. "If my vegetables killed those ladies, how come nobody else got sick?"

On the landing, a small table displayed two framed pictures. A red rose in a bud vase sat in front of each picture. An elderly woman with a kindly smile looked out of one. That must be Miss Lacey. Bev Montgomery's face gazed out of the other. Pearls encircled her neck, and her hair had been styled. Cam had noticed her dressed up only once, at the wake for Bev's son, Mike, last June. Bev hadn't been at all happy to see her at the time.

"Poor Bev," Cam said softly and then turned. "Pete," she gasped, startled. Pete, in a tie and sport coat, stood a couple of feet away.

"Sorry. I didn't mean to alarm you." He started to extend an arm toward her. Before it reached her, he let it drop back by his side.

"Don't sneak up on me like that." She patted her chest. "Are you here investigating?"

He nodded slowly. Lines pulled down from the corners of his eyes.

"How's it going?" Cam stuck her hands in her pockets again. And then realized how warm she felt with her coat on. She slid out of it and draped it over one arm.

"Not much progress, I'm afraid."

"What about this Miss Lacey? Did Bev's murderer kill her, as well?"

He glanced up and down the hall, but nobody stood nearby. "We're waiting on lab results. Can't say at this point."

"A woman downstairs called *me* the murderer when I came in. Nice."

"Sorry about that." He sighed.

"Are you? Aren't I still a suspect?" Cam was being neither nice nor tactful, but she didn't possess the energy to try. And was starting not to care.

"Cameron—" He held out both palms.

"Oh, and the director said he wouldn't buy my vegetables next summer. Because it would upset the residents or something. Pete, you guys have to find the real killer. And soon."

He opened his mouth and then shut it again. He jiggled change in his pocket. "We're doing the best we can. And you know I can't talk about it with you. Take care of yourself, all right?" He walked with a heavy step down the stairs.

She watched him go. He did not glance behind him. She walked slowly toward Albert's room, feeling both somber and agitated. The walls were decorated with paintings of musical scenes, along with flat sculptures of instruments. A metal cutout of a violin hung at a jaunty angle next to a Degas painting of an orchestra in action. At a junction of two outer walls, Cam paused. A hairline crack next to the corner ran from floor to ceiling. She frowned. The building seemed fairly new. It shouldn't have cracks in it already.

She knocked on Albert's door, but he didn't answer. *Funny.* He said he'd be here at this time. She opened the door a crack and called. When he still didn't answer, she pushed the door open. She'd make sure he hadn't gone into the bathroom, and then she'd go search for him in the common room.

The bathroom door stood ajar. He wasn't in there. She stepped farther into the main room. She didn't see him, but she spied his red plaid lap blanket in a heap on the floor near the foot of his bed. It would be nicer for him to come back and find it folded on his chair. She picked it up and cried out. It had covered Albert's feet. He lay prone on the floor on the far side of the bed.

He wasn't moving.

Chapter 11

In two more steps Cam knelt at his side. She was about to place her hand on his neck to check for a pulse when he shifted slightly and moaned. His eyes remained closed.

"Thank God you're alive." She looked frantically near the head of the bed. Where was the emergency buzzer? There, on the wall. She reached up and slapped the round red button. Then hit it again two more times.

She glanced back at Albert. She didn't see blood anywhere. He must have passed out and hit the floor. Or maybe he'd been resting and had fallen out of bed. But would he have landed on his back if he'd fallen out of bed?

Oscar rushed into the room, followed by a woman in a blue smock-like jacket with a stethoscope around her neck.

Cam stood. "I found him here on the floor only a minute ago. He's breathing, but he isn't conscious." She stepped out of their way, her heart thudding, her throat thick. She almost tripped on one of Albert's crutches, which lay half hidden under the bed.

Oscar turned away and spoke into a kind of two-way radio.

"I'm the facility's nurse." The woman took Cam's place, kneeling. She listened to Albert's heart. She pried an eyelid open and shined a little flashlight in his eye. She measured his pulse. She gazed up at Cam.

"His vitals aren't bad. We'll get him to the hospital to be checked out. I can't tell right now if he had a stroke or what. Until he wakes up." She glanced around and picked up the blanket. She stretched it over him, then leaned in close to his ear.

"Mr. St. Pierre? Albert. Can you hear me?" She gently patted his cheek.

Albert didn't move.

The nurse sat back on her heels and then stood in a fluid motion. "You sit there and talk to him until the EMTs arrive," she said to Cam.

Cam knelt by his side again. "Uncle Albert. It's me, Cammy. Can you hear me?" She found his hand under the blanket and squeezed. "Uncle Albert?"

His eyelids fluttered open.

"I think he's waking up." Cam glanced at the nurse to make sure she'd seen Albert's open eyes.

The nurse smiled and nodded. Cam looked back at Albert.

"It's okay. You'll be fine." Cam tried to keep the tremble out of her voice. "You had a fall."

Albert's eyes widened. He moved his head a little from one side to the other. He moaned and shut his eyes again.

"What's going on in here?" Pete Pappas stood behind the woman. "I heard the alarm."

"I found Albert lying here," Cam said. "He just woke up a little."

"He must have fallen," the nurse said to Pete. "His pulse and blood pressure are stable, though. It doesn't appear to be a cardiac event."

Pete frowned, with hands on hips. "I'm glad."

Two EMTs strode into the room. One carried a large red bag. "Mr. St. Pierre?" asked the female EMT.

The nurse nodded.

"Wait a minute," Pete said. He held one palm face out and extended his ID with his other hand. "State police detective Pappas. This could be a crime scene. We've had two unattended deaths here in the last forty-eight hours. This might be an attempted murder."

The male EMT whistled under his breath. "How do we proceed? You realize we need to get this gentleman to the hospital stat."

Pete nodded. "Try not to touch anything you don't have to. That goes for all of you." He included Oscar and Cam in his gaze.

The nurse briefed them on Albert's condition even as the female EMT gave Cam a look that sent her scrambling to her feet. She hurried out of their way and stood near the bathroom door on the other side of the room. The other EMT repeated the nurse's steps of assessing Albert's health.

"We'll have him out of here in a minute," the female EMT said on her way out of the room. "The gurney is in the hall."

"As soon as you can, please assess any wounds on him, especially on his head," Pete said. "I'll be over to talk to the doctors. Are you taking him to Anna Jaques?"

"Yes," the female EMT said.

"Add a note to his chart that he might have been attacked."

"Got it." The EMT nodded.

A flurry of activity ensued, ending with Albert, strapped to a gurney, being wheeled out of the room.

"I'll see you over there, Uncle Albert," Cam called.

He nodded his head almost imperceptibly. Oscar and the nurse followed the others out of the room, leaving Cam and Pete alone.

"He's in good hands," Pete said. He took two steps to stand in front of her. "I'm sorry that happened." He glanced behind him. They were alone in the room. He opened his arms to Cam.

She let him wrap her in his care. A sob escaped her before she choked it back. The image of someone whacking Albert over the head filled her brain. She stepped away and wiped her cheek of tears.

"Do you really think someone attacked him?" she asked.

"It's possible. Perhaps he saw who poisoned Bev Montgomery. Or had been asking too many questions. Which is why I don't want you getting all detective on me. You could be in danger, as well."

She nodded slowly. "When he opened his eyes, I told him he'd fallen. He looked a little alarmed and tried to shake his head. He might have been saying no."

"Interesting." His eyes narrowed.

"I'm headed over to Anna Jaques." Cam grabbed her bag from where she'd dropped it on the floor.

"Good. Be careful." Pete turned away and spoke into his cell phone, asking for a crime scene team.

The television in the emergency department waiting room at the hospital blared some inane talk show. The woman seated next to Cam coughed again, a deep, thick rattle that sounded infectious. Cam rose and moved to a chair in the hallway, on the way dosing up her hands with sanitizer from a dispenser on the wall. The last thing she needed was to get sick. She could still see the door to the reception area from here.

She'd been waiting for news for an hour. They wouldn't let her go in to see Albert yet, even though she was his only relative anywhere nearby. Her stomach grumbled. She checked her phone, which read almost one o'clock. She hadn't eaten since seven that morning. But she didn't plan to go in search of the cafeteria, in case she missed the doctor.

She wanted to see Albert so badly, it ached. That look he'd given her in his room. Did he try to tell her he had not fallen? Which would mean Pete's suspicions about an attack might be true. And then Pete's embrace . . . What did that mean? It had to be because his feelings for her hadn't changed. He needed to follow regulations about not consorting with a person of interest. But how could he turn his emotions off and on so easily? She was incapable of doing that.

As she waited, the movie of her finding Albert on the floor replayed in her head. Funny that Oscar had arrived first. He wasn't even one of Albert's care providers. He must have been tending to one of his own residents.

A white-coated woman about Cam's age came through the door. "Cameron Flaherty?" She carried a tablet device.

Cam stood. The woman walked over to her. Her coat read DR. FUJITA. Her eyes and shiny black hair matched her name. "You are Albert St. Pierre's great-niece?" She extended her hand.

Cam nodded as she shook hands. "You're the doctor who saw me after my accident last fall, aren't you?"

The doctor cocked her head. "Mild concussion? That's right. No lingering effects?"

"No. How's my uncle?" She clasped her hands behind her so they wouldn't tremble.

"He hit his head hard on something. He did wake up for a while, which is a very good sign, but we need to admit him. He seems basically healthy, although the hospital record indicates a history with diabetes."

"That's why he lost his foot. But he's been very careful with his diet, and he swims for exercise."

97

"Any history of heart disease, heart attacks, angina, that kind of thing? That you know of?"

"I don't believe so."

"Good." The doctor frowned and checked something on her tablet. "There's a note in his chart about a possible assault. Do you know anything about that?"

"Not really." Cam paused, then decided not to mention Albert's head shaking. "The state police are investigating a murder, possibly two, at the facility where he lives, though. I'm sure they'll contact you."

"You can visit him for a minute before we take him for more tests, but you should know he is sedated."

"Are you the doctor who will be in charge of him?"

"I am. Give me your cell phone number. I'll call you as soon as he's in his room. It could be a while, though."

Cam scrabbled in her bag, eventually finding one of the farm's business cards, which bore her cell number, along with the street address and the address of the Web site.

Dr. Fujita thanked her. "Don't worry. We'll take good care of him." She reached out and patted Cam on the arm. "Follow me."

A minute later Cam stood in a bay, at Albert's side. He wore a blue-print johnny, a white blanket covering him to the chest. Tubing and cables connected him to an IV bag and several machines that blipped and ticked. The fluorescent lights shaded his skin a tinge of green that echoed the walls, and the air nicked her nose with the sharp tinge of disinfectant. His near hand lay flat, the age spots more visible than ever. She held it and squeezed. She leaned down and brushed her lips across his forehead.

"Uncle Albert, you're going to make it. We have a dinner date, don't forget." Her throat constricted. She could barely say those last, most important words. "I love you."

A muscular male nurse hurried in. "You need to leave now. I'm taking him for tests."

She slid around him toward the opening to the central area.

The nurse lowered the guardrail on one side of the bed and busied himself with tubing and settings.

Cam blew Albert a kiss and then wandered with blurry vision toward the exit, one hand over her mouth, as if that would keep her anguish from spilling out.

Chapter 12

After she arrived home twenty minutes later, Cam felt like she moved in slow motion, as if she were walking underwater. She fixed herself a sandwich, poured a glass of milk, sat at the table. While she ate, her mind stayed with Albert and with all the questions arising. She couldn't help at the hospital, but she didn't want to be at home, either. She ate slowly. Preston reared up and rubbed against her knee, then purred as she petted him with her free hand.

She moved to the desk and started the computer. Usually, if she wrote things down, they became more clear. Her mind worked best when she could see a problem in front of her. This particular set of problems wouldn't be solved with the logic statements of a computer language, but at least if she listed everything she knew, she could examine it all in one place.

She opened a file and named it "The Moran Affair." She typed, "Did someone hit Albert on the head?" She typed, "He didn't have any enemies. Had he seen something suspicious around the residence and asked the wrong person questions? He seemed nervous after Miss Lacey's death."

She added lines for Bev's death. And for Bev's difficult relationships with Ginger, Oscar, and Frank. She typed, "What was the poison that killed her? How had the police or the medical examiner or Pete even thought to test for a poison?" Before this morning she could have called Pete and asked him, but that door was closed for now. She wiggled her cold toes in her slippers, then glanced up to see the curtains stirring as cold air seeped in through the leaky windows.

She included what Ellie'd said about Oscar working in the kitchen. Cam didn't know a thing about poor Miss Lacey, but she added a line for her death, as well. Next time she went over to Moran Manor, she'd ask around, see if the deceased woman had shared any friends with Bev, or enemies, for that matter. She saved the file. Sure enough, getting everything down in black and white had calmed her nerves. Opening a browser, she navigated over to the farm Web page. Someone had left a comment on the page titled "Community." She peered at it.

"Are the eggs you sell from vegetarian chickens?"

"As if," Cam said aloud and began to type a reply. She'd discussed this issue with DJ in the fall, anticipating this moment.

"Chickens are omnivores. Our free-range birds feed outside all day in their natural habitat, which includes worms, bugs, and insects. Another farm might confine their hens and give them only nonanimal feed, but not this one."

Her phone buzzed. She posted the comment and then connected the call. Lucinda spoke.

"You all set for tonight, *fazendeira?*"

"Tonight?"

"The forum. At my school's library."

Cam swore. "Um, sure, all set."

"You don't sound that sure."

Cam filled her in on Albert's situation. "But it appears he'll probably be okay. And I did a bit of preparation for the forum last night. So yeah, I'll be ready." *I hope.*

"Wow. Well, give him a hug from me. I like that old guy. He's a class act."

Cam said she would. She got directions to the school from Lucinda and disconnected. Then groaned. The forum. The last place she wanted to be tonight. But a commitment remained a commitment.

She checked the clock on the monitor. Two thirty. She'd better spend more time preparing, checking her research, finishing her slide presentation. She would swing by the hospital on her way and visit with Albert, or at least sit with him if he was asleep. She'd need to leave at around five to fit all that in and still get to the school early. Make it four thirty. She hated being late.

Shivering a little, she shoved her chair away and went to check the thermostat. She'd set the room temperature to seventy, but with the frigid wind outside, the old boiler in the basement couldn't keep up. Even though the thermostat read sixty-six in the room, the air felt colder than that. She threw on a heavy wool sweater and wrapped a scarf around her neck. And then lit the burner under the teakettle.

On her way back to the computer, she checked her digital indoor-outdoor thermometer. No wonder her boiler couldn't keep up. The display on the device read five degrees. Good thing she'd kept all the beds in the hoop house covered.

Her phone buzzed again. Felicity was on the other end.

"Cam, I heard about Albert. Is he going to be all right?"

"That's what they say. They are admitting him to Anna Jaques, but he doesn't need surgery, and it didn't appear to be a heart attack."

"Someone told me he fell in his room. Did he have a stroke? Or did he just trip?"

"I don't know. They're doing more tests." She kept quiet about her, and Pete's, suspicions of someone striking Albert.

"Well, I hope he heals soon."

"Thanks. I'll tell him when I go back over there," Cam said. The teakettle started to whistle.

"I also wanted to let you know that my father keeps talking about something he saw. As you know, he has dementia. And he often doesn't make a bit of sense. But he says he saw Bev's killer."

"Really?" Cam felt a whoosh of excitement. "Who did he see?" The kettle split the air with its needle of urgency. Cam let it go. She moved into the far corner of the living room.

"That's the part I can't get out of him." Felicity sighed. "I wondered if you'd stop by and see him next time you're around. He seemed to like you a lot the other day. Perhaps a fresh face would prod his memory. What's that sound, Cam?"

"The teakettle is boiling. Cover your ear. I'm going to go turn the burner off." Cam dashed into the kitchen, where steam raced angrily from the cherry-red kettle's spout toward the ceiling. She turned the burner off. "Sorry about that. Anyway, I'd be happy to stop by and see your dad. But I may not get over until Albert is released from the hospital. Which I hope will be soon. You should let Detective Pappas know, too."

"Good idea. I'll call the station," Felicity said. "Let me know when you'll be by, and I'll meet you there to talk to Dad."

"Will do. Listen, I think it's best that you don't tell anybody else that your father thinks he saw the killer," Cam said. "We wouldn't want anything to happen to him."

"Yikes. I never thought of that. What a terrifying prospect. Somebody stalking Dad. He's nearly helpless."

Cam squeezed her eyes shut in a grimace. She'd never gotten the hang of being tactful. "Don't worry. I shouldn't even have mentioned that. I'm sure he's fine."

"I hope so." Felicity's voice quavered. "I know he's losing his mind, but I still love him dearly."

After they said good-bye and Cam disconnected, she said aloud, "Nice move, Flaherty. Now Felicity is scared, as well. When will I learn?"

She fixed herself that cup of tea, since she'd gone to all the trouble to blow out a few auditory nerve cells, and brought it to the desk. She sat and stared at her monitor for a moment. Then she typed a line that read, "Nicholas Slavin saw Bev's killer?"

She checked the wall clock. Four fifteen. She glanced in the mirror one more time. Her hair, which was longer than she liked to wear it, curled around her ears. During the warmer months she sported a short cut that needed little care. But during a winter like this one, having longer hair made her head seem warmer, even if it wasn't. She wore a power outfit from her previous career, a tailored black jacket over a scoop-necked green sweater and a gray wool skirt that fell just below her knees. If she planned to butt heads with the agrochemical industry, she wanted to feel as powerful as possible. Flat knee-high black boots would keep her legs warm, and they actually had a decent tread on them for navigating icy pathways.

She checked her bag and added plenty of farm brochures and business cards. She grabbed a granola bar and a packet of almonds, which would have to take the place of dinner. Time to hit the road for the hospital and then the academy. She bundled herself in her good coat and beret. Picking up her scarf, she spied an empty egg carton on the table.

No. She'd forgotten all about the hens. She swore and grabbed her bag. On her way to the coop, she dumped the bag in the truck and strode around the corner of the barn. The hen yard appeared empty, so at least they'd had the sense to huddle inside. Then she saw TopKnot standing at the top of the ramp.

"You goofy chicken. Get in there where it's warm." Cam made her way into the enclosure and made shooing gestures. "Get out of this cold."

The hen didn't move. Cam walked closer. She reached out a hand, and TopKnot still didn't budge. Cam touched her, and the bird toppled over onto the ground.

She lifted the hen in her gloved hands. The poor girl was frozen. She blew on her face. The red beads of her eyes were filmy. Cam wondered how to check for a chicken's heartbeat. She carried her into the barn and set her on the hood of the truck. She pulled off one glove and tried to feel the chicken's skin under her feathers. But TopKnot seemed cold through and through.

"You stupid, sweet bird." Cam had loved watching her antics over the months since she'd acquired the hens. She kicked herself for not checking on the birds earlier. She found a plastic bag, wrapped TopKnot in it, and laid her in the chest freezer. She'd figure out what to do with her later. She pulled her glove on again and headed out to the coop, hoping the rest of the hens were alive. She opened the people-sized door and checked it out. The air felt a lot warmer in there than outside, and the hens were puffed up and clustered in one corner. They'd be all right. She left the incandescent bulb on for the bit of heat it provided and latched the door. She also closed the solid door over the rubber flap to the small entrance. If she'd done it earlier, TopKnot would still be alive. *Damn.*

Twenty minutes later she stood at Albert's bedside. He looked better than he had earlier in the day, with color in his cheeks, although his eyes were still closed. And he seemed to be attached to fewer devices. The one that displayed a green waveform on a wall-mounted monitor beeped at a reassuringly regular pace. Cam stroked the back of Albert's hand. Its warmth also reassured her. After a minute, his hand turned under hers until they were palm to palm. He squeezed softly.

"Uncle Albert, it's me, Cam."

His eyelids opened a crack and then more. The edge of his mouth tilted into the shadow of a smile.

"You look much better." She touched his cheek.

He nodded a little. He murmured something Cam couldn't make out.

She leaned down. "What did you say?"

"Quite the accommodations."

"Are you comfortable?"

"Pretty much." He closed his eyes. "But the party's too loud."

Cam frowned. "Right," she said, having no idea what party he was talking about. Now didn't seem like the time to ask, though.

"I'm going to let you rest. I'll be back tomorrow. Love you." She patted his hand and kissed his forehead. He raised his hand slightly and kept the faint smile on his face.

On her way to the elevator, once again with tears threatening to spill onto her cheeks, Cam passed the nurses' station. *Uh-oh. Here comes trouble.* She blinked away her worry for the moment. Pete faced Dr. Fujita, who stood with arms folded. Pete waved one hand in front of him, like he couldn't get why she didn't understand something so obvious. He glanced around with an expression of exasperation and saw Cam.

"Cameron." He waved her over. "Will you tell the doctor what Albert did when you found him? And why I need to talk with him?"

Cam approached and greeted both of them. "When I told

him he'd fallen, he looked alarmed, and he tried to shake his head. I thought he was telling me it hadn't happened that way." She stayed a few feet away from Pete. If she smelled his scent, if she felt his warmth . . .

"I told you we've had two suspicious deaths at the assisted-living residence." Pete, glaring at the doctor, tapped his pen on the counter next to him. "Mr. St. Pierre could have been attacked. Someone might have tried to kill him. I need to ask him what happened."

"And I told you, Detective, that he's only beginning to recover. I will not have you in there harassing and upsetting him. Come tomorrow, and we'll talk more then. He's on the mend, I assure you."

A wave of relief washed over Cam. Albert seemed to be getting better, but she welcomed hearing the news from the mouth of an expert.

"Did he receive a head wound?" Pete asked.

"He presented with a contusion, but it did not break the skin."

"Could it have been from someone swinging a heavy object at him, or could he have fallen and hit his head?" Pete stuck his hands in his pockets.

"We can't tell. I'm sorry."

"Doctor, a minute ago Albert said something about the party being too loud," Cam said. "What was he talking about?"

"There haven't been any parties going on, I can assure you. Has he shown any signs of dementia?"

"Absolutely none. He's sharp. He has his own blog. He plays Scrabble. No, his mind is fine."

"Well, sometimes the elderly find being hospitalized very disorienting. He might be exhibiting temporary dementia. It will likely clear once he returns to familiar surroundings."

"Great," Pete said. "So whenever you do let me question him, he might not make sense. Is that what you're saying?"

Cam stared at him. Pete didn't seem to care about how Albert was faring, only when he'd be ready for an interrogation.

"Detective, I have other patients to see. We'll talk tomorrow." Dr. Fujita turned away, balancing a tablet on her left hand, tapping something into it while she walked.

Pete gazed at Cam. His face softened. "How are you holding up?"

"How do you think? Over at the Manor they believe I'm a murderer. My favorite relative is in there, injured and newly senile. My favorite chicken just froze herself to death. And my new boyfriend can't consort with me and doesn't seem to care how Albert is doing, only when he can question him. Oh, and I'm off to debate a representative of an agrochemical giant. I'm having a really awesome day." She turned toward the bank of elevators down the hall.

"Cam," Pete called out.

"Your rules," she said without turning toward him. She was nervous enough about the debate and would be lucky to get through the evening intact. She didn't need her relationship troubles to mess with her head. They'd already messed with her heart.

Chapter 13

Despite the discussion having gone on for forty-five minutes, the attendees in the packed library at Hamilton Academy listened closely, several sitting on the edges of their chairs, others nodding or frowning. Cam's presentation had gone well, she thought, despite how nervous she'd been at the beginning. She'd had to keep reminding herself to breathe.

Paul Underwood stood at the podium to her left, her opponent on the forum. He had prepared well and several times had included the usual defense of "The EPA approved this chemical as safe for use on food crops." He wore an immaculate gray suit with a perfectly knotted green tie. Cam was glad she'd gone with her own power outfit.

She'd stressed the importance of increasing organic material in the soil through the addition of compost and maintaining a diverse environment with insects, plants, air, and water in balance. It appeared to go in one of Paul's ears and out the other, but it gained vocal approval and encouraging nods from the audience.

Lucinda stepped in and opened the floor for questions.

"Please either use the microphone in the center aisle or speak loud and clear. I'll repeat the question before our speakers address it."

A man around Cam's age stood. He had black, curly hair pushed away from his forehead and a lively expression on his face. He made his way to the microphone.

"What we need is to feed our soil correctly. Organic doesn't matter if the plants can't be healthy because their soil is lacking in nutrients. And when the plants get healthy, they can withstand pests and diseases, so farmers don't need to apply pesticides and herbicides. Bionutrient-dense feeding is the wave of the future. And that future has to happen now. We can build a healthy, sustainable food supply without chemicals of any kind." He sat. A ripple of applause went through the room.

"Did everybody hear that?" Lucinda asked. At the roomful of nods, she gestured toward Paul and Cam.

"That sounds very interesting, although it's new to me," Cam said. "I do a soil test, of course, and amend accordingly with minerals like greensand. Let's talk afterward. I'd like to learn more."

Paul leaned into his mike. "Nothing to add."

A white-haired woman in the audience stood. "Where can I learn more about composting? And I'd like to know, why isn't the school composting their food waste from the kitchen and the cafeteria?" Lucinda repeated her questions for the audience.

"I can't address the second comment, but of course I am in favor of composting," Cam said with a smile. "As for the first, you can find how-tos on the Web. And if you check out the Northeast Organic Farming Association, you'll find links for local workshops and probably even videos. If all that doesn't work, come on down to the farm this spring and I'll be happy to walk you through it." At the ensuing applause, she added with a smile. "You can all come. Composting is a big part of my operation."

This was going better than she'd expected. No one had asked her forum partner a question yet, and people seemed happy with what she'd offered.

A ruddy-faced man in a plaid shirt stood. Cam thought she might have seen him at the Haverhill Farmers' Market when she sold there last summer.

"If I didn't spray my crops, I'd have nothing to sell," the man boomed. "Paul here knows all about the pros and cons of using his products. Like he said, there's nothing wrong with using them on your vegetables and your fruit trees. And you're not going to feed the world population on a few dinky organic farms. It's fine for you locavores"—he said the word like it was an obscenity—"but it's not efficient."

Scattered applause broke out.

Paul waved at the man. "Thank you, George. Eliminating world hunger is one of our company's goals." Cam watched him smooth the lapel of his jacket, like he thought himself the company president.

"And aren't you the lady farmer who had a couple murders on your farm up to Westbury?" the ruddy-faced man continued. "What? You killing them off with all your fancy organics?"

A collective gasp resounded.

Cam swallowed. "A poor man was killed on my farm last June, it's true. I had nothing to do with it, and neither did my growing practices." She started sweating under her jacket.

The woman who had asked about composting looked at Cam and started clapping. Others in the audience joined in. But not all.

A man with a full head of dark hair streaked with white stood. He waited for the applause to die down.

"I'm Luca. I own Wolf Meadow Farm, an artisanal Italian

cheese company." He spoke with a lilting accent. "We make organic mozzarella, ricotta, and other southern Italian farm cheeses from local organic milk. Like back home in Molise. My customers would have it no other way." He sat.

Lucinda took the mike. "All right, everybody. Are there any more questions pertinent to the topic?" She surveyed the room and nodded at a man, who stood.

"My name is Louis Dispenza. Studies show there's a link between glyphosate and Alzheimer's disease," said the man. Appearing to be in his early forties, he sported a tie and a tweed jacket. He spoke in a loud and clear voice. "How can you, in good conscience, continue to sell your herbicide G-Phos?" He stared at Paul Underwood.

Paul tapped his pen on the podium. "We've been over that ground. The EPA has approved our products for use on food crops."

"Does your company ever reconsider? What about the ethics of giving dementia to people with a career in landscaping or farming? Don't you personally care about that?"

"I have nothing more to say." Paul raised his chin.

The man shook his head and sat down.

"If there are no more questions, we've set out refreshments in the rear," Lucinda said into the microphone. "I'm sure our guests will stick around and continue the conversation." She thanked them both. "Let's give them a big hand."

Cam remained at her podium, trying to stay smiling, during the applause. She was exhausted, and Lucinda still expected her to schmooze. The guy in the tweed jacket approached her, his dark hair contrasting with patches of silver at the temples. He stood a few inches taller than Cam.

"Great information, Ms. Flaherty. I'm Lou Dispenza. I'm a science teacher here at the school." He held out his hand, with smile lines branching out from green eyes over rosy cheeks. "My students call me Mr. D."

"Nice to meet you, Mr. D." Cam shook his hand. *Warm skin and a firm grip.* "Call me Cam, please."

"And I'm Lou. Assuming you're not enrolling in class here." He chuckled.

Lucinda approached. "Glad you two have met. Nice job, Cam."

"Thanks. Sounds like you both read the same study about Alzheimer's and glyphosate."

Lou nodded. He glanced at Paul, who was talking with a small group clustered around him. "Not that it's going to change their practices."

"Come and take some refreshments," Lucinda said, gesturing to the rear of the room.

Cam girded her proverbial loins for more socializing and walked toward the food, still chatting with Lou. She accepted a glass of cider from Lucinda and spent several minutes thanking people for coming and answering questions about organic practices. When the crowd thinned, the man who had mentioned bionutrient-dense feeding approached her.

"I have to run, but let's talk sometime soon. My organization offers workshops, as well." He handed her a card.

Cam thanked him and said she'd call. The room began to empty out. Lucinda started to tidy the refreshment table, and Lou returned to Cam's side.

"I, uh, wondered if you'd like to grab a bite to eat sometime. It appears we have a lot in common." He smiled a little tentatively.

A bite to eat? Was that a date? She was temporarily free of romantic entanglements, after all, thanks to Pete. "Sure. That sounds like fun."

With his left hand Lou held up one of the farm brochures she'd left on the table Lucinda had provided for information. He did not wear a wedding band. "I have your number. I'll give you a call soon," he said, his smile now more sure.

"I look forward to that."

As he walked away, Lucinda looked after him and then at Cam. "Nice work, *fazendeira*," she said in a low voice, with a wicked grin. "He's smart. And one of the hottest bachelors around."

Cam made it home by nine thirty and threw a thick sweater on over her outfit. She'd accepted an invitation for a "bite to eat" with Lou. How wise was that? Then she scolded herself.

"He didn't make a marriage proposal. It's simply dinner with an interesting man. That's all. Right, Preston?"

He jumped onto the couch and nestled next to her. She stroked his head as he purred. The heck with a few cat hairs on her skirt.

She couldn't believe the G-Phos rep had gotten away with saying what he did. He'd kept repeating the same line. "The EPA blah-blah-blah . . ." He obviously had supporters, like the man who had said he couldn't feed his customers if he couldn't spray his crops. With chemical fertilizers and pesticides, undoubtedly.

DJ would have had a better response than hers, which had been no response. He would have asserted the value not only of organic but also of permaculture-designed farming. Cam remembered reading about a one-hundred-acre farm in Wisconsin that used organic permaculture methods successfully, and about farms in Australia that were hundreds of acres in size doing the same. She chided herself for not coming up with those examples on the spot. She had smarts, but she wasn't quick on her feet when interacting with people. One of the many reasons she avoided public speaking.

She checked her phone, hoping the hospital hadn't called. That kind of news could only be bad. Nothing from Anna Jaques, but Ellie had rung her. Cam glanced at the time. Ellie had first texted and then had called at around six. Cam must have been either driving or visiting Albert. And she'd turned her phone off during the debate. The text read only,

Have smthng to tell u.

She listened to the voice mail message.

"I heard something on Sunday. I didn't want to tell you in front of my mom. Call me."

Cam saved the message and disconnected. Ellie'd heard something, on Sunday, the day Bev died, that she didn't want her mother to know she had heard. After nine was too late for Cam to return her call. Cam would try to find her after school let out for the day tomorrow. Ellie should be able to find a place to talk where her mom couldn't overhear. Cam felt a little uneasy about Ellie hiding information from her mom, but Cam could always tell Myrna if necessary.

She pulled the sweater close around her neck with cold fingers. Some rummy cider would warm her up. In the kitchen, she extracted a half gallon of local cider from the fridge and poured three-quarters of a mug full. She added a cinnamon stick and two whole cloves to the mug and nuked it in the microwave. The cider would be a lot tastier mulled at a low heat for a couple of hours, but by then she'd be asleep. She added a generous splash of Turkey Shore rum and a little Cointreau. She topped the cider with a dusting of cinnamon. When she raised the mug, the fumes made her eyes water.

She swung her feet onto the couch and sipped the toddy, its heat warming her hands, as well as her insides. If Pete knew about the text, he would urge Cam not to try to do his job. Ellie trusted Cam, though, in a way she clearly didn't trust

Pete. Once Cam knew the story, she would pass it on to Pete. She supposed. Being a person of interest criminally had transformed her into a person of no interest romantically, at least for Detective Pappas. She had to accept it, but she didn't have to like it.

Bev's service tomorrow morning would involve another onslaught of socializing. For now, Cam needed to relax and be alone. She gazed at the lace curtains Marie had hung years before. Were Marie and Bev sitting in heaven, playing cards together right now? Marie and Albert were Catholic. Cam wasn't sure she shared their view of an afterlife. She tended more toward the carpe diem school of "right now is all we have." Unfortunately, she'd seen more than one dead person. It had been clear each time that after death the essence of the person evaporated from the shell of the body. Was it the soul that left? Did it migrate into a newborn baby somewhere or gather on heavenly clouds or merely dissipate? Cam didn't know. But it was certainly comforting to picture all those who had gone before gathered in a pleasant place, doing whatever they liked without fear of sickness or death.

Chapter 14

Cam called the hospital in the morning to ask about Albert. The male nurse on the floor said Albert's health had improved, but he still seemed confused about his surroundings.

"He will likely be discharged today or tomorrow."

"Can I talk to him for a minute, please?" Cam asked. The nurse said he'd connect her to Albert's room.

After Cam had waited over a minute, someone picked up. Cam heard a shuffling noise and then, at last, Albert's voice. But he sounded faint, like he was speaking from a long distance.

"Uncle Albert? Are you there?"

"Who is it?" Albert said.

Cam could barely hear him. Then she heard the nurse's voice. "Mr. St. Pierre, it's your great-niece. But you're holding the phone upside down. Here."

"Cameron?" This time Albert came in loud and clear.

"It's me, Uncle Albert. How are you this morning?"

"Well, I've been better. The party went on all night long."

"The party?" So he was still confused. Maybe she could reach the doctor and ask how long it would last.

"They were making a ruckus right next door. Talking and carousing. I asked them to keep it down, but they didn't pay me any mind a-tall."

"That's too bad." Cam kept her voice sympathetic. He was probably misinterpreting what he heard the nurses and aides say among themselves. "Listen, I wanted to tell you I'll come by and visit a bit later today. I'm going to Bev Montgomery's funeral this morning."

"Why, I must go, as well. Listen, son, I need to be getting out." His voice became more distant. He had to be talking to the nurse. "Beverly was good to my Marie, and to me. Have to pay my respects."

Cam didn't catch what the nurse said, but then he came on the line.

"Sorry about that. Your uncle is a bit agitated."

"Please tell him I will represent him at the service for his friend. And that I'll come see him directly afterward."

Poor Uncle Albert. She only hoped his confusion would clear once he returned home. She checked the clock. Bev's funeral would begin at eleven o'clock. Cam still had a few hours for work.

The air still tasted bitterly cold outside. Inhaling hurt, and she slid on the iced-over snow packed on the paths. Preston followed but didn't have a problem keeping his footing.

"You're lucky to have four feet instead of two, Mr. P. Although you could have stayed in that warm house, you know."

Preston didn't reply, instead dashing off to chase a slate-colored junco off its perch on a fence post.

Cam checked on the chickens first thing. All the remaining birds were still alive and accounted for. She freshened the hens' food and drink but kept them closed in with the light on. She checked the lettuce flats she'd planted, started two more of spinach, and added water to the trays under the flats so it would wick into the cells. All the beds in the hoop house were still covered. She threw her own kitchen scraps into the worm bin.

As she worked, she thought through the recent events. Why would the doctor be thinking of discharging Albert already? It could be an insurance issue. The forum last night had gone passably well, aside from her being called a murderer. Again. Lou seemed kind of interesting. She would have to see how their dinner went, if in fact he called her. She liked Pete, but she found it hard to stomach that he needed to shun their relationship for work reasons. She missed the closeness they'd developed. She wondered if he missed her in return.

In the barn office, she checked the list of what she had to offer in the shares on Saturday. The portions looked scant. What else could she include? Cheese would be nice. An image of the guy who had spoken last night, the cute Italian, appeared in her mind. Luca of Wolf Meadow Farm. A ball of his cheese in each share would be perfect. He'd said he used local organic milk. Maybe he'd give her a wholesale price. If she left early, she could stop by the store on the way to the funeral.

When she finished working and went into the house, Preston came along. Even with his two layers of fur, he didn't want to stay out for long in this kind of cold. Cam showered, then dressed in her outfit from the night before. She donned her good black wool coat and headed out to buy some cheese.

"Welcome," Luca said. He came out from behind the cheese counter with a big smile and open arms. "What can I help you with?" The shop was empty except for the two of them.

"I was hoping to buy some cheese from you to give to my shareholders."

"How about some samples before you decide?" He returned

behind the counter, then drew out three wedges of cheese and a slender knife. "This is many people's favorite, the aged truffled farm cheese." He sliced off a piece and laid it on a square of paper.

"Mmm," Cam said, savoring the nutty flavor.

"But our specialty is mozzarella." The sounds that rolled out of Luca's mouth made Cam feel like she was in Italy instead of Westbury. He fished a white, squishy ball out of a bin of water and offered her a slice.

"Wow. That melted in my mouth," Cam said when she finished it. "That's nothing like what we get in the supermarket. Would you give me a wholesale price on thirty balls of it? I distribute shares on Saturday."

"We're both local. I am happy to. I make it fresh on Friday and deliver to your farm. *Bene?*"

Cam smiled and thanked him, then said good-bye. Luca said something she didn't understand as she climbed into the truck, and she drove off with Italian echoing in her ears. If she ever saved enough money for a vacation, she'd head straight for Italy.

Almost no spaces remained in the parking area of Oneonta Congregational Church. Cam squeezed the truck into a spot that hadn't been well plowed, crunching the snow-piled berm with the truck's nose. She made her way into the church with only minutes to spare, glad of the tread on her boots. An organ played a kind of dirge, one of the reasons Cam had stopped attending any kind of religious service in her teen years. Her idea of worship was more about being outside, under God's sun and sky, than about sitting on an uncomfortable wooden bench and listening to depressing tunes.

The sanctuary was nearly full and smelled of incense mixed with overly sweet flowers. On an easel in the front sat an enlarged copy of the same picture of Bev that Cam had seen at

Moran Manor. Two vases of tall flowers flanked it, but she didn't see a coffin. Ginger sat in the front right pew with several others. Two had to be her brothers. Richard Broadhurst sat in one of the forward pews on the other side of the aisle. Oscar sat in a rear pew, with hands in his lap, his head bowed.

Cam spied Ruth in a pew halfway toward the front on the left and slid in next to her. Ruth, in dark slacks and a soft purple sweater stretched over her hefty figure, squeezed her hand. A moment later, Alexandra and DJ slid in from the outer aisle on the other side of Ruth. They brought a whiff of fresh air. Cam leaned toward them and gestured a greeting. Alexandra smiled in return, while DJ closed his eyes and crossed his legs meditation-style on the bench, laying his hands, palms up, on his knees.

"So this isn't really a funeral?" Cam whispered to Ruth. "No casket."

"Right. The state couldn't release the body yet, but the family wanted to hold the service now."

So the receptionist had been right. *Good.* She had been to one open casket funeral and hoped never to have to repeat the experience. Knowing in her mind that someone had died was enough. She didn't need visual proof.

The organ music changed to something stirring, and the minister came to the altar. He spoke several platitudes, he led them in a song, and then he read from the Bible. Cam cast a glance around, noticing community members she had seen in the Food Mart but didn't know by name. She spied Felicity in a pew on the other side. Jim Cooper, the Moran Manor director, sat across from her. Then a thin man edged into a seat behind Felicity. Frank Jackson.

Cam nudged Ruth and pointed. Ruth's eyes widened. She sighed and gazed back at Cam, who could only imagine the thoughts and feelings roiling in Ruth's head.

A man rose from the front row and made his way to the podium.

"I am Bill Montgomery. My brother Tom and my sister, Ginger, and I would like to thank you all for coming. Our mother was taken too young, but I want to share some of my memories of her."

He went on to talk about Bev's childhood, her marriage to their father, and their farm.

"When my brother Mike died last year, it kind of took the wind out of Mom's sails, and we hoped she'd be happier at Moran Manor. But she had a hardworking life and was good to the people she loved." He swallowed hard and wiped a tear from the corner of his eye. "Let's remember her for that."

The minister stepped to the podium. "Let us hold Beverly's soul in our hearts as she journeys on. If anyone present would like to stand and share a memory, please feel welcome."

The music started again, quietly this time. If Albert were here, he would offer his story of how good Bev had been to him and Marie. Cam could tell his tale for him, but after the forum last night, she felt about all shared out.

A woman who said she had been a Grange friend of Bev's told of how they'd worked together to keep the rural nature of the town alive, and she made people laugh with a tale of a Halloween party they had thrown, with both of them in costume, one as a carrot, one as a stick.

Someone else rose to speak of how her family had been close to Bev's and what a good mother she'd been.

Cam studied her hands, trying to muster the energy to speak on Albert's behalf. Ruth nudged her.

Frank stood. "Bev and I were in the same, um, club. She was a good friend to me. She didn't deserve to die the way she did. May she rest in peace."

A murmur rustled through the room. The club had to be the Patriotic Militia, a violent anti-immigrant group they'd both belonged to. Cam assumed Frank still did. Hardly a social club. And he was the first to mention how Bev had died. Cam felt she had to counter that, for Albert. She stood and took a deep breath.

"I am Albert St. Pierre's great-niece. He couldn't be here today, but I know he would want me to share with you how kind Bev was to him and his wife, my great-aunt Marie, when she lay dying a few years ago. Not only did Bev cook and care for Marie, but she also did farm chores so that Albert could be at Marie's side. He has told me this more than once, and I know how much it meant to him." She sat. Ruth patted her hand.

The minister stepped forward again. He appeared about to speak when Richard Broadhurst stood. He began to sing "Amazing Grace." The minister appeared startled. Richard turned sideways and opened his arms, his hands inviting everyone to sing along. Several others stood and joined him in the song. Ginger rose and began to harmonize. The minister smiled and gave a nod to the organist, who played along. Soon the entire church was singing in unison.

Cam's throat thickened. Something about singing in a group always got to her, especially when it entailed such a beautiful song in a spiritual place, despite what she thought of organized religion. She pictured Albert and willed him to recover so she could tell him about this moment. And so his service wouldn't be the next in line.

Chapter 15

"Here goes," Ruth said twenty minutes later in the church's reception hall. "Wish me luck." She headed in Frank's direction.

Cam sipped from a plastic cup of sherry. She surveyed the spacious room that adjoined the sanctuary. Most of those who had come to pay their respects to Bev had adjourned to the reception. Finger sandwiches, a raw vegetable platter, cookies, cider, and an urn of coffee sat on a long table. Many had opted instead for the small plastic cups of sherry a young man offered from a tray. Bev's children stood in a row, greeting the guests. A poster board featuring a collage of pictures leaned on an easel near the door.

In her peripheral vision, she caught sight of a familiar figure. She turned her head. Sure enough, Pete was walking toward her, carrying a cup of coffee.

"I didn't see you in the service," she said. He came close enough to touch. She kept her hands to herself, even as her conflicted heart reached out.

"I stood in the rear. I'm working, as you can imagine." He wore a dark suit with a pale green tie. Although his clothes were clean and pressed, his face showed the stress of the past few days.

"Getting anywhere?" Even though Cam had seen Pete every day this week, a rush of longing swept through her. She clenched her fists to tamp it down, deny it.

"Not anywhere good. You look nice," he said, but his gaze was on Frank and Ruth.

Cam gazed in the same direction. The couple stood close and talked intently, heads leaning in. She couldn't hear any raised voices or see any angry gestures.

"See any other murder suspects?" Cam asked.

"It's possible." Pete put his hands in his pockets, scanning the area.

Cam followed his eyes. Oscar, in a dark sweater over a white shirt and a brightly colored tie, talked with Jim Cooper in a corner. Oscar glanced toward Pete and then turned his back. Pete might suspect Oscar. She had, herself, after all. Ellie had said he'd delivered Bev's meal to her room. Her last supper, as it turned out. She had opened her mouth to ask Pete when Richard ambled toward them.

"Farmer Cam, lovely to see you again," he boomed. "Who's your gentleman companion here?" He smiled and winked. He wore the same turquoise vest he had when Cam saw him at Moran Manor, this time with a tweed jacket and black slacks.

"This is Pete Pappas. State police detective Pappas, actually. Pete, Richard Broadhurst."

Richard kept on his broad smile while he shook Pete's hand. Richard stood only an inch or two taller than Pete, but he projected a much larger profile, and his meaty farmer's hand definitely dwarfed Pete's.

"Mr. Broadhurst." Pete extracted his hand. "I believe my office has been trying to contact you in recent days."

"Oh? Have I done something that needs detecting?" Richard raised his eyebrows nearly into his hairline.

"It's in the matter of Mrs. Montgomery's death. You haven't been responding to your messages."

"Lost the damn cell phone somewhere. And I canceled my landline a couple of years ago. No longer necessary these days. So am I a person of interest? That sounds exciting."

"I wouldn't be so sure. I understand you were in negotiations to purchase Bev's farm."

Cam could tell Pete was struggling to keep irritation out of his voice.

"Purely a business deal. Nothing suspect about it, I assure you," Richard said. "I need to go and speak with Ginger and her brothers. Those poor children." He shook his head with a sorrowful expression on his face and headed for the end of the reception line. He launched into another aria, this time singing more softly than when he sang in the Moran Manor lobby.

"Those poor children, my ass," Pete said, watching him go. "Excuse my French, but that man is a load of hogwash."

"He's a bit over the top, I agree," Cam said. "Do you think he was telling the truth about losing his cell phone? I can't imagine someone with a business not having a working cell phone. It puts you back in the Stone Age."

Pete was opening his mouth to speak when Felicity materialized at Cam's side.

"Oh, Cam, I've been trying to find you." She sounded breathless.

Cam introduced Felicity and Pete, and Pete greeted Felicity.

"What's up?" Cam frowned. Felicity didn't appear her usual calm, beaming self.

"I told you my father believes he saw something. He's getting more adamant about it. Could you come by and talk to him sometime soon? That would set his mind at ease."

"Felicity's father lives at Moran Manor," Cam said to Pete.

Pete glanced from one to the other. "He thinks he saw something connected to Bev's death?" He took his turn frowning. "And you didn't tell me, Cam?" He folded his arms.

Cam sighed. "Felicity mentioned it to me, what? Yesterday?"

Felicity nodded. "And he has Alzheimer's disease, so he might be entirely unreliable." She smiled, but the look was a faint, worried echo of the expression Cam usually saw on her face.

"I'll need to interview him," Pete said.

"Would it be all right if Pete and I talked to him together?" Cam glanced at Pete. "You can be kind of scary on your own, you know."

"Why not?" Felicity said.

Pete's nostrils flared. "Who's running this investigation, anyway? I've asked you to keep out of it, Cameron."

Cam opened her mouth. And then shut it. Now wasn't the time to get into an argument with him.

"My father feels comfortable with Cam," Felicity said. "He might not talk to you on his own."

"Fine, then."

Cam checked the time on her phone. "After I pay my respects, I'm heading over to the hospital to see how Albert is. I should be able to be at Moran by two o'clock. Meet you there?" She looked at Pete.

"It's a date," he said. "In a manner of speaking," he rushed to add.

"I'll get in the reception line with you," Felicity said.

As the two women waited to greet Ginger and her brothers, Cam saw Pete head in Oscar's direction. That looked like trouble. Trouble she was happy not to be part of.

* * *

127

Cam had one hand on the door of her truck in the church parking lot when Ruth hailed her. Cam waited until she came closer. "How'd it go?" she asked.

Ruth leaned on the truck, next to Cam. She folded her arms over her red wool coat and stared into the snowy woods across the road.

"He's lost it. He sounded pretty rational in the service, except for calling his militia group a 'club,'" Ruth said. "But to me during the reception? He ranted on about starting a new life, about making amends. He wasn't making much sense. His so-called amends didn't include apologizing to his daughters for leaving them, I noticed."

"He's even skinnier than he used to be."

"Yeah. And he split as soon as he could." Ruth shook her head slowly, a sad look on her face. "I guess it's time to file for divorce. I don't know what I was waiting for."

"Hang in there, girlfriend." Cam slung an arm around Ruth's shoulders and squeezed. They were nearly the same height, although Ruth carried a lot more padding on her big-boned frame. She'd always said it gave her more credibility in a department where she was the only woman. The guys could see that she wouldn't be easy to push around physically, and she definitely wasn't a pushover emotionally, either.

"Thanks." Ruth smiled with a pull to her mouth. "I always do, don't I?"

"And let me know when you're good for that glass of wine," Cam said. She detached herself and fished in her bag for her keys.

"Let me check with my mom, see if she can take the girls this weekend. How does Sunday sound?"

"Good, I think. I'm heading over now to visit Albert in the hospital. Did you hear what happened to him?"

Ruth nodded. "Detective Pappas doesn't seem to know yet if someone hit him or if he fell."

"Yeah, the doctor didn't know, either. But when I called this morning, they said he was doing well. I hope he'll be able to talk about what happened soon."

"I need to go home and get ready for work. Pulled second shift this week. I don't know what I'd do without Mom's babysitting services." She blew out the sigh of a single mother. "Give Albert a kiss for me, will you?"

Cam said she would. They exchanged a hug, and Ruth headed for her car. Cam climbed into the Ford and started the engine. She sat for a moment, letting the engine warm and giving her brain time to process everything. So Pete's team had been trying to reach Richard. *Interesting.* But of course they would, since he and Bev had been talking about a financial transaction. And if Richard hadn't lost his phone, why would he lie about it?

Chapter 16

Finding Albert became a scavenger hunt. After Cam left the church, she drove to the hospital.

She rounded the corner into Albert's hospital room, hoping to see him sitting up and feeling like his old self. She stopped short. The bed lay empty and appeared freshly made. Nothing occupied the bed tray, and no machines clicked or buzzed. Where had Albert gone? Had he had a relapse? Maybe they'd moved him to intensive care. She felt a welling of emotion. He had to be all right. They'd said just this morning he was improving.

She made her way to the nurses' station. "Excuse me. Where did Albert St. Pierre go?"

"And you are?" A nurse in hot pink scrubs gazed up from the desk.

"I'm his great-niece."

"Ah." She checked a monitor. "He's gone home."

"Home?" Cam gaped.

The nurse swiveled on her chair to paperwork on the opposite desk. "Where he lives."

So they'd released him already. Cam drove to Moran Manor and went straight up to Albert's room. Which showed no sign of his presence. Another neatly made bed, no lights, no laptop humming on the tidy desk. The white windowsill still bore traces of a dark dust, which, Cam thought, must be fingerprint powder. Where was he?

She reversed direction, headed down the stairs to the reception desk, and asked for him. The middle-aged man on duty directed her to go downstairs.

"What's downstairs? I am downstairs."

"He's in the care unit. Downstairs." He pointed her to the elevator.

She waited for the elevator, which seemed to take a year to arrive. She could ask the man what the care unit was, but she was too anxious to see Uncle Albert. She tapped her hand on her thigh on the ride down. The elevator opened to a counter labeled SKILLED NURSING. Now she remembered Uncle Albert talking about this area.

"Is Albert St. Pierre here?" she asked. Only a distant whine of television programs emitting from a couple of the rooms disturbed the quiet. An older woman in a green flowered top, whose name tag read JUNEY, stood behind the counter. She wore dozens of braids, which were pulled back with a green scarf.

She nodded. "He's in room six. And none too happy about it," she said in a Caribbean accent. When she shook her head, the beads at the ends of her braids clicked with the motion.

Cam headed in the direction the woman had indicated. "Uncle Albert?" she called, poking her head into the room.

"I'm here, consarn it." He sat in a wheelchair near the window, with a blanket covering his lap. He wore pajamas and a robe, and a book lay open on the blanket.

"You look much better." She approached him, smiling, and perched on the end of the bed next to him. "They let you out so soon."

"Yeah, rush around here and there. My head hurts, I'll tell you that much."

"Sorry to hear that. You hit your head pretty hard yesterday morning."

"No, it was last week." He started to move his head and then winced. "That's why I can't understand why they won't let me go upstairs to my own room."

He thinks he fell last week? She patted his hand, the age spots standing out among ropy veins. "I'm sure they'll get you out of here soon. I bet they want to keep an eye on you for a few more days. Make sure you're steady."

"I don't know about that."

"Do you remember what happened? When you hit your head?"

He narrowed his eyes at her. He gazed out the window for a moment and then back at her. "Well, I almost remember, and then it's gone. I'd been reading and . . . and then . . ." He searched an empty memory. "And then I have no idea what happened."

"It'll come back to you." Cam smiled again. She hoped the memory would return, and soon.

"Can you ask Juney out there to take those cats out of here?" He gestured to a plastic bag hanging from a cupboard handle near the door. "They've been fighting in that bag all day."

"Cats?" Cam glanced at the bag. It held something, but the bag was not moving. She was willing to bet it held socks and underwear brought down from Albert's room. One hundred percent inanimate.

"Oh, they've been making quite the racket."

Cam swallowed. "I'll tell her."

He chuckled. "She's kind of cranky. Go easy on her."

"Yoo-hoo," a voice called out. Marilyn moved into the room, leaning on her walker, a high-class model that featured brake levers, a bright yellow plastic flower tied to one of the handles, and a seat in the front. "How's my main squeeze?" She cocked her head and smiled at Albert.

"A lot better now that I can see your beautiful face." Albert beamed. "Come sit down."

Cam stood and made room for Marilyn, who locked the wheels on the walker and then slowly moved around to the front and sank into the seat.

"Hello, Cam. How's he doing?" Today she wore a red sweatshirt embroidered with flowers.

"A lot better than when he was in the hospital," Cam said.

"I'm 'he,' and I can answer for myself, thank you very much." Albert frowned at Cam. "I wish they'd let me get back to my own place."

"I'm sure they will soon. Listen, I'll let you two visit. I have to talk to someone upstairs. I'll stop down here again before I leave, all right?"

He nodded. He reached for Marilyn's hand, eyes only for her. But before Cam entered the hallway, he called out, "Don't forget to tell Juney about the cats."

Cam found the stairway and slowly climbed to the second floor. She hoped Albert would regain his faculties once he returned to his own familiar surroundings. It was odd that he made sense most of the time. But the business about believing he'd hit his head last week instead of yesterday, and about complaining about the party at the hospital and the cats fighting in a bag—that stuff seemed like hallucinations.

For now, she needed to figure out what had happened to him. Emerging into the second-floor hallway, she checked the time on her phone. Residents might be in their rooms at this time. She had an appointment to meet Pete and Felicity at two, but a few minutes remained until then.

She walked down to Albert's room and then backtracked one room. She didn't recognize the name above the memory box on the wall outside the room. She knocked on the door, anyway. No one answered.

She moved to the door beyond Albert's, which stood ajar. She hadn't met this resident, either. She rapped on the door-jamb.

A woman's voice called out, "Come in."

Cam pushed open the door to a room arranged in the mirror image of Albert's. A woman in a pink fleece top sat in an easy chair facing a television set. Her hands were busy crocheting with variegated yarn in the blue-green spectrum.

Cam introduced herself, saying she was related to Albert. "I'm sorry for bothering you, but I wondered if you might have seen anyone out of place in the hall yesterday morning, before lunchtime."

"You're Albert's great-niece, then?" The woman turned her head toward Cam. "I'm Belinda Colby."

"Nice to meet you."

"I heard Albert took a fall. How is he?"

"He's downstairs in skilled nursing now. He's much better. I'm sure he'll be back up here before long."

"Good. He's a lovely gentleman. Reminds me of my late husband, Ralph."

Belinda still hadn't answered Cam's question. She tried again. "I'm trying to find out if anyone visited Albert yesterday, before his accident. Did you happen to see anyone?"

"Oh, no, dear." Belinda's laugh was a peal of bells. "I'm

blind, you see." Her hands kept working in unison on the project in her lap.

Cam realized Belinda, in fact, wasn't looking at her crocheting.

"And I'm a bit hard of hearing, don't you know, so I usually have my television turned up."

Cam's heart sank, but she thanked the woman and left.

She tried two more rooms. One resident said in a shaky voice that he'd been downstairs, playing bingo. The other door stood open, but the room held no occupant. It smelled of cleaning products, though. She hadn't thought of asking the housekeeping help. She shook her head at her own cluelessness. She glanced to her left, down the hallway, and then to her right. At the end, where it took a turn, she spied the edge of a cleaning cart. *Perfect.* She headed in that direction.

The sound of a vacuum came from a doorway. Cam knocked and stepped in. A young woman in dark blue pants and a matching polo shirt continued vacuuming near the far window. Cam moved farther into the room.

"Excuse me," she said, trying to be heard over the noise.

The woman whirled. The wand hit a chair, and the vacuum fell silent. She placed her hand over her heart.

"I'm sorry. I didn't mean to startle you," Cam said.

The woman pulled out her earbuds. "No problem. Can I help you?" She had a broad face and high cheekbones. Her dark blond hair streaked back into a ponytail.

"I'm Albert St. Pierre's great-niece."

The woman smiled and nodded. "Albert. Very nice man." Her smile turned to a frown. "How's he doing?"

"He's much better. He's in skilled nursing."

"Downstairs."

"That's right. I wondered if you saw anyone near his room yesterday morning. Somebody who didn't belong there."

The woman's eyes widened. She shook her head, fast. "Nothing. Nobody."

"Are you sure? Had someone—"

"Excuse me." She stuck the earbuds in again, switched on the vacuum, and turned away from Cam, pressing the wand back and forth on the carpet with excessive force.

Cam stared at her for a moment before leaving the room. She walked away, the sound of the machine echoing in her ears, masking the truth.

Chapter 17

"I'm in the lobby with Felicity. Where are you?" Pete's voice coming out of her cell phone a minute later rasped harshly in Cam's ear.

"I'm heading down the stairs. Be right there." She disconnected. He had a lot of nerve to be short with her. True, Cam had said she'd be available at two o'clock, but she was only a few minutes late.

She clattered down the stairway. He stood with Felicity in the hallway leading away from the lobby. Felicity wore the same silk jacket with Japanese styling she'd had on at the memorial service.

"Oh, good. There you are, Cam," Felicity said with a smile. "We're going to go into the Neighborhood. Come along."

Pete didn't smile at Cam, although she thought she caught a glimpse of a message in his face. Longing returned? Asking forgiveness? Sorrow? She couldn't tell. He gestured with his hand for her to precede him while they followed Felicity through a wide doorway. The door clicked shut behind them.

"You need to use a code on that keypad to get out," Felicity said. "It's so the dementia residents don't try to make a break for it." She laughed, leading the way at a brisk pace.

Two women sat slumped in wheelchairs in a small sitting room. A man shuffled toward Felicity and asked if she had a deck of cards. Felicity greeted him and said she didn't have any.

The man saluted. "Yes, ma'am." He moved past them.

"I think it's best not to tell Dad that you're with the police, Detective," Felicity said, gazing at Pete. "If you don't mind. I don't want to upset him."

"No problem," Pete answered.

In a spacious room at the end of the hall, a large-screen television blared. The aroma of freshly baked cookies mixed with a faint smell of urine. Several residents sat in chairs facing the TV. A caregiver sat opposite a woman in a wheelchair, feeding her pudding from a little cup. Another woman sat next to Nicholas and sang "Silent Night" in a clear voice. She and Nicholas held hands.

Felicity said hello to her father and kissed the top of his head. She also greeted the woman next to him.

"I brought visitors to see you," Felicity said, gently disengaging her father's hand from the woman's. "Let's go somewhere a little quieter and talk."

He nodded, and she turned his wheelchair around. After pushing it to the far end of the room, she positioned him at a table.

"Come sit down." She waved Pete and Cam toward chairs and sat. "Dad, this is my friend Cam. You met her the other day. She's the farmer."

"The farmer. Nice to see you again." He smiled at Cam.

"And this is Pete Pappas."

Pete extended his hand across the table to Nicholas. The two men shook.

"Any friend of Felicity's is a friend of mine," Nicholas said.

His voice quavered, and his eyes were rheumy, but he looked at Pete straight on.

"Dad, tell Cam and Pete what you told me. What you saw on Sunday."

Nicholas's face took on a lost look. "What happened on Sunday?"

"Remember? The day our friend Bev Montgomery died. You told me you saw somebody go into her room."

"When I was looking at the pictures." He nodded slowly.

"What pictures were those, Dad?" Felicity asked.

"The music ones."

"And you saw someone enter Mrs. Montgomery's room." Felicity's soft voice was full of caring.

"That I did. But I don't quite recall who I saw now."

Pete cleared his throat. "Man or woman?"

"Somebody in trousers. I'm sure of that." Nicholas's gaze drifted to the action on the big screen. "It was an Indian."

"An Indian?" Pete said. He tapped a finger on the table.

Pete's habitual tapping didn't distract Nicholas. Cam glanced at the screen. Fred Astaire was twirling Ginger Rogers in black and white. Nicholas hummed the tune they danced to as he swayed with the music in his chair.

"Dad?" Felicity touched his shoulder. "Daddy, we're still here."

"That's lovely, dear." He kept his eyes on the movie.

"What did you mean by 'an Indian'?" Felicity asked.

"An Indian?" He kept watching the screen.

"What was the person's hair like?" Cam asked Nicholas.

He kept humming and then asked in a faint voice, "What person?"

The three stood in the lobby a few minutes later. Felicity spread her palms.

"I'm sorry. I guess that wasn't very helpful. Trousers, right? Who doesn't wear pants these days?" She glanced down at her own denim skirt. "Well, besides me."

"What do you think he meant by the pictures?" Cam asked.

"He played classical violin in the North Shore Symphony for many years. He loves those pictures on the second floor, the ones of the orchestras and such. And the cutouts of instruments."

"Bev's room was on the second floor." Pete scratched his head. "What would your father be doing on that floor? Is that even possible?"

"An aide wheels him around the residence sometimes, you know, for a change in scenery."

"If a caregiver was taking him around, she must have seen the same thing he did," Pete said. "I'll get an interview with her. Or him. This could be the break we need."

"I have to run. Good luck, Detective." Felicity shook his hand. "Bye, Cam. Let me know if you need any help on the farm."

Cam said she would. Pete also turned away. Cam reached out and caught his sleeve. He paused, facing her.

"I have something to tell you," she said. She glanced around the lobby. A woman about her age was signing in with her two young children. A caregiver held the outer door open for a stooped resident who was moving at tortoise pace with her walker toward a van waiting outside.

"This isn't a good place to talk about us, Cam." The lines around Pete's eyes held care and sorrow.

"It's not about us." She lowered her voice. "I asked a member of the housekeeping staff if she'd seen anybody near Uncle Albert's room yesterday morning."

"You just happened to ask her?" He shoved his hands in his

pockets. "Cameron, you know you shouldn't be doing that. Asking around could be dangerous."

Cam waved a hand. "Relax, Pete. I was only asking a few questions. I wondered if a resident saw the person who pushed him. I'm curious, okay? And he's my dear old uncle." Her throat thickened for the second time that day. She hadn't planned on that. She cleared her throat and glanced away.

"I know how much you care for him. And this might be connected to the murder." He rested his hand on her arm for a few seconds. "Tell me what the maid said."

"Well, she said she hadn't seen anything or anybody. But she looked and sounded alarmed."

"What was her name?"

"I didn't see a name tag. But she looked Russian. Or Slavic. You know, blond, high cheekbones. Younger than me."

"We'll find her. We couldn't interview every single employee here or every resident. And, tough as this sounds, our focus has to be on finding Bev's murderer. We're not even sure someone attacked Albert. The doctor said the nature of his injury was inconclusive."

"And Albert says he doesn't remember. He was reading, and after that his memory is gone. I'm going downstairs now to see him again. I'll keep asking him."

"Let me know if he remembers anything."

Cam nodded. "How's Dasha doing?" She surprised herself by asking.

"He's fine. A bit lonely." He sighed. "Not a great week for me to be on a new case."

"I suppose I'm still technically a suspect?" She supposed she was since he hadn't said otherwise.

Jim Cooper chose that moment to pop out of his office. He walked by them right when Cam said the word *suspect*. Jim frowned and pursed his lips. He glanced at her and Pete out of the side of his eyes and hurried past.

"I suppose you are. But let's not talk about it here. For obvious reasons," Pete said, tilting his head in the direction Jim had gone. "I'm still on the clock, and my to-do list is huge. I'll be in touch."

Cam said good-bye and headed downstairs. When she got to Albert's room, he was sleeping in the bed, the red plaid blanket now pulled up under his chin. Marilyn sat reading in a chair next to the bed.

"I came down to say good-bye," Cam said. "Good that he's sleeping, though."

"Can you stay for a minute?" Marilyn asked.

"Sure. Thanks for keeping him company." Cam leaned against the bureau.

Marilyn smiled. "I'm getting quite fond of him. I hope you don't mind."

"Not at all. I'm glad to see you both happy." Cam smiled at her. "So was he still talking about the cats in the bag after I left?"

"I'm afraid so. The same thing happened to my late husband when they hospitalized him once for pneumonia. I'm sure Albert will be fine once he has returned to his own room. Don't worry, dear. It's part of being old."

"Have you heard when he'll get out of here?"

"A doctor stopped by in the last hour and said Albert should be able to go back upstairs tomorrow."

"Great news." Cam frowned. "I guess. But what if he isn't safe in his room? What if he's still . . ." *In danger.* She clamped her mouth shut. She wanted to add that she was worried. Whoever had whacked him on the head might appear again and finish him off. But she didn't want to alarm Marilyn and kept it to herself.

"Oh, dear. Do you think he wouldn't be safe up there?" Marilyn asked. "I suppose he could fall again."

Cam realized that Marilyn was giving *safe* a different meaning than she had. "I could have him stay at the farm with me. I could take care of him there. At least until we clear this up." *Oops.* "I mean, until he improves."

"But would he be able to get around with his chair and his crutches? Is your house handicapped accessible? Do you have a ramp?"

"No, of course not. It used to be Albert's house, but that was before he lost his foot."

"Something to consider, dear." Marilyn glanced at the snoring Albert with a fond smile. "He gets very good care here, you know."

"I'll go home and check the house from his perspective. He might not want to come, anyway." She pushed her hair off her forehead. "Did he tell you anything else about his fall?"

"No. But if he does, I'll give you a ring. What's your number, Cameron?" Marilyn pulled an iPhone out of her handbag.

"You're up on the latest technology. I'm impressed."

"You know, I can enlarge the numbers and the print on it so it's easier to read and type. And this way I can text with my great-grandchildren. We really enjoy our little shortcuts. Like *lol.*"

"You mean 'laugh out loud'?"

"No, no. It means "lots of love." Isn't that cute?" Marilyn poised a finger bent from arthritis over the phone and looked up expectantly. "Now, give me your number."

Chapter 18

Cam held the pen above the sign-out book and then paused. She glanced at the clock on the wall behind the receptionist's desk. It read three o'clock. She didn't need to get home to the chickens yet. There had to be someone who knew what had happened to Albert. Pete's priorities were with the murder case, as he'd made clear. If anybody was going to figure it out, Cam would have to be the one.

She had never paid much attention to the caregiver staff beyond Albert's and didn't know whom she could ask. The high school kids, including Ellie, wouldn't have been around in the mornings. The housekeeper had been unhelpful to the point of hostility.

"Heading home?" The man behind the desk smiled brightly at Cam.

Oscar walked down the hall, pushing an empty wheelchair.

"Not quite yet." Cam laid down the pen and set out after him. "Oh, Oscar," she called.

He looked over his shoulder with a quick glance, then disappeared around a corner.

Cam hurried after him. She rounded the same corner. The wheelchair sat abandoned. A door swung back and forth with a quiet swish at the end of the hall. The kitchen door. Cam hurried down and pushed it open.

The stainless-steel counters sparkled, the floor shone, and an enormous Dutch oven simmered on the ten-burner industrial stove, but the room was empty. Cam sniffed. Mixed with the aroma of dinner was the scent of fresh air. She navigated through to the rear door, which was propped open a few inches.

Oscar stood on a covered open-air porch with arms folded, a lit cigarette between the fingers of one hand. He saw her, then took a drag.

"Good afternoon, Ms. Flaherty." His breath mingled with the exhaled smoke and seemed to hang in the frigid air.

"Call me Cam." She joined him, then hugged her own arms around her, which was feeble protection from the cold. The porch consisted of a roof over a concrete deck with a wide apron and three stairs leading down to a parking area.

"Cigarette, Cam?" he asked, his tone as cold as the icicles hanging from the eaves.

"No, thank you." Cam remembered his temper from the first day she'd met him. Maybe this wasn't a good idea, after all. But she should be fine. They stood right by the kitchen, and the door was propped open.

"Are you chasing me down or something?"

"I wanted to ask you a question."

"I seem to be very popular for being asked questions these days. I'm getting a little tired of it. Tall black man who delivered the poisoned dinner is everybody's favorite suspect." His mouth pulled down in displeasure.

"I'm actually trying to find out something different. And I

don't suspect you of anything." He'd never talk to her if she let on that she considered him an attacker.

"All right. Let's have it." He took another long drag. He dropped the butt, ground it out with his heel, and then slipped it into a sandwich bag he drew out of his pocket. He glanced at Cam. "Not supposed to smoke anywhere on the grounds. Good thing there's no camera out here."

"You know my great-uncle had an accident yesterday morning. I wonder if someone might have pushed him or hit him on the head. Did you happen to be in the hall where his room is? Did you see anybody go in or out of his room? I mean, somebody who didn't belong there?"

He gazed out over the snow-covered field beyond the parking area. "No. Didn't see anyone. I was on the second floor, collecting breakfast trays, too." His voice grew more gentle. He gazed at Cam. "You know, he's old, and he's missing a foot. He probably fell."

She sighed. "I suppose. I'd hate to think he's still in danger, though. If someone hit him once, perhaps hoping he'd die, they could come after him again once he's back in his room."

"I'll try to keep an eye on him. Listen, I've got to get back to work. The gentleman who needs a chair will be wondering where I am." He popped a breath mint, then held the door open and followed her through.

Jim Cooper stood in the kitchen, speaking with Rosemary, whose hands disappeared into a deep bowl full of dozens of carrots submerged in water. She made scrubbing motions.

Jim frowned at Cam. "What were you two doing out there?"

"Just having a chat, Jim. No worries," Oscar said. He disappeared into the hallway.

"And you, Cam? I'm not sure I want you hanging around here. The residents are nervous enough as it is."

"I'm trying to figure out if somebody hit my great-uncle on the head or if he fell. Nobody else seems to be looking into—"

"Certainly he simply fell," Jim said.

Cam frowned at his interruption. "How can you say that? We don't know what happened in his room."

"Perhaps he had a TIA."

"TIA?"

"Transient ischemic attack. A ministroke."

Cam glanced at Rosemary, who now chopped the carrots with a gleaming knife and quick motions.

"The doctor didn't say anything about that." Cam looked at Jim.

Jim pressed several fingers on his left eyebrow. "Well, from now on, when you come here, please try simply to visit Albert and then go home, or I'll consider revoking your visitation privileges." He bustled out of the kitchen.

Cam stared at the door, shaking her head. "What a . . ."

"Not the easiest man in the world," Rosemary said.

"Can I ask you a question?" Cam leaned a shoulder against the wall and watched the cook at work.

"You just did." Rosemary didn't look up from her cutting board.

She ignored the jab. "You know I brought over clean organic produce for the dinner. Would you put in a word with Detective Pappas that the food I delivered couldn't possibly have had toxins in it? I'm still considered a person of interest, and it's ridiculous."

Rosemary snorted. "You're not the only one. He's suspicious of me, as well. You think my word would carry any weight with him?"

"He suspects you?" Cam asked.

"I didn't have a reason in the world to knock off that poor lady, cranky though she was. But I made the dinner." She glanced up from the growing pile of orange-colored bits. "And how do I know what was in your produce? No, I won't be putting in a word for you. Let them catch the real killer and we'll all be off the hook."

Chapter 19

Cam arrived home and changed out of her nice clothes into jeans and an old sweater, glad to be home alone again. It'd been a long day, spent mostly talking to people. She'd read an article once about introverts and extroverts. Being around others fed the extroverts. For her, socializing and being in the company of folks, even those she knew and liked, drained her and made her hungry for solitude.

School should be out by now. She pressed Ellie's number, but the girl didn't pick up. She took a minute to walk through the farmhouse, with an eye to Albert navigating it in a wheelchair or on crutches. Marilyn was right. Not only would he have to get up the outside stairs, but also the only bedrooms were on the second floor. The couch in the living room wasn't a sofa bed, and she couldn't expect an elderly man to sleep on those narrow, sagging cushions. But if he wasn't safe at Moran . . .

She shook her head. After grabbing the egg bucket, she stuck her phone in her pocket and headed outside. What with Albert's health, plus a murderer on the loose, she didn't want to be without the lifeline of a cell phone even for a few minutes.

In the coop, in air becoming fragrant with the sharp tang of fresh chicken poop, she gathered all the freshly laid eggs from the past few days. She would clean up the droppings later in the week, when the weather warmed to double digits again. Definitely not today, though. She fed and watered the hens and closed them in, grateful the birds were all still alive, then carried the bucket to the barn to wash the eggs before she stowed them in the egg fridge. She slid open the wide barn door a few feet and slipped inside, then switched on the light and closed the door behind her.

"What the heck?" On the floor in front of her were two cat carriers. And the carriers were emitting the funny gargling speech of chickens. "Who's leaving me more hens?" An envelope sat on top of one carrier. She extracted a piece of paper and read.

Our donation to your farm! We find we can't keep these hens in our backyard, after all. We didn't realize how much work they are, and we're headed to the Bahamas. Thanks for giving them a good home. Their names are Eunice, Sylvia, Ruffles, and Linda. Thanks.

The note had been signed "M&M." *Great.* She had no idea who M and M were. The hens in the coop behind the barn had been rescued from certain death last fall. She supposed these had been headed for the same fate, except for different reasons. These were the fault of irresponsible owners who'd thought a few gallinaceous pets would be fun, until reality sank in.

She filled the egg bucket with water, then knelt and opened the door to one of the carriers. It held two birds. She was surprised they weren't wearing little name tags. The other carrier held two more. They were interesting-looking breeds. The silky golden one with a beard might even be an Ameraucana, the stupid but winter-hardy breed with the blue eggs. If she put them in the coop tonight, they might start fighting. If she left them in their cages, they could peck each other's eyes out or feathers off. And if she let them loose in the barn, they could end up eating something they shouldn't or getting stuck under the tiller. Plus, the air wasn't at all warm in here. But what if her current flock didn't like the new girls on the block? She sighed and pulled out her phone. She pressed DJ's number.

After she explained what she'd found, she said, "Will it be all right to put them in the coop with all the others?"

"It should be fine. They might peck at each other a little. But it's better than keeping them in those carriers—that's way too small of a space."

Cam thanked him. "Plus, we're down one, anyway." She told him the story of TopKnot's freezing death.

"No worries. These things happen."

"Speaking of hens, somebody left a comment on the farm Web site, asking if our eggs were vegetarian. That is, if the chickens are."

"We talked about that, right?"

"Right. I was glad I had an answer, and wanted to thank you. Some people are just clueless."

DJ laughed. "Hey, while we're talking, let me tell you what my brother said about Ginger Montgomery."

"I'm all ears." She perched on a salt marsh hay bale away from the door.

"I told you Eddie worked on that housing development she did in Newburyport. He says he'll never work for her again. She cut corners, even with safety stuff, just to spend less money. She used cheap building materials and told them not to bother fixing stuff like cracks in the foundation. Said to just cover it up."

"Sounds like bad business practice to me. That's got to bounce back at her one of these days," Cam said.

"You'd think so, right? One time he overheard her talking on the phone to somebody about a loan she was supposed to be repaying. Eddie said she didn't seem particularly happy with whatever she was hearing on the other end of the line."

Cam thanked him and disconnected. After she washed the eggs and refrigerated them, she carried the new members of her chicken family out to the coop. When she opened the door of the first carrier inside the coop, the birds didn't want to come out. She left the carrier on the floor with the door ajar. After she opened the other carrier, those two marched right out and started exploring. Hillary hopped off her roost and went to greet them with a few pecks. She cocked her head, as if studying their résumés, then returned to her nightly resting spot. The new ones apparently passed the test of membership. Cam had no idea which named hen was which. When their personalities emerged as time went on, she'd rename them. She reached into the carrier on the floor and pulled out the two shy chickens, one by one. The second, larger one squawked and tried to peck Cam's wrist, but when she set it down at the food tray, it stopped complaining.

She shut the coop again, dumped the empty carriers in the barn, and trudged to the house. Once inside, she cranked up the heat. She'd find a way to pay for the heating oil. Maybe next winter she'd put in a woodstove or one of those pellet stoves. For now, she wasn't willing to sit around wearing gloves and a hat indoors.

Her stomach complained bitterly of emptiness. She rummaged in the freezer until she found the single serving of lasagna she knew she'd stashed, and started heating it in the microwave. She poured a glass of red wine and munched on crackers while she washed a couple of handfuls of her own salad greens. Which reminded her of what Rosemary had said, that Pete thought Rosemary was also a person of interest. True, Rosemary had made the salad. She could have easily added poison to an individual plate of greens. *But why?*

Ten minutes later Cam sat down to eat, the local *Daily News* spread out on the table. She idly flipped through the paper, noting that the Westbury Winter Festival was this coming weekend. It featured sledding and skating on Mill Pond, hot chocolate in the shed, and a snow person contest, weather permitting. So far it certainly appeared that there would be plenty of snow and plenty of frozen pond. December's relative warmth had given way to January's old-fashioned New England winter weather. With global climate change, who knew what February would bring?

Her cell phone rang. She didn't recognize the number but connected, anyway.

"Cam? This is Lou. From the debate."

Lou. "Hey, Lou."

They chatted for a couple of minutes.

"Let's set that dinner date," Lou said. "I mean, if you still want to."

A stab of guilt hit Cam. She'd rather be arranging a dinner date with Pete. But she couldn't, could she?

"I'd love to."

"Friday at Phat Cats Bistro? I can make a reservation."

"I've heard about that place. Small, in Amesbury, right?" Ruth had mentioned dining there with her mother. Delicious and creative dishes, an intimate setting, friendly owners.

"Right. You'll love it. In fact, you should sell vegetables to them. They like to use local produce."

"I'll check into it." So far she'd batted zero, or whatever the sports metaphor was, in her attempt to secure a new contract for supplying locally grown veggies. But she might as well keep trying.

"Pick you up at six thirty?"

She agreed and said good-bye. She'd get a good meal out of the evening and some intelligent conversation. She wasn't marrying the guy or anything. And it could be that a little competition might make Pete realize what he was missing. Or maybe that was rationalizing her guilt.

She returned to the paper and paused on a short article below the announcement about the Winter Festival. Richard Broadhurst had applied for a small business loan to expand his orchard at Cider Valley Farm. *Interesting*. Did he believe he was still going to be able to buy Bev's land? With Bev's death, the property would surely go to Ginger and her brothers. Cam fully expected to see several roads lined with overly large homes on the property by next summer. Overly large and shoddily built, if what DJ's brother had said was true.

After she finished eating, she refilled her wine and carried it to her desk, running her finger along the smooth stem. She checked the farm's Web site, then paid a few bills and recorded the number of eggs she'd gathered. All that was under control. She rose and paced the length of her house and back. A killer roamed free. Albert might still be in danger. She hated the feeling that she couldn't do anything about it. She couldn't even talk over the case with Pete, as she had after the murder in the fall. Then he'd asked for her help in keeping her eyes and ears open in the community.

She needed to lose herself in something. She moved to the couch, clicked on the television, and started to watch an episode of the latest BBC mystery drama. It reminded her too much of the current mystery, and she switched to a cooking show. That shouldn't present any reminders of real life. But it

featured a chef assembling *une salade composée*. The plated sal
ads reminded her of Rosemary. Cam's mind jumped right back
into Bev's murder. She switched off the TV.

Her sleuthing at Moran Manor had gotten her exactly
nowhere. She searched her brain to figure out what else she
could do. She found her phone and called Alexandra.

"Hey, I heard about Albert," Alexandra said after greeting
Cam. "Is he all right?"

"He will be. He's back at the residence. He's still a little
confused, but he should recover. What we don't know is what
actually happened to him. With the murder and all, I'm worried that he was attacked."

"What does your detective say?"

My *detective. Not exactly.* Cam sighed but kept the thought to
herself. "Detective Pappas said he doesn't have the resources
to pursue that line of inquiry, especially since the doctor
couldn't say if Albert hit his head in a fall or if somebody
bopped him one."

"I'm glad he's okay. But they should follow up on Albert.
Maybe your friend Ruth can look into it."

"Good idea," Cam said. "Have you talked to Hannah, the
one who is Richard Broadhurst's stepdaughter?"

"I meant to call you. I talked to her this morning. She said
her mom and him separated a few months ago. She said he's
not good with money. He likes to go down to Foxwoods, you
know, the casino in Connecticut. She said he always returns
with less money than what he took with him. Sometimes way
less."

"Boy, I totally don't get gambling," Cam said. She sipped her
wine. "Betting money on a game of chance seems crazy. And
hanging around a big, noisy place with no natural lighting, to
do it among a bunch of strangers who are drinking? Even
worse."

"No possible way I'd do that. Plus, I don't have any extra money to throw away. But back to Hannah. She didn't seem upset about Richard not living with them anymore. I don't think she ever liked him much."

"So he and her mom are getting a divorce?"

"I'm not sure," Alexandra said. "Hey, tell me how the hens are doing with this cold snap."

"Oh, I have bad news."

"More bad news?" She sounded horrified.

"This is small-scale bad." Cam laughed and then related the story of TopKnot's demise.

"The poor bird. But don't worry about it. You can make stew out of her. Invite Lucinda over."

"That would be local food, all right." Cam laughed again.

"The rest are fine?"

"In fact, four new ones arrived last night."

"You're kidding me."

"No." Cam told her about the "donation" she'd received, and that DJ had said she could go ahead and integrate them.

"Some people are just incredible," Alexandra said. "I can't believe they would abandon their pets. Like, what if you hadn't found them? They could have frozen to death. Or killed each other in those close quarters. Who did you say signed the note?"

"They signed it M and M. No idea who that is."

"Hey, I gotta split, Cam. Me and DJ are going to a movie. Tell Albert hi for me when you see him."

Cam disconnected. Richard wasn't good with money. And from what DJ had said, Ginger might not be, either. She moved back to the computer and opened her "Moran Affair" file. She added the information about Richard's gambling and Rosemary being a suspect. She typed a line about Ginger's shoddy building practices.

156

Preston ambled over and leaped onto her lap. Alexandra had mentioned chickens killing each other in close quarters. Moran Manor fit the description of close quarters, too. Cam gazed with satisfaction around her solitary abode, shared with exactly no one except a cozy cat.

Shivering in the barn office the next morning, Cam checked the thermostat one more time. She'd switched on the space heater when she came in, but the temperature had risen only to sixty, even though it felt marginally warmer outdoors this morning than it had been. The clock on the thermostat read 7:15. She pulled her scarf more snugly around her neck and yawned. Her sleep had been troubled by what seemed like hundreds of thoughts and images. She'd awoken at least five times during the night and then had lain awake, restless, before sliding back into sleep. Her last dream before waking an hour earlier had first involved a banana farm on an island mountaintop and had devolved into Cam at the wheel of a vehicle packed with people, where she couldn't quite reach the brake pedal. The car had rolled backward into an ocean, and she couldn't stop it. She'd opened her eyes, grateful to be alone in her bed in Massachusetts in the middle of winter, despite feeling like her life reeled out of control.

She shook off thoughts of her restless night and checked the seedling flats. The newly planted seeds were already sprouting in their warm beds. Maybe setting up the seed-starting station in the barn had been a bad idea, though. The tiny plants would want warmer air than fifty-five, but keeping the electric space heater running around the clock wasn't safe. She always found something new to learn about farming, which was a science experiment in action, with Cam as the lab technician. Or the mad scientist. A shame some of the experimental results ended up being failures.

She watered the flats gently and then sat at the desk. She'd scheduled this Saturday as winter share pickup day. She examined the list of what would go into the shares on Saturday. It still seemed a little scant, even with the addition of a ball of fresh mozzarellà to each shareholder's portion. The share would be similar to what she'd brought to Moran Manor for the dinner. The cost of which she doubted Cooper would reimburse her, and she had no payback to expect in the future, either. She could offer winter squashes, greens, leeks, the ubiquitous kale, rutabagas, parsnips, and carrots. Onions and garlic. She'd run out of the Corey farm apples she'd bought in the fall, and Meg had said she couldn't supply any more bushels this winter.

What else could she add? She'd met a maple farmer last summer whose syrup production wasn't far north into New Hampshire. What had the woman's name been? It'd sounded like a man's name. Ronny? Benny? No, she was named Dani. Dani Greene. She'd been about a foot shorter than Cam, but they had shared a bottle of wine at a farmers' market potluck and had swapped farming stories. Cam might be able to wangle a wholesale price from her on a bottle of syrup for each share. She found Dani's e-mail on her cell and sent her a message.

Cam's gaze fell on the phone list tacked above the desk. It'd been Albert's list of contacts: seed companies, a soil amendment supplier, fellow farmers, even a small-engine mechanic for when the tiller broke down. Richard Broadhurst's name topped the column labeled FARMERS. He lived right here in Westbury. He might give her a bulk price on stored apples, and she could include a pound or two for each subscriber. If she kept buying products from other farms, her bottom line was going to suffer. But if she didn't satisfy her customers, who'd paid a premium price for their winter shares, she'd lose them. She had considered this financial balancing act when she acquired the farm, and had known it was risky. She had decided to take the plunge, anyway. Albert had alluded to the hard work she could expect when he gave her the farm, but he hadn't touched much on the costs. Of course, he had farmed conventionally and had never considered trying to keep crops going all winter long.

She squared her mental shoulders. She was smart. She would find a way to make it all work. She tapped Richard's number into her cell and saved it. She was about to call him when she pulled her finger away from the phone. Even early rising farmers didn't call each other before eight in the morning.

She switched off the space heater and headed out to get some work done. Peering into the coop, she saw that the new hens appeared to have retained their feathers and were settling in like part of the flock. *Good.* She opened the coop's small door. The weather was not quite as frigid as this morning, and the sky was the color of a slate roof. She sniffed. Snow was on its way.

The largest of the new chickens pushed out onto the ramp leading down into the yard. The hen lifted her head and straightened her body. She let out a full-throated "Er-er er-errrr."

Cam stared. That she was a he. Those people had left her a rooster. It, *he*, must be the one they'd named Ruffles. Ruffles was the only non-female name on the list in the note they'd left—well, the only name human females didn't normally go by—but what a silly thing to call a rooster. She peered at him. His comb stood a little taller than those of the hens, and his wattle was larger as well. She hadn't planned on acquiring a rooster and didn't want one. DJ had said males were pushy and noisy, although he'd also mentioned that they could help keep the hens in order and protect them against predators.

She supposed she could sell the eggs for a higher price now that they would be both organic and fertilized. Or she could slaughter the fellow. Except she had no idea how to go about that. Did one simply sharpen the old ax and chop his head off like in the cartoons about Thanksgiving turkeys? She sighed. For today, at least, good old Ruffles there would enjoy the run of the yard.

Chapter 20

The wind turbine on the hill above Richard's farmhouse spun lazily against the metallic sky, a stark contrast with the stylized sunny valley full of trees and the close-up of a smiling, winking apple on the sign reading CIDER VALLEY FARM.

Cam had left Richard a message at eight. Even though he hadn't responded, she had driven over to the orchard at nine, anyway, and had pulled into the open parking area in front of the house. The space had been poorly plowed, with icy ruts and hillocks of snow mixed in with bare spots of gravel. He could be outside or in his barn, working, doing whatever orchardists did in the dead of winter. This was her first visit to the farm. The house perched on the side of the hill. The Greek Revival style of the white farmhouse hinted at origins in the mid-1800s, but an addition that stuck out from the right side had clearly been built recently. White housewrap covered the new section, and each window still bore its manufacturer's sticker. Richard should have put on the siding before winter hit. It must be cold in there. But if he had a gambling habit, he might have run out of funds to finish off the project.

A barn with a corrugated metal roof sat to the side of the house. A rusty tractor stuck out of the snow next to an old refrigerator with rounded corners and no door. Down the hill in front of the house and barn stretched acres of bare-branched apple trees in the eponymous valley.

She climbed out of the cab of the Ford and called his name. They'd never talked about their personal lives, except for him telling the story about his former career as an international opera singer. She wondered if Hannah and her mother had lived here at the farm, or if Richard had maintained the farmhouse while living at Hannah's mother's place.

When she knocked on the door, no one emerged from the house. Cam couldn't see a doorbell. She wandered toward the barn, whose wide sliding door stood closed. She hauled it open, fighting with the rust and the grit in the tracks, which prevented it from sliding smoothly. The overcast sky didn't lend much light to the inside, but she glimpsed rows of wooden apple crates four feet square stacked on top of each other, a small battered forklift, and a heavy door with a cooler-type handle off to one side, likely a walk-in cooler for the apples. The space appeared tidy and tickled her nose with the smell of apples and sawdust, but she didn't see a soul until a yellow cat streaked past and out the door.

"Richard? It's Cam Flaherty," she called. "You in there?"

When only silence answered, she pulled the door mostly shut, leaving it open a few inches so the cat could make its way in again. She gazed down the hill toward the orchard itself. A figure in red moved between the rows. Richard must be out there pruning or something. She pulled her hat a little lower on her head and stuck her hands in her pockets. She walked across the parking area toward the trees. A car started somewhere on the other side of the house. An engine revved.

A black sedan streaked with road salt emerged. It picked up speed, spinning gravel. The car headed straight for Cam.

"Hey!" Cam yelled. She took a quick step back. Her front foot slid on a patch of ice. She fell backward on one of the mounds of snow, landing on her rear. Her heart raced.

The car kept coming. She tried to push herself up but slipped again. She waved her arms in front of her. Surely the driver would see her. Surely he would stop. The vehicle blasted straight at her. She tried to scramble out of the way, but she had run out of time.

Heat off the engine warmed her face before the car swerved away from her at the last second. It tore down the drive toward the road. Cam stared at the license plate and said the combination of numbers and letters aloud a couple of times. The car also bore a bumper sticker with the word *Jewelers* on it, but Cam didn't get a chance to catch more than that. She'd seen that car before somewhere. She pulled one glove off with her teeth, extracted her phone from her pocket, and tapped the license plate number into a notes app before she forgot it.

She hoisted herself off the ground and leaned down to retrieve her keys from where she'd dropped them next to the mound she'd tripped on. She took a deep breath and started toward the orchard all over again. When she got within shouting distance, she started to hear singing. That had to be Richard working.

"Yo, Richard," she called. "It's me, Cam Flaherty." She waved.

From halfway up a ladder leaning against a tree, he glanced up the hill and motioned her toward him. When she approached a minute later, he climbed down, holding what looked like a small chain saw on the end of a pole. He greeted her, then set the tool on the ground and tugged his gloves off. He pulled a cigarette pack out of his pocket. He extended it toward Cam.

"Smoke?"

"No thanks."

He lit a cigarette. "What's new?" he asked after inhaling and breathing out the smoke with his chin tilted toward the sky. A navy blue watch cap sat on top of his large head, and wiry salt-and-pepper hair waved out from beneath the sides of the hat. Above a straggly gray beard his cheeks were pink from the cold. His work-stained red jacket resembled Cam's own work coat: mended, frayed around the edges.

"I'm all right, thank goodness," Cam answered. "Somebody almost ran me down when I started walking into the orchard. Up there in front of the barn." She pointed. "I thought I was dead meat."

He grimaced. "That must have been—" He caught himself and closed his mouth, exhaling. He continued, "It was, uh, my friend. Sorry about that." He frowned.

"He seemed to be in a crazy big hurry."

Richard nodded. He said nothing else.

"And you?" Cam asked. "What are you working on out here in the middle of January?"

"Pruning, pruning, pruning. Has to be done before the buds form."

Sure enough, small branches littered the ground under the trees in one direction from where they stood, and the shapes of the trees were more open, cleaner.

"Is that really a chain saw?" She pointed to the tool.

"Yup, cordless pole saw. Makes the work go way faster than using loppers and pruners. So, what brings a beautiful woman like you out on such a gray day?" He lifted his eyebrows, drawing on the cigarette, and then blew smoke out the side of his mouth.

"Don't be ridiculous. It does look like snow, though, doesn't it? And it tastes like it."

He gazed at the sky and sniffed. "Should start around mid day, I'd say."

"I came by because I wondered if you have any storage apples I could buy at a wholesale price. I need to pad out my winter shares, or the subscribers will start complaining."

"Any particular varieties you're wanting?"

"I don't know much about apples. I've heard of Baldwins. And I love to eat Macouns in the fall. What do you have?"

"Let me give you some Spartans," Richard said. "They're great keepers and have the most marvelous flavor. An antique variety."

"That sounds great. And the locavores will be happy."

"Can't get much more local than five miles distant from your farm."

"Your apples aren't certified organic, are they?"

He shook his head. "I follow organic practices, as much as I can. But I am a CNG."

"What?"

"Certified natural grower."

"A new term."

"It's a much smaller certifying agency than the USDA, which is a bloody bureaucratic nightmare for a libertarian like me. Certified naturally growing farms are peer evaluated. My customers are satisfied. They don't care about a USDA sticker on their fruit."

"I'll check it out." Cam suspected the fees were lower and the standards might be, as well. "Do they allow woodchuck bombs? I had a terrible time with those critters last summer."

"They do. But I have a better solution." He lifted his arms, with one extended in front of him, palm up, and the closer hand in a trigger configuration. "Blammo."

"You shoot them?" A shudder went through her. Woodchucks were extremely destructive, but the thought of taking a gun to one horrified her.

"You bet. I trained as a sharpshooter a long time ago. I blast their little heads off. Pop them off, one, two, three." He winked at her. "Say, I heard you changed your farm's name back to Attic Hill?" He took a drag on his smoke.

"I did. The name Produce Plus Plus turned out to be really annoying. And I had to explain it all the time." She shrugged.

"Such explanation being?"

"Well, as my volunteer Lucinda put it, the name represented vegetables, plus local, plus community, or something like that. I used to write software, and the language we wrote in was C plus plus." She folded her arms. "Anyway, Attic Hill Farm is a better name, and it means something to the community because of my great-uncle. So do you have time to get me a few bushels of those Spartans?"

"About time I took a break and warmed up these old pegs. After you, my dear." He bowed with a courtly gesture.

As they trudged up the hill, Cam said, "Looks like you didn't complete your addition."

"Oh, that. I ran out of time before the fall, and then I didn't have a minute to spare. We had the best crop ever this year. Conditions were perfect."

"Must be cold in that part of the house."

"I'm not using it at present. It's not finished on the inside, either, so I closed it off."

"It was such a good season. Have you thought about hiring somebody to complete the job?"

"Oh, no." He spread his hands expansively. "I do all my own work."

"So, awful news from Moran Manor. Bev Montgomery dead, and then another woman died, too."

Richard gave her a sharp glance. "Of the same cause?"

"No idea. Pure coincidence, I'm sure. What I'm trying to figure out is, of all the people who didn't get along with Bev, why somebody would go so far as to kill her."

"An extreme measure, certainly. But surely that is the purview of the police, your detective Pappas and his cronies, isn't it?"

"Of course," Cam said. "But since somebody in the state police seems to believe I might have poisoned Bev myself, which of course I didn't, I have a vested interest in figuring out who did."

He nodded.

"I heard that Bev planned to sell you her land." Cam glanced at him while they walked. "That deal must be off now."

"It's early days yet." He waved a hand of dismissal in the air. "I've been trying to get hold of her daughter, Ginger, but she doesn't return my calls." He increased his stride and kept his gaze on the barn ahead.

But Richard had told Pete he'd lost his phone. He must have either found it or bought a new one.

Chapter 21

By the time Cam got home with the apples, it was nearly eleven. Richard had to be the world's biggest schmoozer. He had shown her the cider press and the walk-in cooler. He'd gone on and on about his fall sales, which had bordered on bragging. He'd even introduced her to his cat, Zipper. Richard hadn't elaborated on the friend who'd been in such a big hurry in the black car, on the unfinished addition, or on acquiring Bev's land.

But now she had three bushels of Spartans in the rear of the truck. Driving home, she'd munched a perfectly crisp one and savored the fruit's deep, winey flavor. Richard had said he left them on the trees as long as he could into the cold weather to sweeten them up. Cam's customers were going to love these apples.

A little shudder ran through her when she remembered the car coming straight at her. Such a close call, but Richard hadn't shown much concern. She should give the license plate number to Pete or Ruth, have them check out the car's owner.

She pulled into the barn and unloaded the bushel baskets. She went out and slid the wide door shut behind her, glancing over at the chicken yard. The gate in the shoulder high fence stood ajar. She must not have latched it securely earlier. She let herself into the enclosure and shut it behind her. At least the hens wouldn't want to be hanging around outside in this frigid weather. She peeked into the coop. Everyone seemed to be present and accounted for. Letting herself out again, she headed for the house. When she rounded the corner of the barn, Ruffles ran down the drive at her at full tilt. When he reached her, he started pecking at her shin. His sharp beak poked through her flannel-lined jeans to her skin.

"Hey, that hurts." She pulled one glove off and swatted down at him. "Shoo!"

Rearing up, he flapped his wings, which made him look twice as big, and kept pecking.

"Ruffles, stop it." She kicked her leg sideways, but he simply switched to her other shin. She needed to get him into the chicken yard again. She strode toward it. Luckily, he followed her, still trying to peck her leg. She opened the gate and stepped in. He stood outside the gate, stretched tall, and crowed twice, then sauntered into the yard. She batted at him with her glove, pushing him toward the coop, then stepped around him. She hurried out, latching the gate firmly behind her. The last thing she needed was an attack rooster.

"If I ever find you, M and M, whoever you are," she said, hurrying toward the house, "that rooster won't be the only one getting his neck wrung."

Inside she placed a call to the skilled nursing center at Moran Manor and asked for Albert. Worry about his safety gnawed at her, especially since she couldn't keep him both safe and comfortable at her house.

"Oh, he's not here anymore," the woman told her. "He's gone back upstairs."

"That was fast. Is this Juney?"

"It is, mum."

"This is Cam, Albert's great-niece. Did his dementia go away?"

"Close enough. The doctor, she came by this morning and said he was okay to move to his room. Mr. St. Pierre, he was glad to go."

"That's great news." Cam thanked her and disconnected, then pushed the speed dial for Albert's room.

Marilyn answered. She said Albert was just in the bathroom and would be out in a minute.

"Marilyn, has he stopped hallucinating about the cats?" Cam asked.

Marilyn didn't speak for a moment. "Well, not completely. Oh, here he is," she said in a bright tone.

"Cameron, my dear," Albert said a moment later. His voice lacked its usual vitality. "You heard that they released me from the dungeon?"

"I did. But, Uncle Albert, you know you were in skilled nursing. It couldn't have been that bad. How are you feeling?"

"A bit of a headache. But I'm fine."

"I'm glad. Listen, I want to propose something to you. Why don't you come and stay here on the farm with me for a week or two? I could cook for you and . . ." "And keep you safe," she wanted to add.

"What? That's sweet of you, but it's a harebrained idea. Why, I'd have the devil of a time with those stairs and such. No, I'm used to my room here. I'll be fine, Cameron."

She'd expected this answer, but she didn't like it. How could she guarantee he wouldn't be attacked again? She decided not to ask him over the phone if he remembered any more details about his fall.

"Listen, they're having some damn fool birthday party here

this afternoon," Albert said. "It's for everyone with a January birthday. They told us to invite our relatives. And since you're it for me, consider yourself invited."

"That sounds fun. What time?"

"It's combined with happy hour. And a good thing, too. I'm going to need a drink to sing 'Happy Birthday' to a bunch of old people. See you at four o'clock?"

"It's a date. I'll come early and visit with you. Now, promise me you'll rest. Yes?"

He sighed, said he would, and hung up. *Good.* She could try to gather more information while she visited the residence, and could also keep an eye on Albert.

She switched on the computer and checked her e-mail. It included a reminder about getting her bulk order submitted, a money-saving service NOFA/Mass offered to members. Going in with other farmers when ordering soil amendments, seed potatoes, onion sets, and cover crop seeds, among other items, cut down the cost for everyone. She finalized the order, then made sure there were no comments to moderate on the farm's Web site. After navigating to the Attic Hill Farm Facebook page, she added a reminder about the weekend's share pickup hours. She glanced at the collage of pictures that comprised the page's banner. Ellie appeared in one, showing off the Girl Scout Locavore badge she'd earned the previous summer.

Ellie. She still hadn't talked with Ellie about what she'd remembered. The girl hadn't returned her call last night. Now Ellie was in school again. Cam would call her again this afternoon, for sure. In the meantime, she was still a farmer with paying customers to satisfy.

In the barn a few minutes later, Cam checked the seedlings in the office and swore. One flat had dried out. The tender shoots lay listless on the soil. She brought water from the sink in the main area of the barn and watered them, then turned down the heating pad under that flat. The others looked fine.

As she closed the office door behind her, she cocked her head at a faint noise that sounded like it came from outside. It didn't recur, though. Preston darted into the barn from the cat door in the rear wall, its flap whapping back and forth after him. Her carpenter had installed the door in the new barn so Preston could go in and out at will. She'd hate for him to follow her in and then get trapped inside when she left. And he was great at keeping the barn's mouse population to a minimum. He often batted at the door before he came in.

She went over the list of chores in her head. She needed to move a bucket of the worm castings onto the hoop-house bed where she planned to plant out the lettuce seedlings. Cut and bag enough mizuna and tatsoi for the Saturday shares. And dig more leeks.

As she walked toward the wheelbarrow, she glanced at one corner of the barn and noticed the doors to the root cellar were open. She'd designed the cold storage room and added it belowground when her carpenter, Bobby, constructed the new barn. The cellar featured wooden racks off the ground and away from the wall, a cement floor, and a gentle slope to the wide stairs so they were easy to traverse when carrying a bushel of potatoes or carrots while either descending or ascending. At Cam's direction, Bobby had situated the cellar in a corner under two outer walls of the foundation on the north side. She didn't remember leaving the doors open, but she must have done it the last time she had gone down to bring up winter squash.

She strolled over to close the doors, which were like outdoor bulkhead doors. She smiled at the memory of Ruth referring to those kinds of doors as "Dorothy doors" after they'd watched *The Wizard of Oz* together for the umpteenth time as children. She paused. This would be a good time to check the condition of the storage crops, as well as how much she had left to give out. She flipped the light switch.

The room below remained dark. Cam frowned. How could that be? The compact fluorescent bulbs in both pendant fixtures down there were brand-new last summer, and they were supposed to last for years. The barn had passed its electrical inspection, so it couldn't be a wiring problem. The barn's main floor provided enough light to illuminate the top of the flight of eight stairs. One of the bulbs could have loosened in its socket. Both of them doing so at the same time seemed odd. How much was it going to cost her to fix this? She needed to get a flashlight. With a killer on the loose, no way was she going down alone into a dark cellar.

As she gazed down into the darkness, strong pressure on her back sent her tumbling down the stairs. Crying out, she managed to break her fall with her hands. A loud clunk sounded, and half the light disappeared. One of the doors had fallen shut. Another clunk closely followed. *What?* She lay on the floor in darkness. She heard a heavy scraping noise.

"What the—" Shouting, Cam pushed herself to her feet. She felt her way to the stairs and scrambled up. She tripped and crashed onto her shin. She cursed, reaching for the doors. They didn't budge. She knew the doors didn't have any locks on the outside, only two handles to grasp them with. Whoever had pushed her had somehow locked the doors shut. She beat on them with her fists.

"I'm in here! Open the doors."

Who had locked her in? Maybe the person was still waiting in the barn. Maybe they were spreading gasoline around, lighting a match. . . .

"Let me out of here, whoever you are," Cam yelled. "What do you want?"

No response. Then, faintly, she heard the wide barn door slide slowly shut. She had to get out. She braced her feet and pushed on one of the doors with her shoulder. Whatever the doors were latched with made a noise but did not give way. And her shoulder stung. She was truly trapped.

She slumped on the stairs, rubbing her shoulder. Somebody wanted her out of the way. It had to be Bev's killer or Albert's attacker. Cam, exactly as Pete had feared, had been asking questions and snooping around to the best of her ability. She felt a chill unrelated to the root cellar. If the person returned to attack again, she would have trouble defending herself. She had nothing but a couple of kabocha squash to hurl at him. Or her. Another thought occurred to her that made her heart race. What if whoever had shut her in had taken Preston? He'd been kidnapped before and then drugged. She sent out a little prayer that he'd be all right.

She wallowed in self-pity for a couple of minutes. And then got mad. She made her way back down the stairs until she stood on the cement floor. She would not die down here, after all, or not very soon. When she designed the root cellar, she could have controlled the environment with electronics. Instead she'd installed three-inch-diameter pipes to the outside, one low and one high, to let in fresh, cool air and let out the stale air, which included the ethylene gas ripening vegetables gave off. At least she'd be able to breathe. She sniffed the air. She detected no odor of smoke, unlike the previous time she'd been trapped in the barn, and exhaled with relief.

She could breathe and didn't appear to be in imminent danger of burning. If she heard any noises in the barn, she would yell as loudly as she could. In the meantime, she needed to stay alive. She could eat carrots. She could—

She could use her phone. Her laugh shook, but at least she could still laugh. She drew it out of her pocket and pressed the button on the side that made it come alive. She'd never been so glad to see those glowing numbers and icons. The clock-face display on the front read 12:10. She pressed the green phone icon, the numerals 911, and SEND. It didn't ring. She waited. It still didn't ring. She pulled the phone away from her ear and peered at it.

The little half pyramid in the top corner was displayed in white. No bars. No signal. No connection with a cell tower. No way to contact the outside world. Her heart raced, and her hands numbed. She felt her way up to the doors again. Still no connection.

If she couldn't figure out how to get out . . .

"Damn it, no. I'm smart, and I'm healthy. Plus, I have people who will come searching for me." She carefully felt her way down again and paced to the end of the space, holding one hand out until it touched the wall, then turned and retraced her steps. Or almost. She cried out when her shin hit one of the lower shelves, the same shin she'd hit on the stairs. She revived the phone again and found the flashlight app. Turning it on, she shone it around the cellar. Half the shelves held boxes and baskets full of winter squashes and various root crops, like rutabagas, parsnips, and beets. Carrots sat in sand in a bucket near the wall. Three bushel baskets in the far corner were full of potatoes: Purple Peruvians, Adirondack Reds, Satina Golds.

The light extinguished itself. She pressed the WAKE-UP button again and groaned when she saw the battery display, which showed only one third charged. And she remembered that the flashlight app exhausted the battery power fast. She'd have to save it for when she needed it. Dejection raised its sorry head again. Someone had to come by after missing her. But who? And how long would it take? She didn't have any water. She wasn't sure munching carrots would provide her body with enough fluid.

She tried to muster the anger again to energize herself, but it stayed at bay. All right, she would use logic instead. She paced, but more cautiously now. Today was Thursday. She couldn't expect a shareholder to arrive until forty-eight hours from now. She'd told Albert she would come to Moran this afternoon. Surely he would worry if she didn't show. But if he was still confused because of the fall, as Marilyn had hinted, he might not even remember her promised visit. Or might think she was coming tomorrow or had visited yesterday, which, of course, she had.

Who else would miss her? Pete? Not if he stuck to his guns about not seeing her until they found the murderer. Sometimes Lucinda dropped by to help prepare the shares, but Cam didn't expect to see her until after work on Friday or even Saturday morning. She had a date with Lou Friday night. When he came to pick her up and she wasn't there, he'd just think she'd stood him up. Cam pressed her back against the wall and sank to sitting, chin on arms, arms resting on knees. She knew she wouldn't freeze, since the below-ground temperature stayed at a nearly constant forty degrees. But cold from the concrete seeped through her pants, and she didn't carry a lot of extra padding in that area. The humidity in here stayed high by design, so the air felt not only chilly but damp, too. Hypothermia was a real possibility.

When a whimper escaped her lips, she shook her head hard and said aloud, "No whining, Flaherty. You'll never make it out of here by feeling sorry for yourself."

To keep warm, she rose and paced the length of the cellar and back, over and over, counting the laps aloud until she reached a thousand. She activated the phone. Almost an hour had passed. Still no bars. She had to do something. She wished she'd had the carpenter add an exit to the outside, but she hadn't asked for one. Maybe he'd built one, anyway, without telling her. Her hopes soaring, she creaked to her feet. She pressed the flashlight icon again. Searching for a way out merited using up part of the battery life. She examined every inch of wall. Behind the shelving. Behind the stairs, which didn't even make sense, since they weren't on an outside wall. Behind the mostly empty wine rack.

And her hopes crashed again. Bobby hadn't built a door. No escape. She switched off the light and made her way as far up the stairs as she could before bumping her head on the doors. She beat on the unforgiving wood and rattled the doors. But they were as solidly jammed in place as they'd been an hour before. She held the phone as close to the top as she could. Still no bars. She swore, descending into the cellar again.

Her stomach growled, but she wasn't ready to start eating sandy carrots to survive. She sniffed the air again. She'd had a particular terror of burning buildings ever since she'd been rescued from one just in time as a child. The incident last summer hadn't helped. But the air was still fresh. Still no smoke.

Fresh air. From the inlet pipe. Of course. She used another few seconds of light to find the PVC pipes. They were set into an outer wall of the barn and angled upward toward the outside. The inlet pipe had been placed about a foot above the floor, and the air outtake had been inserted at eye level. If she got the phone closer to fresh air, she'd be that much closer to being picked up by the closest cell tower. She eyed the size of the opening. Her arm might fit. She shrugged her bulky coat off her right arm and pushed her sweater sleeve as far as it would go toward her shoulder, grateful for once for her long, skinny limbs.

Her heart racing, she switched the phone to its speaker function. She could call Pete, but what if he felt he couldn't respond? Lucinda would be working. She was afraid that if she called 911, it would be too hard to explain her situation. *Ruth.* She'd call Ruth's cell. Her friend would see the call whether she was on the job or not. She pressed Ruth's number and then extended her arm as far into the outlet pipe as she could. It stopped at the elbow.

Her smile almost hurt when she heard the phone ring and then Ruth's voice say, "Cam?"

"Ruth, I need help. I'm trapped in my own root cellar in the barn."

"What? This is a terrible connection."

Cam raised her voice. "I need help. I'm locked in." The phone started beeping. The battery was almost dead. Despite the damp cold, Cam began to sweat.

Ruth laughed. "How did you manage that?"

"Just come and get me out." Cam didn't know if she should scream or giggle. Her voice sounded like a mix of the two.

"Problem is, I'm at work. I won't be off until three today. Can you wait? And where are you again? You sound like you're in a cave."

"Ruthie, I told you. I'm in my root cellar."

"Say again. The reception is breaking up."

Cam's heart sank. She could hear Ruth perfectly. Why wasn't it reciprocal? She breathed in deeply and spoke as clearly as she could, whether that made sense or not. "Somebody pushed me into my root cellar here. In my barn. They locked me in and left."

"Oh." The laugh disappeared from Ruth's voice. "That's serious. We'll be right over."

"We?"

"It sounds like a crime scene to me. I'm bringing backup."

Cam was about to tell her to hurry when the phone went dead.

Chapter 22

"**W**as that your shovel they wedged through the door handles?" Ruth gazed at Cam. They sat in the barn's office half an hour later with the door closed and the space heater on.

"Yes. I planned to check on the stored crops in the root cellar. The lights down there didn't come on." Cam hugged herself. "Believe me, I wasn't going down there without a flashlight. But someone pushed me down the stairs. Then the doors shut above me, and I heard a scraping noise. That must have been whoever it was jamming the shovel handle through the door handles."

"But you didn't hear anybody arrive or drive away? No clue at all about who might have done this?"

"No on both counts. I did hear a small noise before I went down the stairs. I thought Preston was swatting his cat door, because then he came through it. I definitely didn't hear a vehicle arrive or leave."

"How long were you down there?" Ruth tapped something into her iPad and then looked at Cam.

"More than an hour." Cam moved closer to the heater, still

chilled to her core. The illumination from the grow lights and the lamp on the desk had never felt so comforting.

"Why didn't you call earlier?"

"I tried. Don't you believe—"

"Calm down, Cam." Ruth patted the air with her hand in the gesture officers made to drivers who were going too fast. "I'm just trying to get the story, okay?"

Cam swallowed. "I didn't call, because I couldn't get any cell reception. After I paced for a while, I finally thought of extending my phone out the air pipe. I don't know why it didn't occur to me before."

An officer poked his head in. "Nothing much to see. Dozens of prints on the bulkhead doors, the handles, and the barn door, half of them smudged. No way to tell which prints belong to the bad guy."

"Lots of people come through this barn. Including all my subscribers," Cam said.

"Haven't found any dropped objects." The officer shrugged. "The guy was probably wearing gloves. And was careful." He held out two light bulbs in his gloved hands. "Found these in a corner. I'll have to print them. Do you have spares?"

Cam pulled two bulbs out of the desk's bottom drawer. "But what about footprints outside?" Cam asked. They had to find who did this to her. And why.

"We'll look. But with the ice—"

"Got it. Thanks," Ruth said.

He closed the door behind him.

Cam hugged herself. "What if he's still out there? Or she?"

"The guys will check the area. Don't worry about that." Ruth checked her iPad again. "You have no idea who might have trapped you down there?"

"I don't think I have any enemies." Cam set her chin in her palm, her elbow on her knee. "But I have been trying to figure

181

out who could have conked Albert on the head. I asked around at Moran Manor a bit."

"Cam." Ruth sounded stern. "You are supposed to leave that to us. Us and Pete Pappas. Besides, there is no evidence that Albert didn't simply black out and fall."

"I don't believe he fell." Cam stared at Ruth. "And it has to all be tied in with Bev's murder. I'm sure it is."

As she was speaking, the door opened again.

"What are you sure of?" Pete stood in the doorway, wearing faded jeans and a leather jacket, a black wool scarf wrapped around his neck. He held Dasha on a leash. Dasha barked twice at Cam and then sat, panting.

"Dasha," Cam said. Smiling, she reached out to stroke his head. She'd kind of missed him. He sat and soaked up the attention. She glanced at Pete. "Dog time?"

His cheeks were rosy from the cold, and his hair was tousled. In those jeans and that jacket he looked good enough to eat. She reminded herself that a murder investigation was in progress.

"I'm off today, and we both needed fresh air," Pete said. "When I heard your address on the scanner, I came right over. Hope you don't mind, Ruth."

"Not at all."

"Are you all right?" Pete looked at Cam.

Cam nodded. She patted Dasha again. "Or I will be when I can go to the house and drink a cup of hot tea. And eat lunch." She glanced at his snow-free shoulders. "Apparently, it isn't snowing yet."

"Only a few flakes," Pete said. "Supposed to get a pretty good storm tonight, though."

And Cam had to be at Moran Manor in an hour or two. She didn't want to disappoint Albert. She should be able to get home before the storm hit with full force.

"What have you got so far?" Pete asked Ruth.

"The guys haven't found anything. No prints, no other evidence."

"So are we all done?" Cam gazed at Ruth.

"I don't know why you're such a crime magnet, Cam." Ruth sighed.

"I'm not. But right now I need to get warm." Cam stood, nearly knocking over her chair.

Dasha jumped to his feet.

"I think he wants to walk you to the house," Pete said. "May we?"

"Sure. Thanks for the rescue, Ruthie."

"All in a day's work." Ruth blinked at Cam. "Go. I'll let you know if we find anything more."

In the house a few minutes later, Cam set two mugs of steaming tea on the table. "Did you eat lunch?"

"I'm all set. Thanks." Pete remained standing, jingling the keys in the pocket of his jeans.

"Well, sit down, already." She brought a turkey sandwich to the table and sank into a chair.

Dasha moved to Cam's side and lay on the floor at her feet. She swallowed her first bite of the sandwich and sipped her tea before she spoke again.

"So when am I going to be off the person-of-interest list?"

Pete finally sat. He cleared his throat. "Effectively, you are already cleared."

"Oh? And when were you going to tell me?"

The furnace in the basement kicked on with a clunk. Warm air began to blow out from the register behind Cam.

Pete sighed. "Look. I haven't found the murderer, and you're pissed off at me. And now somebody's after you." He drummed on the table with his fingertips. "You can't imagine how I felt when I heard your address on the scanner. I might have sounded casual out there in the barn. But I don't feel casual about you. Not one bit." He reached across the table and covered her hand with his.

The skin of his hand warmed hers. He smelled of aftershave and wood smoke. She took a deep breath and let it out. "Do you want to talk about it? The case, I mean."

"I want to. But the most I can do is ask if there's anything else you have learned. About anybody, anything." His face pleaded for understanding.

"Well, we didn't get much out of Nicholas Slavin. It might be worth talking with him again."

He pulled out his phone and tapped in a few words.

"This morning I bought apples from Richard Broadhurst. Somebody tore out of his driveway," Cam said. "And almost ran me down. But I doubt it's related to anything." She withdrew her hand reluctantly and pulled a pad of paper off the counter behind her. She jotted down the license plate number she'd memorized, then slid the paper across the table. "That was the car. It seemed sort of familiar, but I can't place who drives it."

"I'll check it out. We have to investigate every angle, whether it seems important or not. What else?"

"Let's see. I heard Richard is a gambler."

Pete nodded.

"You look like you already knew that. On Saturday, the day before the murder, he took Bev out for dinner. But they were farmer friends. I'm sure there was nothing wrong with that."

Pete just raised his eyebrows and kept working with his phone.

"I told you about the maid on Uncle Albert's floor."

"Yes. Anything about Oscar?"

She shook her head. "He said he didn't see anybody go into Uncle Albert's room that day. And he was collecting trays on that floor. He said he's being targeted as a suspect because of his skin color."

"He can think what he likes. There are several reasons to check him out, and none of them are to do with his being African." He reached down and stroked Dasha.

Cam watched his hand, the same hand that had stroked her in a different way only a few days ago. Her cheeks grew hot and her body tingled. She swallowed hard and finished her sandwich, washing it down with tea. She felt her cell phone in her pocket. She'd left the charger plugged in on the kitchen counter, near the table. She reached over and connected it to the phone. As soon as she did, the text alert sounded. She peered at the screen.

"It's from Ellie. Shoot, I was supposed to return her call. She must have just gotten out of school. Let me check this."

"Be my guest."

She read the message. Need to tell you smthing. Heard dude in bevs room.

Eyes wide, cheeks suddenly cool, Cam extended the phone to Pete. The power cord popped out of the wall, and the device emitted its low-battery noise. She swore. She stood and plugged the power cord in again, then motioned Pete to come closer. "You need to see this." She held the phone up.

His arm pressed warm into hers. He read the message aloud. "I wonder what dude she's talking about." He drummed his fingers on the countertop.

"Hmm. Richard took Bev out to dinner on Saturday. And Frank Jackson visited Moran Manor on Sunday. Bev didn't want to see him. But he whispered something in her ear, and they both went right up to her room after that." She moved away from Pete. If she couldn't have him, she did not need to torture herself with touching him, no matter how good it felt.

"We've been searching for Jackson, for sure."

"Could he have killed Bev?" Cam asked.

"I wish I knew. So much for my day off. Actually, Ellie could have heard any male. Oscar. Jim Cooper, even."

"Did I ever tell you that Ginger Montgomery arrived after Frank did on Sunday? And she went up to Bev's room at the same time Frank was there."

"Interesting. You could have told me that a little earlier."

"Right." Cam jammed her hands into her pockets. "It didn't seem important at the time."

"I need to act on some of this information. But I don't want to leave you alone here." Lines creased his forehead.

"I'll be fine. I'm heading over to Moran soon, anyway."

"Let me check the house for you."

Cam nodded and followed him around while he examined every corner, opened every door.

"Should I be worried that the person who trapped me is going to come back?" *And do worse than lock me away and then leave.* She shuddered and then shook off the feeling. No, she would not live in fear.

"I hope not. Your house is clear, anyway." Pete turned to her. "Do you want to keep Dasha with you for company?"

"I can't. I'm going over to see Uncle Albert. I'll be okay at Moran."

"Call me when you get home."

Cam nodded.

"Thanks for the tea. And—" He looked wistful.

"Just go. You're welcome." She gave him a little push toward the door. "Let me know what you find out. If you can."

He walked to the door, calling Dasha. "Be careful. Please."

She watched them leave and locked the door, checking it twice. She brought the mugs and her plate from the table to the kitchen. The tea had warmed her but had not settled her nerves. She poured wine from an open bottle of merlot into a glass. Preston flapped in through his cat door, clearly having waited until the dog left.

If Ellie had been frightened before, how must she be feeling now? She pressed Ellie's number. It rang three times. Four. When Cam was about to disconnect, Ellie answered in a breathless voice.

"Cam? Did you get my text?"

"I did. We should talk about it. Are you okay? Where are you now?"

"I'm good. Just on my way to work."

"At Moran Manor?"

"Yeah. I couldn't stand not going in."

"How's your mom feel about that?"

Ellie didn't answer for a moment. "I'll call her when I get there. Vince is giving me a ride."

Cam sighed. "You didn't tell her you were going."

"No. She'd only get upset. It'll be okay, Cam." A low voice rumbled in the background. "Hey, Vince says hi."

"Hi, Vince. Listen, Ellie, I'm going over to see Uncle Albert at four. If you get a break, find me and we can talk about what you overheard. How are you feeling about that?"

"I'm down with it." Her voice stayed light. Vince's voice sounded again, and Ellie laughed. "I gotta go, Cam. See you at the Manor." Ellie lowered her voice and warbled the last two words like a horror film announcer.

"See you soon, then." Cam disconnected. *Rats.* She'd planned to tell Ellie that Pete had read the text. He'd want to talk with her about it, certainly. Well, she'd see her in an hour. At least the girl didn't seem freaked out about what she had observed—another example of her resilience.

Cam sipped her wine and munched a couple of cookies. She wandered throughout the downstairs. She needed to shower off after being trapped in the root cellar, and get over to see Albert before the snow started. She checked the door lock one more time.

Chapter 23

Fairy flakes were falling when she pulled onto the road thirty minutes later. The snow remained light and dry from the cold. Mostly, the flakes just flew around, but a layer formed on the trees and the berms of the country road. Switching on the headlights, she drove slowly and checked the edges of the road for tire tracks or any other signs of her attacker, but came up empty. If there had been any tracks in the old snow, the thin new layer of white had obscured them.

Cam stayed in second gear all the way down the steep slope of Attic Hill Road until it joined Bachelor Street. Bachelor had evolved over the centuries into a wider thoroughfare, and plenty of locals treated it more like a speed track than a rural lane. So far no one had raced past her. She passed the ball fields on the left, the tops of the outfield fences barely sticking up out of the accumulated snow, the scoreboard bereft of numbers. From spring to fall this park bustled with children in baseball or softball pants and cleats, parents holding the ubiquitous traveling coffee mug, and younger siblings running and sliding on the playground beyond. In summer the gazebo near the public senior housing hosted a Thursday evening outdoor concert, which was attended by all generations. It echoed a warm, safe season. Not how this winter was going for Cam, exactly.

Now the park lay empty save for one energetic soul clicking his feet into a pair of cross-country skis. She slowed. That man could be the one who had locked her away. She peered at him. It didn't appear to be anyone she knew. *Get real, Flaherty.* She'd go crazy if she thought any random cross-country skier had malicious intent. Plus, he'd be long gone by now. She watched him head out on the trails that led into the town woods. Cam would do the same in her own woods at home tomorrow if this didn't end up being a three-foot storm. Breaking trail in thigh-high fresh snow took a ton of work, not the kind of labor she cared for.

As she stopped at Main Street, the light snowfall became a squall. The Ford's wipers could barely keep up. But she knew how to drive in wintry conditions. She'd grown up in Indiana, and she'd often visited Albert and Marie at Christmas.

She waited, peering in both directions, until the way was clear, and made her left. A quarter of a mile later she rounded the bend, heading toward the small town center. A wide, low boat of a car, like one her grandmother had driven, approached from the other direction. Cam could barely see the driver's head above the steering wheel, and not because of the snow.

The car started to slide toward the middle of the road. The driver could be her attacker. Cam swore. She eased her truck toward the right as far as she could go. The car kept coming. Hitting the brakes wouldn't help. Neither would stepping on the gas. She'd just go into her own spin. She maintained a slow, steady speed, at one point scraping the curb.

At the last second before impact, the nose of the old car turned away. It straightened out. Cam watched its tail fins come toward her, but the driver corrected out of the fishtail and vanished around the bend.

Cam, sweating, glanced in the big side mirror. What stroke of luck had produced exactly no cars following her? Plus, the driver of that car was more likely to be a senior citizen than the person who'd locked her in. She let out a whistle of thanks at escaping a collision and then swore again. She wrenched the steering wheel and turned into the Westbury Food Mart parking lot. She'd almost forgotten to get something for Albert for his birthday, which didn't fall until the nineteenth. He was alive, though, and that was something to celebrate. Every day, if need be. And for today, she was alive, as well. She hated to picture having survived being shut in her root cellar, only to be run into by a senior citizen and to land in a snow pile, or worse.

Warm air and smells redolent of baking and spicy meats welcomed her when she pushed open the door to the small grocery store. The new husband-and-wife owners, a French-Brazilian couple, had recently added a small bakery to the rear. Georges, the husband, baked baguettes worthy of a Parisian bistro. Patricia, his wife, created delectable savory turnovers stuffed with spiced meat and vegetables, as well as desserts that featured egg yolks, sugar, and coconut. Cam wasn't sure how they managed also to run the store, but they seemed to have won over the mostly white, extremely provincial local population with their fresh-baked offerings.

She grabbed a plastic shopping basket and headed for the pastry aisle. A couple of those meat turnovers would be just the ticket for Albert. His doctor had forbidden him from eating sweets because of his diabetes, but he was always complaining about the food at Moran. When Cam had joined him for dinner, she'd never had a bad meal. She supposed the routine of institutional food could wear on a soul, though. She used the available tongs to slide three still-warm turnovers into a bag labeled *PASTEIS* TURNOVERS and then into the basket. He could warm them in the toaster oven in his room. She had no idea why they were called *pastéis*, but they were delicious enough for it not to matter.

When she came around the end of a row by the registers, she nearly ran into Ginger Montgomery, who faced a man wearing a trim dark beard. His jeans and Carhartt barn jacket nailed him as someone who worked with his hands.

"Eddie, this is no place to be having this discussion. See me in my office tomorrow." Ginger folded her arms and pursed her lips.

"I'm not coming into your office ever again. You want to cheat people, you can do it with another carpenter." His voice rose. "And this is a great place to have this discussion. Everyone in town should know about the unethical way you do business."

Cam realized the man speaking had to be DJ's brother. That was why he looked familiar. Eddie, who had worked for Ginger. A man standing in the checkout line turned his head, as did the woman behind the register.

Ginger saw Cam. Her eyes blazed. "What are you looking at?"

Cam held a palm up. "Simply doing some shopping, Ginger."

Ginger turned and marched out of the store, head high, her ire trailing behind her.

"Eddie, I'm Cam Flaherty," Cam said to the man. "You're DJ's brother. He's been helping out at my farm."

Eddie threw one last glance after Ginger, then turned to Cam. "You bet. DJ's my baby brother. I've heard a lot about you, Cam." He smiled and offered his hand. His hair was brown, whereas DJ's was light, and his build was a little stockier, but their voices and heights were similar, as were their genuine smiles.

"He also mentioned something about Ginger Montgomery's

business practices." Cam lowered her voice and cocked her head.

"Yeah. It's a rotten situation. I've had it with working for her."

A plump woman walked toward them, holding a tray full of turnovers. Short dark hair curled over huge green eyes and the widest smile Cam had ever seen. She balanced the tray in her left hand and held out her right.

"I am Patricia Cook," she said. "I am one of the new owners. You like the *pastéis?*" She gestured at the bag of turnovers in Cam's basket.

Cam examined the label. "The turnovers? I love them, and so does my great-uncle. I'm Cam Flaherty. Very nice to meet you." She wanted to ask how a Brazilian got a last name like Cook, but didn't. The previous owners, longtime town residents, had maintained the market, but the place had needed an update after they retired, and these owners had turned out to be a good fit.

"So nice to meet you, too."

"This is Eddie, um—"

Eddie broke in. "Eddie Johns. And I'm a big fan of those turnover things." He winked at Patricia.

"Good to meet you, Eddie."

"Do you happen to know my friend Lucinda DaSilva?" Cam asked Patricia. Their accents were similar, although Lucinda was more fluent in English every time Cam saw her.

Patricia's face lit up. "You are the *fazendeira*. We will buy some of your stuff in the springtime. You know, strawberries and lettuce, and vegetables."

"I'd like that. I'll stop in with samples in May or June, once the growing season gets going. Thanks." This could take the place of the failed Moran Manor idea, if it worked out.

"Very good, very good." Patricia bustled away.

"Are you going to have trouble finding work?" Cam asked Eddie.

"No. People know I'm good at what I do. I tried to get her to change the way she operates." He pursed his lips and gestured with his chin toward the door. "But she wasn't having it. She'll be lucky if someone doesn't sue her."

Cam pulled into the Moran Manor parking lot at exactly four o'clock. She hadn't managed to arrive early, but she was here. Being shoved into and trapped in the root cellar had rattled her, as had sliding in the snow. The parking lot was particularly full, probably because of all the relatives joining in the monthly birthday party, but she found a slot to back into. The sudden snow squall had passed, and while white flakes continued to fall, the volume was still as light as a sprinkling of powdered sugar. Carrying a pair of loafers in her bag so she wouldn't need to wear her snow boots once she arrived indoors, she trudged past a black sedan and then stopped. The sedan was streaked with white dashes of road salt. And bore a bumper sticker that read JEWELERS DO IT WITH STUDS. She reversed her steps and peered at the license plate, her snort at the bumper sticker's message mixing with a zing of excitement at finding the car that had nearly hit her at Richard's this morning. *Now to find the driver.*

Inside, she removed her coat and shook the snow off it before hanging it on the guest coatrack. She changed into her shoes and then signed in, gazing once more at Frank's portrait of the residence. The way he'd captured shadows and light made it a fine piece of art. She turned toward the common room. The sound of conversation mingled with glasses clinking and soft notes from a classical guitar. Albert emerged from the elevator in his wheelchair, with Marilyn leaning on her walker at his side.

"Cameron, you made it." He waved and gestured her over. He was still more pale than usual and seemed diminished somehow. But a big smile split his face, and his eyes crinkled with pleasure.

Cam leaned over to embrace him. "You're looking great. Nice to see you, Marilyn." She smiled at the older woman.

"Shall we go in?" Albert didn't wait for an answer. He spun his wheels and headed for the party.

Marilyn winked at Cam. "I can't tell you how glad he is to be in his own room again."

She ambled behind him at Marilyn's pace. "What about the confusion?" Cam kept her voice low.

"He hasn't said anything goofy in a couple of hours."

"So it must have been disorientation from being in the hospital. The doctor said it would clear with time."

Marilyn nodded.

They entered the busy room. Albert sat at an empty table. Other residents clustered with younger family members at tables and in a row of chairs around the perimeter of the space. A long sideboard displayed hot and cold appetizers, and another held bottles of red and white wine, cider, and sparkling water. Twin boys about the age of Ruth's daughters sat with their mother and grandmother. One boy read a book, moving his lips, while the other played on a small digital device, his feet kicking the legs of his chair. At the far end Ginger Montgomery sat picking out a classical guitar tune. So she could play more than old sing-along favorites.

Marilyn pulled out a chair at Albert's table, maneuvered herself from her walker, and plopped down with a satisfied sigh.

Cam set down her handbag. "What can I get you both?"

"I'll take a glass of red, Cameron," Albert said. "Strictly for my health, you understand. Cider for you, Marilyn?"

"I might try half a glass of red, as well." Her cheeks pinkened. "Just to keep you company."

Albert whistled. "That's quite a bit of company coming from a teetotaler like you, my dear." He raised his eyebrows and patted her hand.

"Oh, hush. A girl can try something new, can't she?"

Cam left them to their sweet talk and brought back two glasses of wine. She went back for another for herself and then brought three plates full of food to the table. She sat facing away from Ginger. She didn't need any more anger from her, not even a glowering look.

"This place goes all out, doesn't it?" She tasted a small pastry. "They must have gotten Patricia to make these little meat pies. Oh, and I brought you some, Albert, but I left them in the truck. Rats." She started to stand.

"Sit down, now. They'll keep."

She obliged but figuratively smacked herself on the forehead for forgetting.

Albert tasted a pastry for himself. "You're right. This is a tasty piece of cooking. Thank you for thinking of me. They'll freeze nicely out there. I can warm them later."

"Who is this *Pah-TREE-see-ah?*" Marilyn asked, mimicking Cam's pronunciation.

"She's Brazilian and one of the new owners of the Food Mart. That is the way she said her name, but I'm sure it's the same as Patricia. And, man, can she ever bake."

Jim Cooper walked into the room and tapped a microphone on a pole positioned at the front. "Hello, everyone," he boomed. "Happy birthday to our January residents."

Refrains of people saying "Happy birthday" echoed around the room.

"We're so glad you all could come. Before we sing, I want to welcome you to enjoy yourselves as long as you'd like. It is snowing out there, though, so don't delay your departure for long. Now . . ." He gestured to Ginger, who switched to the familiar tune.

When the roomful of people began to sing, Rosemary and Ellie walked in. Rosemary carried a tray of cupcakes, each with a lit candle in its center. Ellie directed her to the birthday residents and set a cupcake in front of each in turn. She leaned down and gave Albert a quick kiss on the cheek when she delivered his. She met Cam's gaze. Cam needed to talk with her about her text. But this was clearly not the time.

When the last refrain had faded away, Jim said, "Don't forget to make a wish." He smiled, but it appeared forced.

Albert exchanged a glance with Marilyn, took a deep breath, and easily blew out his candle. Rosemary brought out another tray of cupcakes, without candles, for everyone else.

Albert, Marilyn, and Cam chatted, sipped, and ate. Several friends of Albert's stopped by and said hello. The little boys began hopping on one foot, counting out loud how many times they could do it before needing to balance themselves with the other foot.

"Happy birthday, Albert," a woman's voice said.

Cam glanced up to see the woman with the red walker. The one who'd called her a murderer.

"Thank you," Albert said. "You know Marilyn? And this is my great-niece, Cameron Flaherty."

"Nice to meet you, Marilyn," the woman said, leaning on the handles of the walker, then pressing her lips together. She shot a look at Cam before wheeling away.

"What's her name? And why didn't she say hello to Cam?" Marilyn watched her disappear around the corner.

"I can never remember her name," Albert said. "And I've met her so many times, it feels foolish to ask her now."

"I know why she didn't greet me," Cam said. "She called me a murderer a couple of days ago. She and a tall woman who walked with her. They both acted like I was coming after them next. With an ax, no doubt."

"Why, that's nonsense." Albert frowned. "I'll give her a word next time I see her."

"I'd rather Detective Pappas found the actual murderer," Cam said. "Then we'd all sleep better."

Cam laid three tiles on the Scrabble board an hour later. "*Sex*. Triple letter for the *x* gives me twenty-four. That's twenty-six, and another fourteen for the plural of *submit*. Forty." She glanced over at the pad of paper on which Albert kept score. "And she pulls ahead."

"Very nice, Cam." Marilyn smiled.

"Not so nice that she used my space," Albert grumbled but winked.

Cam rose and walked to the window of the Moran Manor library. The crowd of visitors had cleared out of the residence pretty quickly after the birthday cupcakes were gone, paying attention to Jim Cooper's directive, no doubt. She'd adjourned to the upstairs library with Albert and Marilyn. They had decided to skip dinner after filling up on the appetizers at the party and had started a game instead. The snow fell steadily now, but the storm so far hadn't included much wind and was still light in volume. The light from a lamppost on the walkway outside showed the path covered in white and unmarred by footprints.

"How's it looking?" Albert asked.

"I should be able to get home with no problem," Cam said, returning to the table. She reached into the bag of tiles and drew out three. "Bag's empty," she announced.

Marilyn pondered her turn, and Albert rearranged the tiles on his rack over and over. Cam watched him for a moment. He seemed good. More tired than usual, but that was expected.

"Have you remembered anything about when you hit your head, Uncle Albert?"

He rested his chin on his hand, gazing at her. He put his hand down and shook his head.

"No. I just don't. I suppose I simply tripped over my own feet. Or foot, as the case may be." He returned his attention to the tiles.

"That's what everyone seems to think . . . that you fell," Cam said. "When I first found you on the floor, I said you'd fallen. And I thought you reacted to what I said and shook your head like you were saying no. I must have been mistaken."

"Couldn't tell you." He pulled his abundant brows together, their white tips touching in the middle. He studied his tiles.

"Bingo and out. Again," Marilyn declared. She laid seven tiles on the board, intersecting with Cam's *x* to spell *vexingly*. She glanced up. "What can I do? It all fit so nicely."

Albert groaned and added her eighty-two points. "You win again, Marilyn. Vexingly so."

"And I lose again," Cam said. "Why am I not surprised?"

Ellie popped her head in the doorway. "There you are, Cam. I just finished serving in the dining room. Mr. Cooper told me to go home. He said it's turning into a blizzard out there."

"That's funny. Only a couple of minutes ago it was snowing lightly."

Ellie nodded. "I can't get hold of Vince to give me a ride home, either."

"I'll run you home." Cam stood. She smiled at Albert and Marilyn and leaned down to give them each a kiss on the cheek.

"You be careful out there, Cameron." Albert frowned.

"You bet. Let's go, Ellie." They could talk while she drove.

Cam and Ellie walked down the central staircase and grabbed their coats from the rack. Jim Cooper stood with his hands in his pockets, gazing out the front door. The snow poured down in the light beyond the vestibule. A gust of wind shot the flow sideways.

"Jeez." Cam pulled on her knit hat and stared at the storm. "It changed quickly."

Jim stared at her. "Don't you follow the weather on television?"

"No, Jim, actually I don't. I rarely have time to watch TV." Cam watched the snow. "And the online weather site didn't predict this at all. Same with the app on my phone."

"It's become a blizzard." Jim sounded almost pleased that Cam had been proved wrong.

Rosemary brushed by them. She waved at Jim. "See you tomorrow," she called, hurrying through the doorway.

Cam looked at Ellie. "We don't have far to go. Should we make a run for the truck?"

Ellie looked up from her phone. "My mom would really like me home." She lowered her voice. "I'm kind of in trouble for not telling her I was going to work." She sounded like a shadow of her usual competent, assertive self.

"Then, let's get you there." Cam swapped out her loafers for her snow boots and flipped her hood over her hat for good measure. She made sure she zipped her coat all the way up and pulled on her gloves.

Ellie wore a puffy quilted lavender ski jacket that fit snugly and didn't even cover her rear end. She tugged off her sneakers, tucked her jeans into a pair of black-and-purple Sorel boots with furry tops, and pulled on a pair of purple knit gloves.

"I'm ready." She pulled up to her full height, still half a foot shorter than Cam.

"The highway patrol has asked everyone to stay off the roads, you know." Jim folded his arms. "I don't think you should leave."

"Hey, if it's not safe, we'll come back." Cam longed to be home, and she hadn't shut the chickens in before she left. But safety came first, of course. "It might only be a squall."

She and Ellie stepped into the vestibule, both hugging their bags to their chests, and then ran into the storm. Cam grabbed Ellie's arm when the wind smacked her in the face. They hurried toward Cam's truck. During the two hours that she'd been parked, several inches of snow had coated the Ford. She used her gloved hand to brush the white stuff off above the passenger door and then opened it. She tossed in her bag.

"Hop in and stay warm. I'm going to start it and then brush off the windshield."

Ellie climbed in but emerged a moment later with Cam's snow brush and the small broom Cam had stashed on the floor.

"I'll help." Ellie kept the long-handled brush and began clearing the windshield from the passenger side. On the opposite side Cam got the engine running and then broomed the snow off the top of the cab. Headlights sprang to life and shone in Cam's face. She held up a hand to shield her eyes. An engine gunned, and the sound of tires spinning filled the air. The vehicle seemed to gain traction. It started to spin.

Cam's heart thudded. She got ready to dive into the snowbank.

The headlights spun away, and the rear of the car swung.

Now the car sat sideways, blocking Cam's truck. The engine cut out. Cam stared. The car was the same black sedan that had almost hit her at Richard's. The one with the jeweler bumper sticker. Cam exhaled.

Rosemary climbed out of the car and slammed the door. "Damn snow." She caught sight of Cam. "Better change your plans. Nobody's going anywhere." She raised her voice to be heard over the howling storm.

"Did you have to block me?" Cam shouted in return. "We were trying to get out."

"I didn't mean to block you. I couldn't control the car. Bald tires are worthless."

"Can't you move it?"

"No. Give it up." Rosemary stomped with bent head to the building.

So it had been Rosemary at Richard's. Twice she'd driven straight for Cam. Accidentally or on purpose? A wild gust blew a new load of snow right back onto Cam's truck, where she'd brushed it off. Ellie's efforts to clear the windshield were almost as Sisyphean as trying to roll a boulder uphill. Cam trudged around to the passenger side.

"We're not going to make it out, Ellie. And if we did, I wouldn't be able to see where I was driving. Let's go in and stay warm. It has to subside sometime. Then I'll drive you home."

Ellie nodded with wide eyes. Cam stashed the brush and the broom in the truck and grabbed their bags, along with Albert's *pastéis*. She didn't bother locking the doors. She didn't have anything inside to steal, anyway.

Chapter 24

Cam and Ellie shed their coats. Cam held hers out in front of herself and gave it a shake to rid it of snow. Ellie followed suit. Snow coated Cam's hat. Brushing it off, she glanced over to see Jim Cooper standing with arms folded, wearing a satisfied look. She turned away from his smarmy face and changed into her loafers again. Ellie went through the same motions. In the few minutes Cam had been outside, snow had blown into her boots, so now her socks were damp.

"Make yourselves comfortable in the common room," Jim said with the magnanimity of the victor. "Help yourselves to tea, hot chocolate, or whatever."

"Thanks, Mr. Cooper," Ellie said. "I'm for some hot chocolate after I call my mom." She turned to Cam. "My uncle can help her if she needs something. He lives next door." She headed for the common room.

"You have one awesome employee there, I hope you know," Cam said. She watched Ellie walk away.

"I know." Jim turned toward his office. "Oh, and the television is tuned to the weather station in there. In case you're interested."

"Thanks a million," Cam muttered to herself as she followed Ellie. Being stranded here for hours to come wasn't her plan for a good time. She yawned. It had been a long, full day, and all she wanted was to snuggle with Preston on her own couch and talk to no one. With any luck, this would be one of those fast-moving storms that blew through and headed out to sea in short order.

In the common room, Ellie already sat in the corner of a couch, with her feet tucked under her, her phone to her ear, a steaming mug on the table beside her. Only a few residents occupied chairs. One man bent over a table, reading a newspaper. Two women sat in easy chairs and chatted softly while they knitted. A television mounted to the ceiling emitted pictures and sound and was indeed tuned to the weather station. Cam fixed a cup of peppermint tea in the snack area. She helped herself to a packet of pretzels and stood in front of the screen. The time in the lower corner read six thirty. A commercial finished, and a chyron for the current local weather appeared.

"This nor'easter has settled in for the night, folks," said a weather woman in a sleek lavender dress. She gestured at the map behind her. Her hand followed the circle of the storm, illustrated with shades of blue, except for patches of purple way out to sea.

Cam groaned. *Blue for snow.*

"We can expect the heavy snow, with wind and drifting, to continue until at least the early hours of the morning," the broadcaster went on, her tone bright and her manner perky despite the dire forecast. "Please stay indoors and safe. Keep those flashlights and batteries handy. If you lose power, never use a generator indoors, and don't grill food indoors, either. We'll be back after the break." She smiled into the camera.

Cam sank into an easy chair near Ellie, who was still chatting away on her phone. Cam munched the pretzels and sipped her tea. *Preston.* Poor kitty was going to be hungry tonight, but he would have enough sense to stay indoors, even though she'd left his cat door open. And with any luck the chickens would stay inside the coop, as well, despite their unlatched door. If Ruffles ventured out and died in the storm, well, he would be one more frozen chicken for the stew. She grabbed a *New Yorker* from the end table and leafed through it, scanning the cartoons, but her thoughts were on those headlights coming straight at her. She wasn't sure she should believe Rosemary's explanation that her car had spun out of control, not after what had happened at Richard's farm. Which had been only this morning. It seemed like days ago. But why in the world would the cook be after Cam? It didn't make sense.

The night promised to be a long one. As soon as Ellie got off the phone, Cam would find somewhere to talk with her in private. Then she could use part of the time she was stuck here to sort out the mess that was Bev's murder. She carried Albert's *pastéis* up to his room, but when she saw he was on the telephone, she left them with a little wave and returned to the common room.

The room began to fill. The residents must have just finished in the dining room. The two suspicious ladies walked in and glanced at Cam, the tall one whispering to the one with the walker. They turned around and left the room. The girl Felicity had introduced as Ray walked in, bent her head down to talk with Ellie, and the two also left. A game of dominoes started among three men at a small table, and two couples began to play cards in the corner. An article on the ethical implications of the latest technological inventions had caught Cam's attention: if someone wearing Google Glass took a video of a person without his or her knowledge, did that violate the person's privacy? She raised her head at a noise.

Jim Cooper stood in the wide doorway, Ginger Montgomery

at his side. He clapped his hands twice. "May I have your attention, ladies and gentlemen? As you know, many of us who do not live here missed our chance to get home safely before the blizzard hit. Ms. Montgomery is one of those, and she's agreed to provide us with another concert this evening. Let's give her our full attention." He turned to Ginger. "Thank you, and take it away."

The man reading the newspaper frowned. "What if we liked it nice and quiet, like it had been?"

Jim scowled at him but left the room without responding. Ginger pulled a stool to the front of the room and extracted her guitar from its case. She started to tune it.

Cam had no idea why Ginger was even still here. She could have left earlier with all the other guests. Her mother was no longer alive. She and Jim seemed kind of chummy. Could be that a romance was brewing there or was already under way. Cam shrugged. Not her business. But she agreed with the man, who now rose, folded his paper, and stomped out. Well, she could read just as well with music in the background. She returned to the article, which raised several intriguing questions.

"Oh, Cam," Ginger called, beckoning to her.

Cam rose with a sigh and walked to Ginger's side.

"I can't seem to find my music. Would you mind getting it out of my car for me? If my hands get cold, I won't be able to play."

"Out of your car? You want me to go out into a blizzard to get sheet music? Don't you know any songs by heart?"

"I promised to make this a special concert, and I need my music."

"What happened to your music from this afternoon?" Cam's voice rose.

Ginger waved a hand. "I'd already put it back in the car before I decided to stay and eat with Jim. Please?" She raised her voice a notch. "I won't be able to produce anything for these nice people with frozen fingers." She threw on a smile and took in the dozen waiting seniors who were listening. Several nodded their heads.

"I suppose," Cam muttered. "I hope you're parked near the door."

"I am. I'll get my keys for you." She walked with Cam to the coatrack.

While Cam suited up again and changed her footwear, Ginger rummaged in the pockets of her winter coat. She produced a set of keys.

"It's the Lexus in the first spot to the right. The music should be on the backseat. I thought I'd put it in my case, but I must have—"

"I'm getting your damn music, all right?" Cam jammed her hat down with both hands until it fully covered her forehead and ears.

Ginger turned on her heel and stalked away. Cam pushed through the inner door into the entryway and then through the outer door into the storm. She glanced behind her into the brightly lit lobby. Ginger was nearly to the common room. The warm, dry common room.

The wind and the snow blew even more fiercely now than they had before. The precipitation fell heavily and stuck to everything. Within seconds the cold penetrated her warm coat and chilled her cheeks. She found the car, which Ginger had, in fact, parked as close to the entrance as it could be. She unlocked the car, slipped the keys into her pocket, then located the music and tucked the folder inside her coat, hugging it to her so it didn't drop. As she fumbled for the keys to lock the car again, they caught on a thread and then came out of her pocket with such momentum that she dropped them in the snow. She tried to fish them out, but it was too cold and dark. She only hoped nobody would think of stealing a luxury vehicle in a blizzard.

She trudged back to the building and grabbed the outer door handle. The door didn't budge. She tugged at it. She rattled it. It wouldn't open. She knew the staff locked the residence after a certain time of night, but she didn't believe they normally locked it until eight or so.

She pounded on the door, but the noise of the storm stole the sound of her knocking. She peered inside. No one moved anywhere near the door. She saw only one woman slumped in a chair on the far side of the lobby, a woman who seemed to doze in that chair every day and evening. Cam started to panic. Her teeth chattered until she clamped her mouth shut. With this cold, she was in real danger out here.

But the place must have some kind of doorbell. She searched the right side of the doorway. No bell button. She moved to the left. A doorbell. Her hands were already thick from the cold, and she couldn't manage to press it with her gloves on.

As she drew off one glove to free a finger, the lights inside went off. As did the outer light. She swore. The residence had lost power. She pressed her face against the glass in the door. Red exit signs glowed. Then a few low lights came on. An emergency generator must have kicked on.

Cam pressed the doorbell over and over. But no one came. Doorbells operated on electricity, she realized with a sinking heart. Surely Ginger would wonder where she was any minute now. But no one appeared.

She abandoned pressing the bell and pulled her glove on again. Her heart raced. She beat on the door again, but nobody came. How would she survive this? Her cell phone sat safely in her bag, which lay next to the chair where she'd been warm and reading only minutes ago. She could sit in Ginger's car She could even start the engine and crank the heater if she could find the keys in the snow. But she'd heard of people dying in cars from inhaling exhaust because their tailpipe was buried in snow. And if she sat in the car without heat, she'd freeze. She didn't know why Ginger hadn't come after her. Unless she'd meant to lock Cam out. Maybe Ginger was involved in her own mother's murder and knew Cam had been trying to find the killer. That was a prospect too terrifying even to contemplate.

But Cam had long, strong legs and a good coat. Oscar might be out on the back porch, having a smoke. The rear door could have been left unlocked. She needed to find that porch. She closed her eyes and tried to picture the rambling building. Which way around would be the shorter? It had to be the right side, since the left side held the extra wing for the Alzheimer's and dementia residents. She pulled her hat down as far as it would go, snugged her scarf around her neck, and began wading through the snow, always keeping the building to her left. She didn't think she should even attempt to find the path that circumnavigated the property. She could end up wandering into the woods that surrounded the facility or, worse, into the stream that ran through the woods. She stuck her left hand out, keeping it in contact with either the shrubs or the building itself. Her right hand she kept in her pocket, which warmed it ever so slightly. The folder of music slipped out of Cam's coat, the sheets scattering into the storm like abandoned wishes. She let them go.

Almost no light came from the windows, only the red glow of the exit signs and a few dimly lit areas. She trudged, struggling through snow up to her knees. She felt like Pa in Laura Ingalls Wilder's *On the Banks of Plum Creek*. He'd held tight to the rope they'd looped over the clothesline between the barn and the house on his way to and from milking the cows. It ensured that he wouldn't wander out on the prairie and be found frozen in a snowbank when the weather thawed in April. Her left hand grew numb from holding it out and from brushing it through the snow on the bushes. The blizzard stung Cam's exposed eyes and cheeks.

The dim light from the building disappeared. She must be at a section with no windows. All of a sudden the shrubs fell away. She reversed a step and found the last one. She cautiously moved forward and felt to her left. The row of shrubbery stopped, but no solid building took the place of the bushes. She stepped back, trying to visualize how the property had looked in October, when she'd pushed Albert in his wheelchair on a colorful fall walk around the perimeter of Moran Manor. She cursed. This had to be the pathway lined with rhododendrons that led out from the building. She'd just plowed her way through a bunch of extra steps. What she had to do now was go around the end of the row and follow the other side of the shrubs back to the building.

As she struggled in the snow, Cam decided that her first task after getting inside and warming up was going to be wringing Ginger Montgomery's slender throat. That satisfying image disappeared when her foot caught on an obstacle under the snow. She lost her balance and fell forward. She reached for the branches but grasped nothing. Two wild, stumbling steps and her head hit something solid. She collapsed in a heap. She shut her eyes. She must have tripped on a root, or maybe on an electrical cable, and hit the building. It felt good to sit here. Her extremities were chilled through, but under her sweater she sweated from the exertion. On top of her exhaustion, now her head hurt. She could just sit here and rest for a while. After all, hadn't Pa survived a different blizzard by digging a snow cave?

A damp cold began to creep up from her rear end. Her body heat melted the top layer of snow and soaked her pants. She pushed herself to standing, scolding herself aloud.

"You can sit here and die, or you can get your sorry self into that building."

At least now she had the solid building to guide her. She slogged ahead, remembering what Ruth had said years ago, when the two of them were hiking in New Hampshire's White Mountains. They'd hit a particularly steep section of Kinsman Mountain.

"Be as a camel," Ruth had said. "One foot in front of the other."

Cam put one foot in front of the other. She kept her left hand on the wall. Her feet were turning into blocks of ice. Not much feeling remained in her left hand. She'd had no idea what a daunting task she'd faced, or what a dangerous one. She could hardly have been more stupid than to go into a blizzard for sheet music to begin with.

"If I hadn't dropped the keys, I could have honked the horn. I should have turned her car on and rammed the building," she said aloud, with lips stiff from the cold, and then giggled. "That would have gotten somebody's attention." The image of ruining both the Lexus and the front door of the residence cheered her, despite her logical side scolding her for even imagining carrying out such an outrageous feat.

She turned a corner and continued. She spied a glow in the wall, and then she touched a window. The glow had to be an emergency light inside. The sill sat right below her eye level, but snow stuck to the screen. She couldn't see in. She beat on the window and yelled. The storm howled around her.

No one responded. She pushed on to find the rear door. But what if she didn't? Maybe the door wouldn't open. She pushed her boots through the deep snow like a farmer wading through a muddy marsh to rescue a stranded lamb. Who would miss her if she died out here? *Preston, probably. Albert, for sure. Pete? Maybe.* With the window behind her, it grew dark again and the blowing snow obscured her vision.

She tripped again and fell forward. Her hands landed on a solid surface a few feet aboveground. The back porch. It had to be. She raised her head. The covered porch faced her. She climbed onto it. The snow, now at least not falling from above, lessened. She found the door and raised her hand to pound on it. She stopped and tried the knob instead. It turned. She'd never been so in love with an unlocked door.

Chapter 25

The door pulled open from the inside. Cam stumbled directly into Oscar's chest. He put out an arm to steady her. "Sorry," she said, gaining her balance.

The astonishment on his face was unmistakable. "What were you doing out there?" He held an unlit cigarette in his left hand.

"I was locked out at the front." Her lips were so cold, it was hard to speak clearly. A shudder ran through her from head to toe.

"And you walked all the way around the building in the storm?" He ushered her in and closed the door, pulling it tight. "I don't know if that's brave or foolish."

She shivered. "I had no choice. It was that or freeze to death."

"Well, get in here and warm yourself." He stuck the cigarette in his shirt pocket and gestured at a chair in the corner. "Sit down. You want coffee or tea?"

"Whatever is the quickest." She removed her hat and threw it on the stainless-steel counter, then sank into the chair. She could not bring herself to shed her coat yet. She inhaled the welcome scents of cinnamon and coffee. Two white emergency lights mingled with the red exit sign above the doorway to cast a soft pink light on the room.

"The java was fresh right before the power went off. I was just having a cup myself." Oscar busied himself with an insulated carafe at the other end of the room. A minute later he set a steaming mug next to her. He added a half dozen sugar packets, three little pods of half-and-half, and a spoon.

"Thank you, Oscar." She poured all the sugar and all the cream into her mug and stirred. This solicitous side of Oscar contrasted with the angry man she'd seen earlier.

He reached into the rear of a cabinet and drew out a bottle of brandy. "For medicinal purposes only, of course. It's Rosemary's private stash." He opened it with a grin pulling at the corner of his mouth. At Cam's nod, he added a couple of glugs to her coffee and a couple to his own, and then replaced the bottle in the cabinet. "She thinks nobody knows about it."

She sipped. The hot, sweet alcoholic drink went down like perfection. The fumes brought water to her eyes. Warmth spread through her, not quite to her toes, but close. She unzipped her coat and slid out of it but kept it draped over her shoulders.

"So what were you doing outside, anyway?" Oscar asked. "Tell me you weren't trying to drive in this."

She explained about Ginger and the music. "What I don't understand is why she didn't wonder what happened when I didn't reappear. Why she didn't come search for me and let everyone know I had disappeared. And why the outer door was already locked. Don't they do that at eight or nine?" She glanced at the big wall clock, which read only 7:15. "I'm surprised the door stayed locked when the power went off, come to think of it."

"I don't know how that stuff works." He leaned his back

against the counter and folded his arms. "I'll tell you, I don't like that Ginger much."

"You're not alone." Cam pulled off her boots and massaged her toes. They tingled when feeling began to return.

"But she and Jim have a thing going on. We're not going to see the end of her anytime soon." Oscar raised his eyebrows.

"I wondered about that."

Rosemary burst, cursing, through the swinging doors. She stopped short when she saw Cam and Oscar.

"So there you are. People have been looking for you, Cam." She set her hands on her hips and glared at Oscar. "And what are you doing in my kitchen?"

Oscar held up a hand. "Calm down, Cookie. Cam was out in the blizzard, if you can believe it, and by some miracle she found the back door. I'm helping her get warm. The coffee was brewed, anyway."

"Don't call me Cookie," Rosemary spat at Oscar. She cocked her head at Cam. "You were in the storm?"

"I was. Long story." Cam frowned, not really seeing Rosemary. The story could have been so much longer. "Ginger Montgomery asked me to get her sheet music from her car. I was stupid enough to agree, and then I couldn't get back in." Her ire rose again.

"That's terrible," Rosemary said, looking horrified. "What? You walked all the way around the building?"

Cam nodded. "I'm never helping her again. You can be sure of that."

Rosemary sniffed the air. "What's in that coffee, anyway?"

"Only cream and sugar." Cam smiled with what she hoped was an innocent expression and gestured at the detritus of packets and empty cream pods on the counter. Oscar leaned against the wall, with a face like the Cheshire cat's. A tall black Cheshire cat.

Rosemary drummed her fingers on the counter. "I hate being stuck here. I need to get home."

"You miss your Ricky?" Oscar asked.

"What are you talking about?" Rosemary's eyes opened wide, and her gaze darted back and forth. With no chef's toque to contain her bottle-blond hair, it curled around her face. Jennifer Aniston layers reached to her shoulders. Her fingers stopped drumming, and she pushed her hair off her forehead with one hand.

"I've heard you addressing somebody as Ricky on your cell," Oscar said. "It sounded pretty lovey-dovey."

"Not tonight, you didn't. Blizzard must have taken out the cell tower. My phone went totally dead a few minutes ago." Rosemary pressed her lips together.

"Do you live with Richard Broadhurst?" Cam said. She sipped the coffee, her toes thawing at last.

"No. I mean—" Rosemary's eyes narrowed. "Well, yeah, I do." She pulled her mouth to the side. "There I go, blabbing secrets again. But how did you know that?"

"You almost ran me down this morning. I was over at the orchard, looking for Richard to buy a few bushels of apples from him."

"I didn't even see you. I was late for work."

"I didn't realize you were the driver, but I noticed the license plate number and the bumper sticker. When I got here this afternoon, I saw the car. I didn't know it was yours until I saw you getting out of it tonight. You know, when you almost ran me over again."

Rosemary cleared her throat. "Sorry about that." She had the grace to appear chagrined.

"Why should your living with Richard be a secret?" Cam asked. "You're both adults, right?" Come to think of it, Rosemary might have a reason to hide the relationship, after all.

Depending on how long it had been going on, Richard might have been cheating on Hannah's mother.

"Not telling." Rosemary tilted her head. "That's what *secret* means."

"So how long have you been with Ricky?" Oscar asked, still sporting a faint smile.

"Don't call him Ricky. We've been hanging out for a while." Her face took on a dreamy cast. "At first I just rented a room from him for my jewelry business. And then we kind of got together."

"So you make jewelry?" Cam cocked her head.

"I do. I like to mix metals—gold, silver, copper." She put her fingers behind her earrings and tapped them. "And I sell them at craft fairs and such. Interested?" She dug a small flashlight out of a drawer, switched it on, and then handed it to Cam.

Cam stood and stepped closer to check out the earrings. The flashlight illuminated elongated triangles of silver with a copper streak and a tiny gold knob offset near the bottom.

"Those are beautiful," Cam said. "But you work as a cook, too?"

"Gotta pay the bills. And I racked up a chunk of debt in the past, which I need to get clear of." She walked over to the cabinet in which Oscar had found the brandy. She drew the bottle out. "Since we're all stuck here, how about a nip?"

Oscar and Cam exchanged a quick glance.

"Why not?" he said. "I'm off duty. Just can't get home."

"Sure. Let me go check on Ellie first," Cam said. She drained her mug and set it down. "I'll be right back."

Cam padded out in her stocking feet and found Ellie on the same couch where she'd been earlier in the evening. With mouth pulled down, Ellie stared at her phone.

"What's up?" Cam sank onto the cushions next to her.

"Phone service got killed." Ellie frowned more deeply. "Where have you been? That Ginger lady was all kinds of pissed off at you for not bringing her music in. After the lights went out, she asked Mr. Cooper to go out and call for you, but you weren't there. And then she stopped playing and disappeared somewhere."

"She was pissed at *me?* I was the one locked out in the blizzard." Cam rubbed her hands together. They were warm on the outside but still felt cold inside.

"What? You were, like, outside all this time?"

"Almost. I made it around to the back door. Barely. The door was unlocked. Oscar gave me a cup of coffee in the kitchen, and I'm finally almost thawed out."

"Being out in a blizzard? That's bad, Cam."

"You bet. I was wondering if Ginger locked me out there herself."

"Do you think she'd do that?" Ellie looked horrified.

Cam rubbed the tops of her chilled thighs. "I sure hope not. Have you seen her around? I'd like to . . . well, at least get the story from her about why she didn't come looking for me."

"Not lately."

"I guess she didn't lock me out if she sent Jim out to search for me. By then I must have been halfway around to the back. I couldn't hear anything with the wind howling. But I'd still like to talk with her."

Ellie glanced at the phone in her hand, and her glum expression returned.

"You don't look happy," Cam said.

"No cell coverage. I talked to my mom again before we lost service, and told her we were, like, stuck here. She's not that cool with it, but what can you do? But I wanted to call Vince, too, and now I can't."

"I'm sure the cell tower will come back online before long."

Cam glanced around the room. The bridge players still sat at their tables, bent over and peering at their games with little flashlights like Rosemary's, and a man slumped, snoring, in an easy chair, but most of the rest of the seats were empty. How long was she going to have to stay here?

"You said you heard a man in Bev's room." Cam lowered her voice. "Shall we talk about it now?"

Ellie nodded. "It was Sunday. I was upstairs, collecting dinner trays from the residents who ate in their rooms."

"I thought Oscar said he collected the trays."

"He asked me to do it after I finished serving in the dining room. I was near Mrs. Montgomery's room when I heard shouting."

"Do you remember exactly what you heard?" Cam checked around to make sure nobody was listening. She leaned closer to Ellie and laid her arm across the top of the couch.

"He said, 'If you don't give me the money, you're going to be killed.' "

Cam whistled softly.

Ellie's eyes narrowed. "So he must be the murderer, right?"

"I don't know. I showed Detective Pappas your message when it came in this afternoon. We'll have to tell him exactly what you heard. Did you recognize the man?"

"It was Frank Jackson, that dude we saw earlier on Sunday, the one Mrs. Montgomery didn't want to talk to. He came out of her room. I pretended I was going to get the tray from Mrs. Benson next door."

"Did you happen to hear Bev's response to what he said?" Cam asked. *Frank. Threatening Bev. Yikes.*

Ellie shook her head. "No. At least Mr. Jackson isn't trapped in here with us tonight. That would be epic scary."

He didn't say that he himself would kill her. *Interesting.* Cam sat back. "How was Bev when you went in to get the tray?"

"I never did. I was scared Frank had gone back in. Oscar must have picked up Mrs. Montgomery's tray later."

"But, Ellie, why didn't you tell the detective this earlier?"

Ellie studied the nails on her left hand, nails with green polish half worn away. "I sort of forgot." She gazed up with worried eyes. "That's not really the truth. I didn't forget I'd heard him say that. But it was just, you know, really scary. I felt like if I talked about it, that made it more real or something. I'm sorry."

"Not a problem. You're not the one on trial here, anyway. And you're safe, Ellie." At least Cam hoped so. What had Frank meant by "You're going to be killed"? Did that mean he hadn't threatened Bev with death himself? That someone else would kill Bev if she didn't give Frank money? And what power had he possessed over her? She could have owed him money from their days in the Patriotic Militia, Cam supposed. Or maybe he'd held a piece of information Bev didn't want made public. Pete needed to know of this new development, but she couldn't tell him now.

Unless they had landlines. Cam spied a phone on a desk in the corner and went over to try it. It was the type that didn't work without electricity, though, so there was no dial tone. She returned to the couch.

Ray walked up and plopped into an easy chair opposite them, slinging one leg over the arm. She sported the same uniform as Ellie—a Moran Manor polo shirt, skinny jeans, and leather sneakers—except her shoes were purple, whereas Ellie's sported black-and-white stripes, and Ray wore a discreet jeweled stud in one nostril.

"How's it going, Ray?" Ellie asked with a smile.

"Work's all done. We're stuck here. No cell. No fun." Her sleek black hair curved down around her chin on one side and was cut above her ear on the other.

"Hey, Cam. Have you met Ray?"

"Briefly, last weekend," Cam said. "I believe I know your parents, Neela and Sunil. I'm the organic farmer up the road."

"They totally love your vegetables." The girl grinned.

"And you don't?" Ellie cocked her head at her friend.

Ray cast a glance at Cam. "You know, with them it's, like, kale this, kale that. They'd totally eat kale ice cream if they could. I mean, really?"

Cam laughed. "Me, I'd draw the line at that one." She stood. "I'll let you girls visit. Ellie, I'll be in the kitchen for a while."

"For shizzle," Ellie said with a wave.

Cam walked away, remembering when she and Ruth would utter a piece of teen slang that left adults bewildered. Yup, she was an adult now.

Maybe she should look for Ginger and have it out with her. But in the dim emergency lighting, the thought of finding Ginger alone made her uneasy. No, that could wait. She'd had enough close calls for one day. For one lifetime.

Chapter 26

Cam joined Oscar and Rosemary in the kitchen again. Rosemary now occupied the chair Cam had sat in, and Oscar perched on the counter, next to the bottle of brandy. Rosemary gestured to a stool.

"Park your derriere, Cam. But first help yourself." She pointed to the bottle.

Cam poured a couple of glugs of brandy into her empty coffee mug, then eased herself onto the stool. She lifted the mug.

"Cheers." She took a small sip of the straight brandy. A trace of her sweet coffee came with it, making it taste like Kahlúa. "Here's to a safe, uncomplicated life." Maybe she could finally relax.

"And here's to electricity and no more snow this winter." Rosemary sipped from her own mug.

"I'll drink to all of that." Oscar reached his mug over to tap Cam's.

"Boy, same here. While I was walking around the building, I kept thinking I should have rammed the residence with Ginger Montgomery's Lexus." Cam giggled. "Serve her right for leaving me locked out in a storm."

Oscar looked at Cam. "That takes balls to even come up with the idea of it."

"I'm glad now I didn't." She snorted. "But can you imagine her reaction?"

Oscar sipped from his mug and eyed Rosemary. "Hey, Cookie. What was up with Richard taking Bev out for all those meals, anyway?"

"Don't call me Cookie." Rosemary shook her head, her hair waving along. "I don't know. He didn't want to talk with me about it."

"He took Bev out a lot?" Cam asked.

Oscar nodded. "Yup."

Cam cocked an ear at a high-pitched whistle. "It's still howling out there."

"Do you have farm animals, Cam?" Oscar asked. "How do they do in this cold and snow?"

"Only chickens and a cat." A sharp pang struck Cam. She pictured the hens and Preston. She was warm, mostly, and comfortable. They were alone and cold, with no fresh food or water. "So far they've survived, except for one extremely dumb chicken who stood outside for too long earlier this week and froze herself to death."

Rosemary laughed, her earrings swinging. She twirled her flashlight around the room, drawing circles on the walls and the ceiling. When the light passed over Cam, Rosemary stopped and shone it on the side of her head. "Looks like you lost an earring."

Cam brought her hands to her ears. "Oh, no." Sure enough, one ear was empty of decoration. "Well, shoot. Those were my favorite eggplants." She fingered the remaining one, a miniature purple vegetable shaped like a real eggplant. Ruth had given her the pair as a farm-warming gift when Cam took over Uncle Albert's business.

"So you need a new pair." Rosemary stood and walked to a closet at the far end of the room. She returned with a zippered bag made of an Asian-looking black damask. She opened it on a clear section of the countertop and laid out several pairs of earrings. "Shop to your heart's content." She waved Cam over, then handed her the flashlight.

"I don't know. I'm pretty short on cash these days." She peered at them. Each pair was unique, but they all contained the same three metals as the earrings Cam had admired earlier.

"They'd be good on you, especially the long, dangling ones with your short hair," Rosemary urged.

"They're lovely. You are very talented." Cam fingered each set. The earrings were hooked into small squares of cardboard bearing a swooping logo that included the initials RC and a tiny silver hammer. "How much are they?"

"For you, twenty. I sell them for up to forty at craft fairs."

Cam sighed and picked up a pair with two long strands each. "I like these a lot. Let me get my wallet. It's in my bag out in the common room."

"Pay me whenever. I know where to find you."

"Thanks." Cam slid her remaining earring out. She fumbled while inserting the new ones. "My fingers haven't yet recovered from being out in the cold." She faced Oscar. "What do you think?"

"Like I can see them? All women look great in the dark, earrings or no earrings."

Cam laughed, sticking the remaining eggplant in her pocket before she plopped on her stool again. This all felt surreal. They were trapped inside, with essentially no power in a dangerous blizzard, and she was buying earrings.

"Hey, Oscar, who is the house cleaner who looks sort of

Slavic?" Cam asked. "High cheekbones, blond hair? I talked to her a day or two ago, but I didn't catch her name."

"Oh, that's 'Tash. Short for Natasha. Her parents are Russian, but she's trying to ignore her heritage." He lifted one shoulder. "It happens. What did you talk with her about?"

"I'm still trying to figure out what happened to my uncle, how he fell. I thought she might have seen somebody go into his room."

"And what did she say?" Rosemary asked. She faced away from Cam and put the rest of the earrings back into the bag.

"She seemed nervous and said she didn't see anything. She wouldn't talk to me after that."

"She's all right," Oscar said. "But I'm not sure if she's documented. Her parents might have brought her here as a young child. Jim Cooper isn't real careful with the cleaning crew."

Cam sipped the brandy again. "So she doesn't want to talk for fear her status will be exposed." She frowned.

"Possible," Oscar said.

Tash had been fine when Cam first spoke to her, though. Only when Cam asked her if she'd seen someone near her uncle's room did the young woman act strangely.

Cam glanced up at the common room clock. Nine o'clock. Would this storm ever end? Ellie and Ray were the only people in the room with her. The girls slept with their heads at opposite ends of a long couch. Rosemary had fixed sandwiches for Cam and Oscar in the kitchen. She'd made a couple more, which Cam had carried out to the girls, who'd eaten and then fallen asleep. Ellie's plate sat on the end table, half a pickle abandoned on a wilted leaf of lettuce.

A care provider pushed a cart slowly down the hallway, its wheels murmuring along the carpet. Yawning, Cam picked up the *Daily News* from the table next to her armchair. The brandy had relaxed her, but not enough that she wanted to snooze. What she wanted was to go home.

She leaned toward the emergency light and peered at the paper. It was folded open to the obituary page. The top item was about Ida Lacey, age ninety-three. The story said she had died of natural causes at Moran Manor. *Good.* At least she hadn't been poisoned by Cam's organic produce. She flipped idly through the rest of the section and then refolded the paper so the front page was on top.

The headline on the first page made her sit up straight: MORAN MANOR RESIDENT POISONED. So the poison had become public knowledge. She carried the paper over to the spot where the most light shone from the emergency bulbs. The authorities were still searching for the killer, the article said. When she got to the words *cyanide salts,* she paused. She'd read mysteries where that had been the murder weapon. The death was fast and painful, at least in fiction. Was it also in real life? *Poor Bev.* Cam read every word of the article.

But where would someone obtain cyanide? Everybody knew it could be fatally toxic, didn't they? She thought she'd read that there was a legal use for the poison, though, even now. Was it in painting? She wasn't able to research it on the Internet, because cell coverage had gone out. She assumed Pete and his team had checked out where a person could obtain cyanide legally. And, of course, Pete wouldn't have told her.

She wandered out to the lobby and pressed her face against the glass door to the outside. The snow still swirled, as if a mad giant waved a snow globe in the air. A huge drift curved up and over where Cam knew a low wall defined the walkway. She tapped her foot. If she couldn't get out of here, what could she do to keep from going stir crazy? Play Scrabble against herself? She snapped her fingers. She knew where she could read about legal uses for cyanide, despite the lack of electricity.

A moment later she entered the library upstairs, which housed not only a dictionary but also an encyclopedia, which a resident must have donated. She was sure it hadn't been published in this decade, and wondered whether they even printed encyclopedias anymore. But she bet that information about cyanide hadn't changed all that much even in the past fifty years.

She peered at the spines of the encyclopedia and drew out the C–D volume. She carried it out into the hallway, where more light illuminated the space, and sank down to the floor, sitting cross-legged. She found the "cyanide" entry and began to read. A few minutes later she closed the book, raised her knees, and rested her arms on them. The article said that it was used to kill ants. And was an anticaking agent for salt. In New Zealand they turned to it to kill pesky mammals. Jewelers used cyanide salts to clean metals. Photographers utilized the chemical in darkrooms. With real film, which was rapidly becoming obsolete but wasn't at the time the encyclopedia was published. She opened the volume again and checked the copyright. 1998. Not ancient, but before digital cameras took over the photography market, for sure. She whistled when she read the last use for cyanide: to increase plant germination. She was horrified to imagine bringing a toxic poison onto her farm to make sure all her seeds sprouted.

She scanned the cyanide entry again. Frank Jackson had emphasized to Jim that he used real film for his art. Like that fall portrait, with its sepia tint. He could have brought cyanide salts to Moran Manor and added a portion to Bev's dinner. But how? And when? It could have been before Ellie delivered her plate, if the plates were left unattended in the kitchen or on a delivery rack, or after in Bev's room. The article described the classic bitter almond scent of the toxin. But it also said that some people weren't able to smell it. Even if Bev could perceive it, the stew could have masked the smell.

Cam's eyes flew wide open. The apple cake recipe she'd provided to Rosemary featured almonds. No wonder Jim suspected Cam. Even if Bev had caught a whiff, she would have assumed the smell came from the dessert. Cam shook her head a little. Her new earrings clinked softly.

The earrings Rosemary had made. The jeweler Rosemary. Who'd also sprinkled the salad with almonds.

"No," Cam scolded herself aloud. "Rosemary had no reason to kill Bev. She barely knew her. At least I think she didn't. It had to be Frank." If only she could call Pete.

She heard a soft sound around the corner from where she sat. A light click followed the noise. The shadows in the corners were instantly darker, more menacing. Her heart raced. She rose and tiptoed into the library. She slid the volume back into its slot on the shelf. Time to get downstairs, where there would be safety in numbers. If two slumbering teen girls counted as safety.

Chapter 27

Rustling. A scrabbling sound.

Cam awoke from a fitful sleep but kept her eyes shut. Her height prevented her from stretching out on the remaining couch in the common room, and she'd wedged herself into it. Her right foot felt numb where it hung over the far armrest. Her left leg sprawled on the floor, and her neck hurt from the angle at which her head rested. She didn't know what the time was. She felt like she must have slept for at least a couple of hours, which made it near midnight. Had she heard a noise, or had it been part of the dream she was having?

She heard the rustling sound again. She opened her eyes and froze. That was no dream. Could a rodent be prowling the residence? Or a person up to no good? Someone cursed under their breath directly behind her head. A rodent who spoke English, then.

Cam sat up and turned sharply toward the sound in a quick move. The crick in her neck pierced her with pain. Ginger Montgomery was bent over the end table next to the couch.

"Ginger," Cam said in a harsh whisper. "What are you doing?"

Ginger's hand flew out of the bag Cam used as a pocket-book, which sat on the small table at the end of the couch.

Ginger straightened. She folded her arms and said in a low voice, "Nothing." She wore what appeared in the dim light to be sweatpants and a man's shirt, which hung halfway to her knees.

Cam stood, trying not to move her head, and grabbed her bag. "What do you mean, nothing? You were searching my bag." Needles jabbed her right foot. She stomped it a couple of times, trying to bring feeling into it.

"I was not." Ginger cleared her throat, then spoke in a low voice. "I can't find my purse. I thought I might have left it out here."

"Right." Cam snorted. "You carry a great big cream-colored leather bag. Looks like a designer one. I've seen it. Mine is a brown canvas messenger bag with crows on it." She clutched the bag, its flap thrown open, close to her. The corner of a piece of paper stuck out. Cam grabbed it, wondering if Ginger had put it there, but the paper was just an old receipt.

"It's dark in here." Ginger shot a glance at the emergency bulbs, whose feeble light didn't quite extend to their corner of the room.

"Well, it's not your pocketbook." Why were the lights so much dimmer than earlier in the night? Cam hoped the generator wasn't running out of gas. But the lights in the hallway were still on. "Why were you in my bag?"

"You're mistaken, Cam."

"No, I'm not." She kept her gaze on the other woman.

"Listen, since we're talking, you can stop snooping into other people's business," Ginger snapped.

"Don't change the subject. You're the one who just went through *my* purse."

"I heard you were asking around about me."

"Hey, if your name comes up in conversation, that's not exactly snooping." Cam shoved the receipt farther down into her bag and slung it on her shoulder.

"That's not how it went down according to my friend. Who heard you talking about me in the Food Mart and called me."

"Eddie doesn't seem to think much of your substandard approach to building. It's not snooping to talk about the effect a local project has on the town." Cam tried to keep her voice down. She didn't want to wake the teenagers across the room.

"You don't know anything about it. And for all I know, he slipped you some false information, a doctored-up photograph, or something."

"Well, he didn't. But here's something I do know about." Cam cocked her head and then winced at the pain from the crick in her neck. "A few hours ago, when you asked me to get your sheet music, I got locked out. In the freaking blizzard. Why didn't you search for me?"

Ginger opened both hands outward. "How did I know you were locked out? I didn't see you leave the building. Maybe you decided you didn't feel like getting my music, after all. Jim went out and called for you, but you weren't anywhere."

"I was halfway around the building by then. In a blizzard, I might remind you. He didn't come looking very soon."

"Well, he eventually located some music another performer had left behind, which I played from."

"What's going on, Cam?" Ellie's sleepy voice sounded from the other couch.

"Nothing, Ellie," Cam said. "Power's still out. You might as well go back to sleep."

"Okay," Ellie mumbled.

Ginger turned toward the doorway.

"Wait a minute, Ginger. I'm serious," Cam said. "Why were you digging in my bag?"

Jim Cooper appeared in the lobby, outside his office. He stood under one of the emergency lights. His hair stood on end like a cartoon character's, and he scratched the back of his head.

Ginger glanced at him and then at Cam again. Despite Ginger being backlit, Cam caught her raising one eyebrow.

"Just looking for dirt. You're a farmer. You should understand that." She strolled toward Jim and hooked her arm through his before they disappeared into his office. In the quiet, Cam heard the door click shut behind them.

Cam stretched her feet out on the coffee table and opened her bag on her lap. She didn't believe for a minute that Ginger had mistaken her canvas messenger bag for her own leather bag. Ginger had been searching for something in it. But what could Cam have that Ginger would want? Unless she really thought that Eddie might have given Cam some kind of proof about Ginger's unethical building practices.

Cam started removing items from her bag one by one. She laid her lip gloss and comb on the couch. Her cell phone. Her wallet. A pen and a stub of a pencil. The scrunched-up receipt for thirty pounds of seed potatoes from the Agway. Her farm checkbook and her personal checkbook. More lip gloss. Nail file. The slim metal case that held farm business cards. A nearly empty pack of sugar-free gum. A few other just-in-case items. She ran her hand along the bottom of the bag's interior and came up with a handful of coins and something soft, which turned out to be a piece of unchewed gum that had escaped its wrapper. She wrapped it in one of the tissues, then upended the bag and shook it. Only dust and a few crumbs from an old granola bar emerged.

She stared at the collection. The previous spring she'd unwittingly brought a bugging device into her house. She wasn't about to be duped like that again. If Ginger had planted a bug

In Cam's bag, she hadn't found it. A listening device was a silly notion, anyway. Or was it? If Ginger was evil enough to kill her own mother, or if she was involved in the crime somehow, surely she wouldn't balk at trying to find out surreptitiously how much Cam knew or suspected about her.

No matter how she rearranged herself on the couch, Cam couldn't fall asleep again. Her neck hurt, her knees ached, and her stomach felt unsettled. Or it could be the interaction with Ginger that was keeping her awake. She sat up, hearing a buzzing noise. Her eyes widened while she scrabbled in her purse for her phone. It showed service bars again. She rose and peered out a window. The snow had stopped. Finally. She wandered back to her couch. The green light on her phone blinked. She had a message from Pete. Several of them, the most recent from twenty minutes ago. She pressed his number. The clock display on her phone read 1:15 a.m., but he obviously was still up.

When he answered, she greeted him. "What's going on?"

"Are you all right? I've been trying to reach you. You didn't pick up at home." The worry in his voice came over the line like a yellow flag.

"I'm fine. Stir crazy but fine. I'm stuck at Moran Manor. A bunch of us are stuck here, actually. Including Ellie."

He exhaled. "I'm snowed in, as well. My little street is the last to get plowed, and since I was off duty, anyway, I didn't think getting me out was an emergency that merited taking state vehicles away from all the real emergencies around the area. But I was worried about you."

"We lost cell service here earlier in the evening. I was visiting Albert, and I didn't leave in time. When Ellie asked me for a ride home, we couldn't even get out of the parking lot."

"Mmm. I miss you," Pete said in a low voice.

Cam shut her eyes for a moment. She wished she were snuggled on a couch next to Pete, with that sexy voice in her ear in person. She opened her eyes and cleared her throat.

"I miss you, too. And I would really like to get out of here. I've been trying to sleep on a sofa, but it's terribly uncomfortable."

"Poor dear. And me in my nice warm double bed." He laughed low and throatily.

"Stop it now. Listen, that text from Ellie? Ellie told me she saw Frank Jackson coming out of Bev's room. And that he threatened Bev. He told her if she didn't give him the money, she would be killed."

Pete didn't speak for a moment, and Cam thought she heard a pencil scratching on paper. "That's serious. Why didn't she tell me earlier?"

Cam told him what Ellie had said. "She feels bad about it."

"I surely hope Jackson isn't also trapped there tonight."

"No, thank goodness. As far as I know." Or was he here? She hadn't seen him anywhere earlier and couldn't think of why he would be at the residence. That didn't mean he wasn't. "I was locked out in the blizzard earlier."

"What? You're kidding."

"I'm not kidding. I found my way around to the rear door, which was unlocked, but being out there terrified me."

"Oh, Cam." Pete sounded anguished. "Are you all right?"

"I am. Took me a while to warm up. I'll give you all the gory details later." Should she tell him about Ginger going through her handbag? She decided to save that news. Nothing had happened, after all, although she was glad Ginger hadn't reappeared from Jim's office, where she must be occupying his long, cushy leather sofa with him.

"You could have—"

"I'm fine. Don't worry. Listen, I learned a few more things, too. Ginger apparently cheats on the buildings she puts up. Oh, and Richard has a gambling problem."

"Whoa, whoa. You learned all this tonight at the residence there?"

Cam laughed. "No. DJ and Alexandra each happened to tell me some stuff. Richard is Alexandra's friend's stepfather. Or ex-stepfather. Her friend's name is Hannah."

"We were investigating Broadhurst's gambling. Remember, we talked about that yesterday? But it's good to get it confirmed. See if you can get the friend's last name, will you?"

"Sure. And DJ's brother Eddie works construction for Ginger," Cam went on. "Or did. He says it's nearly criminal, what she does."

"Also good to know. What's DJ's last name?"

"Johns. His brother is Eddie Johns."

"Good. What's also good is that the weather station says the storm is blowing out to sea," Pete said. "We should all be able to get out tomorrow morning. I mean, this morning."

"I hope my animals survived the storm. And Preston."

"Dasha can't wait to get out for a long walk, too." Pete cleared his throat. "I haven't been able to sleep, thinking about you," he said in a husky voice.

"Because I'm a person of interest?"

"Of interest to me personally. This has been killing me, this week. You know that, don't you?"

"You didn't exactly make that clear to me."

"I couldn't. I wasn't even supposed to be talking with you. But you're in the clear now, as I already told you. We're closing in on the murderer."

"Who is it?"

Pete didn't speak.

"Yeah, you can't tell me." Cam yawned. "I might be able to sleep now, though. See you tomorrow sometime?"

"I hope so. I'm on duty again." He didn't speak for a moment.

The large clock on the wall ticked, as if reassuring Cam that life would someday return to normal.

"Why don't you call me when you get home?" Pete asked. "If you don't mind, I'll stop by to say hello and leave Dasha with you for the day."

"No problem. I'd love to see you. And him. Get some sleep yourself."

"I'll be dreaming—" His voice cut out, and then she heard him again. "Got a work call. Later." He disconnected.

Cam sat with the phone in her hand. She hadn't had a chance to tell him about Rosemary and Richard. She also hadn't told him what she'd learned about the legal uses of cyanide salts. But surely a detective already knew that. She stretched out and fell asleep, still clutching her phone.

Chapter 28

The rattle of a cart in the hallway woke Cam. She sat up and wiped a drop of drool from the corner of her mouth. She still clutched her phone in her other hand. It read 6:50 a.m. She glanced out the closest window. The pale dawn light showed snow everywhere but in the sky itself, which grew bluer as she watched. She looked around the room. The girls still slept.

Cam rose and stretched. She grabbed her bag, made her way to the visitor bathroom, and then followed the alluring scent of fresh coffee all the way to the kitchen, an aroma that put all thoughts of almond-scented poison out of her mind.

"Ah, Sleeping Beauty arises?" Rosemary gestured at an old-style coffee percolator atop the eight-burner stove. "I pulled that out of storage. Grab a mug and help yourself."

"Did the power come on?"

"Nope." Rosemary ran her hands down her white apron. "But with a gas stove and a box of matches, who needs power?"

"Can I help?" Cam gazed at the stainless-steel island, which was covered with several industrial-sized rectangular pans, a couple of bowls, and a mound of grated cheese.

"I'm making a major egg bake. Soon as the potatoes are done, I need to assemble it and get it into the oven. I don't want to waste generator power trying to toast a hundred slices of bread. But sure, you can help. Wash up over there." She tilted her head at the big sink. "And then start cracking eggs into that big mixer bowl."

Cam obliged. Two flats of eggs sat next to a huge metal bowl. She began to crack egg after egg, until dozens of pale yellow orbs swam in their clear fluid. She hadn't realized how accustomed she'd become to her own free-range hens' organic eggs, with their deep yellow yolks and their flavor to match.

Ellie wandered into the kitchen, rubbing her eyes, followed by Ray. Their sleepy faces and rumpled hair made them appear more like children than the almost adults they were.

"Good morning, ladies," Rosemary said.

"Morning," Ellie murmured.

Ray nodded, still looking half asleep.

"Ellie, cell coverage is back," Cam said.

"Thanks. I'll call my mom," Ellie said. "When I wake up."

"Why don't you both freshen up, get yourselves a glass of juice, and start setting up the dining room?" Rosemary extracted a large whisk from a wide crock and began to beat the eggs. "The roads are still impassable. I'm going to need you to work this morning, until the rest of the staff can get in."

Ellie nodded and turned. Ray followed her out of the room like a teen robot.

"I'm all set now, Cam. Thanks for lending a hand. Pop in, in about half an hour, and I'll fix you a plate."

"Will do." Cam topped up her coffee and walked down the hall to the lobby. She heard the scraping sound of a snow shovel on pavement. She gazed out the glass door. Oscar, bundled against the cold, was slowly clearing the walkway. A snow scoop leaned against the wall. Cam donned her coat and hat and swapped her shoes for boots. She slung her bag over her head and one shoulder. No way was she leaving it unattended with Ginger still on the premises. Pulling on gloves, she pushed through both doors.

Oscar glanced at her. Pink overlaid his dark cheeks. "If I told people back in the home country about this, they would never believe me. You here to help?"

"Flaherty Shoveling Service." She smiled at him and lifted the snow scoop. She walked down the few feet of cleared walk and began to push the scoop into two feet of fresh snow. The tool was shaped like a mini plow, with a square-sided scoop and a U-shaped handle. She'd gotten the hang of using the one at the farm. She pushed the scoop until it could hold no more snow, then upended it along the side of the walk, packing the pile of snow before righting the scoop again. The wind had ceased, but breathing the clear air was like inhaling shards of ice. Her exposed cheeks stung, and the tips of her fingers numbed.

They worked together for half an hour, occasionally swapping implements. The one who scooped accomplished more clearing, and the shoveler cleaned up the loose snow the scoop tended to leave at the edges. When they'd cleared the walk nearly all the way to the parking lot, Cam stopped. She could feel sensation in her fingers again, and the hard work mitigated the effects of the cold.

"I need a breather," she said. She glanced around. The sun now bathed every crystal of snow in light, making the universe sparkle. Branches bent low and gracefully under their beautiful burdens. The scene was a winter wonderland at odds with poisoned salads, midnight clandestine searches, and elderly victims.

"How did you pass the night?" Oscar asked. He laid both hands on the shovel handle.

"Uncomfortably. You?"

He stuck the shovel in a snowdrift, then pulled a cigarette out of his pocket and lit it after checking the vicinity. "I figure if they have me working past my pay grade and job description, I deserve a smoke. But yeah, not that comfortable on a short couch in the staff room."

"Tall people like us are at a real disadvantage." She smiled at him again, but it turned into a frown. "I caught Ginger going through my bag last night, at around midnight."

"That lady is a real number." He shook his head and inhaled. "What did she think she was going to find?"

"She claimed it was a mistake."

"Only mistake she made was taking up with Cooper. That guy is no manager. I don't know how he ever got the job."

Cam turned to gaze at the building behind them. "How old is Moran Manor, anyway?"

"This residence was built only two years ago. The place was new when I started here. Before that, Moran Manor had been family run in a big old house in town. I suppose it's still family run, but the owners moved to Florida."

"I saw a crack in the plaster upstairs a few days ago," Cam said. "It might be cosmetic, like somebody put too much paint on. But if it isn't, a building this new shouldn't be showing problems like that. Unless it's just settling."

"Oh, there are other cracks, I can assure you." Oscar took a long drag on his smoke and then ground it out under his heel. He looked around again, picked it up, drew back his arm, and shot the butt high and far into the woods. "It's poorly built. Walls that aren't square. Receptacles that don't work. Drains that back up. And lots of cracks in the walls."

"I wonder if the residents are safe. Have you raised those problems with the director? With Jim?" If Albert survived his fall, only to have a roof collapse on him, Cam wasn't sure she could bear it.

"Cooper does not want to hear about it." Oscar let a breath out. He took the scoop out of Cam's hands and handed her the shovel in exchange. "I've got to finish this job. I'm sure I'm needed inside by now for several cantankerous male residents who want only me to attend to them." He scooped toward the parking lot.

Cam didn't move for a moment. She was willing to bet the farm that Ginger Montgomery had been the Moran Manor developer. And her cozy relationship with Jim Cooper would explain her continued presence at the residence even after her mother's death. Cam hefted the shovel and tackled the walkway in front of the cars parked facing the residence, the first one being Ginger's snow-covered Lexus. At her fourth shovelful, she crunched into something. She dug under it, and there, in the pile of snow, was Ginger's bundle of keys. Cam laughed out loud. She used her sleeve to swipe a spot clean on the car's hood and laid the keys in the middle, resisting the temptation to write, "You're welcome," in the snow on the windshield.

A large yellow vehicle with a wide scoop of its own lumbered into the parking lot from the road. The scoop lowered with a clunk. The machine began to clear the pavement, one swath at a time.

Chapter 29

Cam stood in the kitchen, a hot cup of coffee cradled in her cold hands. Both girls sat on stools. Ray gazed out from under heavy eyelids, and Ellie had a dazed look about her, as well.

"Girls, you're free to go," Rosemary said to the teenagers. "The roads are clear, and the regular staff is arriving."

"Sweet," Ellie said.

"I can give you both a ride," Cam told them.

Rosemary yawned. "And Jim actually told me to head on home soon," she said to Cam. "Apparently, he has a backup cook on retainer. I need to do lunch prep until the guy gets here, and then I am bound for my bed." She grinned. "With my favorite opera singer."

On her way out, Cam found Albert in the breakfast room and planted a kiss on his head. "I'll come over on the weekend to see you."

He glanced up. "Do you mean tomorrow?"

"Today's Friday, isn't it? I totally lost track." At least Albert had his sense of time back. "I'll be here tomorrow or Sunday. More likely Sunday, since tomorrow is share day."

He nodded and tucked into his egg bake. Cam's stomach grumbled at the sight, but she decided to eat at home. One more minute than absolutely necessary in a communal setting and she might start screaming.

Outside the girls helped brush the snow off the truck. Both Ray's red and yellow knit cap and Ellie's purple pashmina scarf were spring flowers against the white snow. Cam dug out around the doors and shoveled away the plowed snow in front of the truck, glad she'd thought to back in yesterday.

When the way was clear, they all piled in. Rosemary's car halfway blocked the way in front, but Cam had room to edge around it. She got directions from Ray and headed toward her house near the river.

"I'm glad it's a snow day," Ellie said.

"If ever one was justified, it's today," Cam said. "Did you let your mom know you were on your way?"

Ellie nodded.

"I'm going to sleep all day," Ray said.

"But both of you slept really well, didn't you?" Cam asked. She could sense their eyebrows rising without even seeing them.

"It wasn't that, like, restful," Ellie said. "Plus, one time I woke up, and that Ginger lady was prowling around. It creeped me out."

"She's super weird," Ray added.

Cam dropped Ray off and then Ellie.

"Thanks, Cam," Ellie said as she climbed out. "Hey, do you need help later? You know, with the shares? Since it's a snow day, Vince could give me a ride over."

"Thanks. I might, but not until the afternoon. I'll text you."

Ellie waved and waded along an unshoveled path toward the house. Cam waited to be sure she got inside safely. Right before she reached her front door, Ellie bent down and then, with a big grin, lobbed a snowball at the truck's window. Cam laughed, flipping on the wipers. She beeped the horn and drove toward home.

Ten minutes later she was stuck in her own driveway. She'd revved the Ford's engine and had swung off the road into her drive. And had promptly stalled out. She restarted the truck but couldn't get anywhere in reverse or plow her way farther in, either. A plow guy had convinced her to hire him, but he clearly had other jobs ahead of her driveway.

She forced the door open and stepped into snow up to her knees. "I'm home," she whooped. She was exhausted, cold, and hungry. But she was no longer shut in with more than a hundred senior citizens and caretakers, plus one shady businesswoman who couldn't keep her hands in her own designer bag. She trudged to the house. She cleared the stoop in front of the back door by sweeping her foot back and forth until she could pull the storm door open. The turn of a key in a lock had never sounded so good. As soon as she entered, stomping the snow off her feet, Preston came at a run.

"Mr. P." She leaned down and stroked him.

He gazed up, over at his empty food dish, and at her again.

"Give me a minute, big guy." She slid out of her boots and into her fleece-lined slippers, then filled his bowl and petted his head a couple of times while he began to crunch the dry bits of food. She turned up the heat, brewed a pot of coffee, and fixed herself a piece of toast. Sitting with her mug of coffee, inhaling its rich roasted smell and gazing out at the snow reflecting off the winter wonderland, she longed to stay in the quiet of her house all day. But tomorrow was share day. And the chickens needed attention. Oh, and she had a truck to dig out. Then she remembered she was supposed to call Pete.

She pressed his number. After she greeted him, she said, "I'm home, but my truck is stuck at the edge of my driveway, and I don't know when my plow guy will get here. No way you'll be able to get in. Try to park at the edge of the road."

"I'll be over in thirty, or as long as it takes me. Still all right to bring Dasha?" The dog barked in the background.

"Absolutely."

Cam poured her coffee into a travel mug before she donned her work coat. Not wanting ever to be cold again, she pulled on snow pants and slid into her boots. If she hurried, she could feed and water the hens and then get her own shoveling done before Pete arrived. At the very least the path to the house and to the barn.

The hens were all alive, Cam saw with relief after trudging through the snow to the coop. Ruffles had lived, as well. He stood on the highest roost but hopped down and pushed the girls out of the way when Cam scooped feed into the tray. She brought water out from the barn to fill their receptacle, then cleared the snow away from the ramp down to the yard. A combination of shoveling and stomping flattened an area at the bottom of the ramp for them. A minute later Ruffles emerged and let out a couple of good crows from the top of the ramp.

Cam had to smile. Ruffles, despite his name, was such a guy. She didn't know if a fowl version of testosterone ran through roosters, but they sure had something that made them act differently from the hens. At least today he wasn't on the attack.

She drained her coffee mug and set it on the bench outside the barn. She shoveled a path from the barn to the hoop house and started on the path to the driveway. She'd made it nearly to the drive when a loud engine noise interrupted the crunching of the shovel and made her lift her head. A big red pickup with a yellow snowplow fixed to the front had pulled in behind her Ford. The truck reversed and came forward again. This wasn't her plow guy's truck.

"Who the heck is that?" Cam said aloud. Someone about to

ram her truck? But why? Her heart began to race. While she watched, though, she realized that the driver wasn't malevolent at all. He was plowing out her driveway. Whoever sat behind the wheel deftly pushed snow to the sides of the drive and cleared the few feet between the road and the Ford. The plower then edged by the side of Cam's truck and cleared the rest of the driveway, banking the snow on the far side, where the perennial garden was now buried under not two, but four feet of snow. The driver wore a dark watch cap, but Cam couldn't discern the person's identity. When the truck made one more forward pass, Cam waved.

The driver rolled the window down. "Thought you might need a little help out here," a woman's voice said.

"Sim," Cam said with a smile. Her plower was none other than Simone Koyama, the local mechanic who serviced Cam's truck. Not a "he" at all. Cam trudged toward her. "Thanks. My usual guy probably won't get here for hours."

Sim winked. "Didn't think you had a plow attachment for that old rattletrap of yours. Actually, your buddy Pete called and asked if I could help out." The sunlight glinted off the silver rings in her nostril and right eyebrow.

"He did?"

"Yeah. I do this for extra cash, anyway, in the winter. When business is slow at the shop."

"Let me pay you, then." Cam started to turn toward the house.

"Forget about it. You helped me out last fall, remember?"

Cam wasn't sure she'd call it helping out, but when Sim had gotten somewhat over-involved after their friend Bobby was accused of murder, Cam had tried to talk her down.

"Go get your keys. I'll push you out of your rut and then plow where you got stuck," Sim said.

"Great idea." Cam hurried to the house. Two minutes later her truck had made it well up into the driveway. Cam climbed out and watched Sim clear the rest of the area.

"Gotta run," the mechanic called, sticking her head out her window. "Lots more driveways on my list. You take care. Let's grab a beer one of these days."

"For sure. Thanks so much, Sim." Cam raised her hand in farewell.

She resumed shoveling the path. The smell of truck exhaust mingled for a minute with the scent of fresh snow and then dissipated. She wished she could click into her skis and head out into the woods on the virgin powder that now coated her ski trails. But first she needed to wait for Dasha and tell Pete more about the night. And get to cutting, pulling, and assembling the shares. Dani hadn't returned her e-mail, so she supposed there wouldn't be any maple syrup for tomorrow. Perhaps she could arrange a few dozen bottles for the next pickup day in two weeks. She hoped she wouldn't go broke paying for it. And then she remembered her broken ski binding. No skiing today.

A beep sounded. Pete pulled up in a dark blue car that looked a lot like a police cruiser, except without the markings or the lights. He parked behind the Ford. Dasha bounded out and nearly knocked Cam over with his greeting. Pete followed at a more sedate pace. He opened his arms to Cam. They stood for a moment in an embrace, not moving, not speaking. Cam closed her eyes and inhaled the delicious smell behind his ear.

When he pushed away, she let her arms drop. "Coffee?"

He nodded. "First this." He laid a gloved hand on each side of her head and pulled her in for a long kiss.

"Mmm," Cam said. "I've missed that."

"How about a rain date for more of the same?" Pete squeezed her hand and held on to it while they walked to the house. "Unfortunately, I'm already late to work. I can't stay long."

"Thanks for calling Sim. She did an amazing job, and it took her only a few minutes. My plow guy gets really backed up."

"You can get a contract with Sim instead, you know."

"Maybe I should. I wish I didn't have to pay anybody, but otherwise I'd either have to shovel it out or buy a snowblower. Winter's tough on a farmer's bank account, at least a snowy winter like this one."

In the kitchen, she poured him a mug of coffee and gave it to him black. "What's that car you're driving?"

He nodded, shrugging out of his wool coat. "It's an official unmarked car. Change in policy. No personal cars while we're on duty." He sat at the table, drumming his fingers. His sport coat fell open.

Cam spied his shoulder holster. "That looks like a different gun, too."

"New service revolver, updated courtesy of the commonwealth." He drew Dasha's leash out of his pocket and laid it on the table. "I don't want to forget to leave you this."

"Thanks." Cam set a bowl of water on the floor for Dasha before joining Pete at the table with her own mug. "So I was out shoveling with Oscar this morning. He said Moran Manor is only a couple of years old and it has a bunch of building issues already. I even saw a big crack in the wall. Do you know if Ginger was the builder?"

"Don't know. I can check into it."

"I saw in the paper last night that the poison was cyanide. You knew that, right?"

Pete nodded again. "I wish they hadn't published it, but the news got away from us."

"And you're investigating legal uses for it?"

"We are," he said slowly. "It sounds like you have been, too. What did you discover?"

"One use is for developing film. Did I tell you about Frank Jackson and the sepia photograph?"

"No." Pete glanced sharply at her. "What picture?"

"It's on the wall behind the reception desk at Moran. It's an artistic portrayal of the residence in the fall. I overheard Jim Cooper and Frank talking about it. Frank said he uses actual film, not a digital camera. And develops it himself. Jim wanted to commission him to do one in each season."

"Why didn't you tell me this before?"

"Pete Pappas. Look at me. Were we talking at all this week?"

"Some." His tone was defensive. "We talked about the case some."

"Anyway, I read last night—while I was snowed in with no cell reception, I remind you—first about the cyanide and then about its use in film developing. And now I'm telling you about Frank's photograph." She reached for his hand.

"Any idea where Jackson is living?"

"No. I told Ruth I'd seen him, though, and we both saw her talk to him after Bev's service, remember? She might have found out by now. If not, she needs to know. He must owe her a bunch of child support."

Pete glanced at the wall clock. He stood and drained his mug. "I'm sorry, Cam. I need to go. I've been saying 'I'm sorry' a lot lately." He pulled a wry smile. "Soon I won't have to."

"You mean—"

He held a hand up. "Soon I won't have to. At least on this case." He leaned down for another kiss, then straightened. "I'll call you as soon as I can."

Dasha jumped up. Tail wagging furiously, he gazed at Pete, then at Cam, then at Pete again.

"Sit, Dasha. I'll be back for you later." Pete slipped back into his coat, stepped outside, and, with a longing glance over his shoulder at Cam, closed the door with a soft click.

Chapter 30

In the hoop house a few minutes later, Cam uncovered the beds, leaving the row cover running in a long pile down the middle. With this kind of sun, and a warmer day, the greens could fry from the heat if she kept them covered. That last bed in the rear might even make it, after all. Lettuce had hearty roots. The rest of the crops had survived the cold snap and appeared healthy. Time to start cutting and digging for tomorrow's shares.

In the barn Cam walked to the back wall to collect scissors, her pitchfork, and a basket. She'd left Dasha in the house, after he and Preston had warily accepted each other's presence. She passed the entrance to the root cellar and kept on going. What if she'd been trapped down there for a couple of days? She wondered if she'd ever figure out who had locked her in. It had to be the murderer. Who else would want her out of commission? But the police hadn't found any clues in the barn as to the person's identity. Perhaps they hadn't searched well enough. She retrieved a large flashlight from the office.

Feeling just a touch like Nancy Drew, Cam knelt near the doors to the root cellar. She ran the light over every square inch. She wasn't sure what she hoped to find. A scrap of cloth caught on a screw, a dropped pencil on the ground, anything that might lead to the person who'd obviously lain in wait and then shut her in.

She sat back on her heels. *Lain in wait.* Where would the person have waited? Must have walked in from the road, because she hadn't heard a vehicle come or go. Must have come in from her neighbor Tully's field. Hidden inside the barn. A creepy thought. But she had enough equipment and dark corners in here that someone could have easily sequestered himself. Or herself. Hiding like that was such a risk, though. Cam would not try to understand the criminal brain, but she couldn't imagine hiding herself in order to hurt someone.

She was about to hoist herself up when the light in her hand flashed on a burst of color. She leaned over one of the bulkhead doors. Snagged on a splinter of wood were a few red threads. Her heart beat faster. This could lead to finding her attacker. "What would Nancy do?" she said aloud and then laughed. Now she was letting her actions be governed by a teenage detective. A *fictional* teenage detective. *The Case of the Red Threads.* She shook her head, and a giggle escaped. Nancy or not, she'd learned enough by now to leave the threads in place for the experts, but she wondered how the team had missed finding the clue.

A day's work still stretched ahead of her. She pressed Ruth's number, and when she didn't answer, she left her a message. Gathering her tools, she slid the barn door closed behind her to resume work where she'd left off. She trudged along the shoveled path to the hoop house, with three-foot-high snowy berms on either side. *Do I now need to start locking the barn as well as the house when I'm not in it?* What a pain that would be. But whoever had trapped her in the root cellar could return and wait for her again.

* * *

Cam didn't make it back to the house until one o'clock. Working in the cold and her lack of sleep from the night on a Moran Manor couch made her yearn to take a hot shower and curl up under a blanket for the rest of the day. She'd made a lot of progress in the past couple of hours, but she wasn't done yet. That plan would have to wait.

Dasha was whining at the door when she got there. Also, a box with a note on top sat on the stoop. The Wolf Meadow Farm logo was printed on the side.

"Hang on, buddy," she called to Dasha. Luca must have looked for her in the barn and not found her. She grabbed the leash out of the house and clipped it onto Dasha's collar. Hoisting the box, she walked Dasha first to the barn to deposit the cheese, figuring it would stay cold enough, and then let the dog prowl around the property. He left yellow marks in the snow here and there. So different from most cats, who didn't feel the need to establish their territory in the same way, unless they were unneutered males. Which Preston was definitely not.

Under a tree close to Tully's field, Dasha set his legs and, looking up, barked over and over again. Cam craned her neck to see what had alerted him.

And then whispered, "Wow." Way up on a branch sat another owl. This one loomed large and mostly white. A snowy owl. It would be unusual for the bird to be this far inland, ten miles from the coast. But she'd read in an article in the *Daily News* that the breed was abundant this year and that there had been other sightings inland, near bodies of water. Her farm wasn't that far from the Merrimack River, after all.

The owl turned its yellow, catlike eyes down on her and Dasha. The round white head remained motionless for several moments. And then it flew. Its broad wings beat silently with grace as it headed north over her house and toward the river.

"How about lunch, Dasha?" Cam said, smiling. Seeing the beautiful bird felt like a good omen. Not that she really believed in such things. But all the turmoil and worry of the week had melted away at the sight of this graceful wild creature. Life would get back to normal. She'd do her work, visit Albert, drink wine with Ruth. And she'd be able to spend time with Pete again. She nudged Dasha toward the house.

Inside, she shed her cold-weather gear. She fixed a peanut butter sandwich and heated up water in the microwave for a cup of tea. As she waited, she glanced at her wall calendar. What had she written in for tonight? It read, "Lou. Six thirty." She squeezed her eyes shut and cursed. Bad timing. Pete had said he would call her later. He was going to come by and get Dasha. He was finally free to see her. And she had a date with another man. A nice, intelligent, friendly man. But this was super, extra intensely bad timing. Her brand-new good mood careened into the compost bucket.

Preston bumped his head against her knee. Cam opened her eyes. The date with Lou was still on the calendar. She reached down to pet Preston. She should cancel the outing with Lou. On such late notice, though? Claiming illness was kind of lame. Just fessing up would be the right thing to do. And the hardest, at least for her.

"What should I do, Mr. P.?" The microwave dinged that the minute was up. She threw an English Breakfast tea bag into the cup and stirred it down while munching on her sandwich. She wandered over to the computer. Avoidance would work for a little while. Bringing up her "Moran Affair" file, she stared at it. Was there anything new she could add?

Sure. Cyanide was the murder weapon. It was used in ant poison, film developing, salt de-caking, jewelry making, even seed germination. She'd meant to mention Rosemary's earring business to Pete but hadn't. She decided she needed to set up a spreadsheet, with column headings of Motive, Opportunity, and Evidence, and rows populated with the names of the people involved: Frank. Ginger. Richard. Rosemary. Oscar. Surely Pete and his team already had this. On a huge whiteboard, if TV crime shows had even a shred of realism. Her wide monitor would have to suffice.

She glanced at her phone. It whispered, "Call Lou."

She brought her gaze back to the monitor. Motive. Well, that was the reason for the names, so she could easily fill it in. Except for Rosemary. The cook had no reason to wish Bev dead. Did she? For that matter, Richard probably didn't, either, unless there was a way he'd benefit from Bev's death that Cam didn't know about. Frank wanted money from Bev, but the way he'd threatened her made it sound like someone else would be the killer. But who? Ginger? The thought of someone killing her own mother gave Cam the creeps. Oscar had had an opportunity, since he'd delivered the trays. Cam had grown to like him. She hoped he wasn't a killer.

Leaning back in her chair, she avoided the call she knew she had to make for just a little longer and examined the screen. Richard and Rosemary. Both of them were trying to hide the fact that they were together. Alexandra had said she didn't know if Richard and Hannah's mother were divorced. That would be a reason to hide another relationship, for sure.

Oh, and the red threads. Ruth hadn't called her back. She added a section to her spreadsheet titled Unsolved Clues. Were there others? Nicholas thinking he had seen an Indian in the hall was a little dubious, but it also could be real. And what about—

Cam stared at the phone again. She took a deep breath and grabbed the phone before she lost her nerve.

"Lou, this is Cam Flaherty," she said when he picked up. "About tonight . . ."

"I was just going to call you," he said in a creaky voice. "I've come down with a bad head cold. I can't make it tonight, after all. I'm really sorry."

Cam told him she hoped he felt better soon, he said he'd call her next week, and they disconnected. She smiled. Saved by the bell, almost literally.

Chapter 31

Cam slid the barn door shut behind her and switched on the light. She set down the basket of parsnips and carrots she'd just dug from their low tunnel inside the hoop house. Drawing off a glove, she checked the time on her phone. At four thirty it was almost completely dark outside, despite the lengthening days. She frowned at the phone display. Pete still hadn't called. She only hoped that meant progress in the case. She yearned for their life together to return to normal.

She put the glove on again and surveyed the harvest on the makeshift table, a long board resting on sawhorses. Richard's apples, enough for a couple of pounds for each member. The parsnips and carrots, their whites and oranges making a pretty mix. A big pale green kohlrabi for each. Red Swiss chard and curly dark green kale. Potatoes, beets, lettuce. The balls of cheese. She would cut Asian greens tomorrow morning, before the shareholders arrived. And she planned to include a butternut squash in each share. She grimaced. The squash still sat in the root cellar. She didn't much feel like venturing down there alone. Which should be ridiculous. She was a farmer, and this was her barn, her root cellar.

Given the recent events, it wasn't ridiculous. But she didn't have to be completely alone. Dasha needed another walk by now, anyway. Cam strode to the house and clipped on his leash. He yipped his excitement and flew down the back stairs.

"Hang on, buddy," Cam said, laughing and struggling to keep hold of the leash. They explored the yard together. After he'd done his business, Cam guided him to the barn, shutting the door after them. She let him off the leash. He busied himself investigating all the corners and smells of a working barn, while she opened the root cellar doors. This time the lights came on.

"Dasha, come here, boy." When he obeyed, she patted him on the head. "Sit. Be my guard dog?"

He lowered himself to his haunches, front legs straight, mouth open, arctic eyes fixed on her.

"I'll be right up. Stay." Amazed at how well trained he was, she took a deep breath and ventured down the steps. The cool air smelled of dirt and something a little sweet, with a touch of rot. One of the squashes must have gone bad. She searched the shelves until she found a kuri with a bad spot. At least the squash didn't touch any of its neighbors. Rot could spread and ruin an entire season's worth of storage. She set the bad kuri on the stairs so she'd remember to take it up and compost it.

She filled a bushel basket with the light tan butternut squashes, which were shaped like elongated incandescent light bulbs. Happily none of them showed any soft spots. She had lifted the bushel and was turning to climb the steps when a rumbling noise reached her ears. She froze. Her heart thudded at the sound of the barn door sliding open. She set the basket down slowly, quietly. Who had entered her barn?

Dasha barked. Would he defend her? He had a sweet temperament. Surely Pete hadn't trained him to attack.

"Hey, Dash," Pete called. "Cam? Are you here?"

Pete. Only Pete. Cam exhaled and mustered her voice.

"Down here." She hoisted the basket and a moment later emerged from the cellar. "You about gave me a heart attack, Detective. I didn't know who had come in here. And, you know, last time I went down to the cellar . . ."

"Sorry about that. I was going to call first, but the day got away from me. In a good way."

Cam lowered the basket to the floor at the end of the table. "Oh?"

Pete stroked Dasha's head. "Yeah. We arrested Frank Jackson for Bev's murder."

Cam moved to Pete's side and squeezed his hand. "Congratulations."

"What you said about his film developing broke the case. We found his apartment over in Haverhill and discovered cyanide salts. He was heard threatening Bev." He ticked the information off on his fingers. "He's almost destitute and needed money for his debts with that Patriotic Militia group he and Bev both belonged to. And several witnesses, including you, placed him in the residence, in fact in her room, near the time of her death."

"Did you ever find the caregiver who was pushing Nicholas Slavin around?"

"We did. It was one of the teenagers, a girl named Raya."

"She's Ellie's friend," Cam said. "I saw her pushing him last Saturday, actually. I didn't realize she did it regularly."

"She admitted that she left him belted into his wheelchair in front of the musical pictures and went off to the restroom to make a quick call to her boyfriend. She was appropriately remorseful. But she didn't see Frank."

"Did Frank confess to the murder?"

Pete frowned. "No. He claims he's innocent. But they all do." He let out a breath, which condensed in the cold air into an evanescent cloud. "Can we talk in the house? It's cold in here."

"I know. It's too big a space for the radiant heating to do much more than keep it from freezing. But I need to stay out here, because I'm not done arranging the shares. Come into the office. It's warmer in there. Oh, wait. Look at this." She pointed to the red threads. "Look what I found. It must be from whoever locked me in the root cellar."

He peered at them. "Good for you for leaving them there. Did you call it in?"

"I called Ruth, but she didn't call back." Cam led the way into the office and perched on the desk. Dasha followed her and lay at her feet with his head on his paws. The smell of cold dog fur mixed with the full aroma of the moist growing medium. The seedlings had sprouted their cotyledons, and the tiny first leaves were happily greening up under the grow lights.

Pete faced her, pulling the door mostly closed. He unbuttoned his coat and stuck his hands in his pockets. "That's better. I have another interesting piece of news."

"You won the Powerball lottery?"

"Close. We acquired a copy of Bev's will. Which she'd changed only last week."

"Right before her death," Cam said.

He nodded. "She left her entire property to Richard Broadhurst. It's notarized and legal."

"What?" She stared. "Not to be sold to him at a discount, but given as an outright gift? Why?"

"We're all wondering that. Didn't you say he took her out last weekend, on the day before she died?"

Cam nodded. "And somebody told me he'd been taking her out a lot recently. Oscar? Ellie? I can't remember who told me."

"She left a note in the will about wanting the land to be

farmed. Maybe she was trying to keep her daughter from developing it. Anyway, it doesn't change the fact that we have a real suspect in custody."

"So I'm now a legally admissible date again?" Cam lifted her chin and smiled just a little.

"You'd better believe it." Pete sidled close to her. When he leaned in for a kiss, Dasha barked and tried to nose in between them.

Pete smiled. "Somebody's jealous." The *Dragnet* theme rang from his pocket. *Dun dahDUN dun.* He gave Cam a quick buss, then retrieved his phone and connected.

"Pappas." He listened for a moment, his gaze on Cam, his face increasingly alarmed. "Yeah. Got it. Send someone over and keep me informed." He pressed a button on the phone and stood in silence.

"What?"

"Someone reported hearing shots over at Broadhurst's farm a little while ago. A neighbor called it in, said she heard gunfire from the house, and then Richard's truck tore out of there."

Cam opened her eyes wide. "Rosemary, you know, the cook at Moran Manor? She said she was going home early today. She lives with Richard."

"You're kidding. She must have lied to us about her address when we interviewed her." He rapped his fingers on the desk.

"She was trying to hide her relationship with him, but when I pointed out that she was the one who had nearly run me down over there, she admitted it. She also makes jewelry." Cam felt her ears. "I bought these from her." She waggled her head, and the earrings danced with the movement.

"Jewelry makers also use cyanide salts." He tapped the fingers of his right hand on the desk and looked uneasy.

"I know. I read about it. Last night." Cam frowned.

"And you didn't think to tell me?"

"You're the detective. I thought you'd know."

"Sure I knew. But I didn't know that Rosemary makes earrings and lives with Broadhurst."

"And I didn't know about the will. Richard could have pressured Rosemary to poison Bev so he'd get the land now rather than later." A cold unease spread through Cam. "But you said you arrested Frank for the murder."

Dasha picked up his head and barked. He jumped to his feet and kept barking.

"Dasha, quiet," Pete said. "Hush, boy." He grabbed Dasha's leash and pulled him close.

"Sounds like you two have things all figured out," a voice boomed, and the door swung open. A grinning Richard Broadhurst, in his red work jacket, filled the space. "Too bad all that information is staying right here."

He slowly swung up his right hand and pointed a gun at Pete.

Chapter 32

Pete had been right about Richard. *Now what?* Cam's breath came fast. The pulse in her neck beat even faster.

"Calm down." Pete held both hands up, with his palms out in front of his chest. He spoke in a low, calm voice. "Put the weapon down and let's talk."

"Nah, I don't think so." Richard's grin was demoniac. "Get your hands up. Straight up, or your girlfriend is going to turn out just like Tosca herself. You, too, Flaherty."

He stood only two yards away. Cam could smell him as she raised her hands above her head: stale smoke mixed with coffee and dirt. What she didn't sense was fear. Except from herself. She'd seen *Tosca* with Great-Aunt Marie. The opera where Tosca famously ends up dead. How were they going to get out of this mess?

Pete dropped the leash and slowly pushed his hands into the air. He glanced at Cam and then at Richard. "So what's this all about?"

"I came over to see Flaherty. Rosemary told me she'd been blabbing about living with me and making jewelry. The woman never could keep her lousy mouth shut. I figured it wouldn't be long before Ms. Computer Programmer here put it all together."

"Put what together?" Cam demanded. She tried without success to keep her voice from shaking. The gun Richard pointed was a big one. A gun he knew how to use from his sharpshooter days.

"You know. Who has access to cyanide. Hearing about the will. Me convincing my girlfriend to add a bit of her precious cyanide salts to Bev's dinner made with your produce. The airhead named Rosemary would do anything for me. Calls it love." He snorted. "And I couldn't risk Cam telling anybody else, especially you, Pappas. But since you're with her, you're a nice little bonus for me."

"Why did you need to kill Bev now?" Pete stared at Richard. "She'd already left you the land in her will."

"Yeah. You know what a tough bird Bev was? She wasn't going to croak for another couple decades. Out of sheer orneriness, if nothing else. And I happen to have some debts that just couldn't wait. Rosemary would have been nailed for it if she hadn't started talking."

"How did you get in without us hearing you?" Cam asked.

"Let's say I'm experienced." Richard waggled his eyebrows.

Cam watched his bravado. He'd been a master of bluff since she'd met him. He wouldn't kill both of them. Anyway, Pete's gun was under his coat. If she could get Richard's weapon away from him, Pete could shoot him in the leg or something. But how could she get the gun? *Think, Flaherty. Think.* She swallowed hard.

"We received a report of a shooting at your house right before you drove off," Pete said.

"Oh, I know. I saw my nosy neighbor staring at the house with her phone to her ear." Richard flicked a piece of straw off his gun arm.

Which was in a red sleeve. The threads Cam had found. It was Richard who'd trapped her.

"Did you kill Rosemary Contini?" Pete asked

"What happened or didn't happen is none of your business."

"It's actually very much my business." Pete smiled.

"It won't be in a few minutes," Richard spat out. His bonhomie from a moment ago had been replaced by a mouth that had tasted bitter fruits.

"You locked me in my root cellar." Cam stared at him.

"You were asking too many questions," he said with vitriol. "Thought it'd be good to get you out of circulation for a while. Not long enough, as it turned out."

Dasha stared at Richard and growled, with his ears laid back and flat against his head. Richard lashed out his foot and kicked Dasha, who whined and shrank away.

Cam gasped. "Don't kick him!"

"I'm doing whatever I want. See this?" He waved the gun while still keeping it trained on Pete. "It's my ticket out."

"You're okay," Pete said, gazing at the dog. "It's okay, buddy." He turned to Richard. "Your ticket expired a long time ago, Broadhurst. My department is fully aware of the miserable state of your finances. It's public knowledge that Ms. Contini lived with you. Bev Montgomery changing the disposition of her estate has no chance of standing up in court. Killing us will only make it worse for you. A lot worse."

"Not if it seems like one of you shot the other. Let's just say Pete accused Cam of murder, and Cam grabbed the gun and shot him, then, in a fit of remorse, turned it on herself. Like I said, just like Tosca, except with the help of a gun."

"That might work on the stage, but nobody will believe it here. And your firearm isn't exactly a police-issue service revolver." Pete started to lower his hands.

"Get those hands back up," Richard barked. "No, this isn't a police weapon. But yours is, isn't it?"

Pete shook his head with a sad look.

"What are you shaking your head for?" Richard asked.

"Not carrying."

Cam's heart sank. They didn't stand a chance if Pete's gun wasn't in his shoulder holster. Why had he removed it?

"What?" Richard switched the gun to point at Cam. He reached over and felt Pete's sides under his coat. "Where is it, then?"

Pete shook his head again.

"Never mind. I'll figure something out," Richard said. "Both of you, move out into the barn. I can't think in that little space."

Cam hesitated. She glanced at Pete, who gave a little nod. They might have a better chance of overcoming Richard out in the open.

Richard waved them through the doorway, first Cam, then Pete. Dasha stayed put, but his gaze didn't waver from Pete.

"And don't try any moves, or I'll blow the closest head off. Could even be Doggy's."

He prodded them a few feet away, into the corner near the wall where Cam hung her hoes and shovels.

"Don't shoot Dasha, Richard," she pleaded. "We're cooperating. And he didn't do anything." Her hands were growing numb from holding them in the air. Her shoulders ached, and her throat thickened with fear. She didn't know how Pete could appear so calm.

"Come on out," Richard said to Dasha but kept his gaze and the gun on Pete.

Dasha didn't budge. He growled again.

"Call your damn dog," Richard said in a deep voice, nearly growling himself.

"*Epithesi*," Pete said in an urgent tone.

Dasha curled himself into a spring. He launched at Richard with bared teeth and a deep, rumbling snarl. His mouth clamped down on Richard's pistol wrist.

"Aii! Let go of me!" Richard yelled.

The gun went off with a blast. Pete cried out. The gun went flying and landed somewhere with a clunk of metal. Dasha swung Richard's arm this way and that, while Richard tried to kick himself free. Pete crumpled to the floor.

Cam yanked at the nearest shovel on the wall, but it wouldn't come off of its hook. She jerked it until it came loose. She shuddered, but she had to do it, and now. She swung it high and smashed the metal head with all her strength into the back of Richard's head. He fell onto his side, and his head hit the floor with a thunk. He didn't move. He was sprawled a few feet from where Pete lay, clutching his left arm with his right hand. Dasha kept Richard's wrist clamped in his mouth and uttered a low, rumbling growl.

Cam tossed the shovel down and knelt next to Pete. His eyes were open, although his face drew in with pain.

"Are you . . . did he . . ." She could barely eke the words out.

"He got my arm." He gestured with his chin toward the top of his left bicep. He kept his other hand clasped there. Blood seeped out through his fingers.

She tore her phone out of her pocket and pressed 911. She laid her hand aside his face while she waited for them to answer, her eyes hot with tears. *Let him be all right.*

"Tie Richard's hands behind him. Turn him onto his front," he croaked out in a weak voice. "Get rope. Hurry. He could come to."

Cam rose, pressing the speaker icon on the phone. She laid it on the floor next to Pete and swallowed hard. She had to stay strong. Richard still didn't stir. Dasha had let go of the wrist, but he stood guard over their attacker, his legs slightly splayed, every nerve at attention.

"Good dog, Dasha. Stay right there." Cam looked more closely at Richard but stayed a few feet away. His chest rose and fell over and over. *Okay. Rope. Twine. Plastic line. Anything. Think, Flaherty.*

As she ran to the section of the barn where she kept supplies, she heard Pete give a terse account to the dispatcher. She returned to Richard with a length of clothesline. Standing behind him, with Dasha on the other side, she pushed with her foot and rolled him over onto his front. When she leaned over to draw his hands behind his back, he grabbed her foot with his big, meaty hand and jerked.

She lost her balance and fell backward, landing on her elbows, crying out. Her left elbow stabbed with pain. She yelled and kicked at him, but she couldn't loosen his grip. He pulled her leg toward him. He began to roll over. She brought her other foot up and stomped down on his hand. He jerked her foot once more. This time she succeeded only in stomping her own shin.

"Dasha!" she yelled.

Dasha growled and leapt onto Richard's back. He bit down on the nape of Richard's neck with that deep, rumbling sound again.

Richard screamed. He released Cam's foot. She scooted in reverse on her rear to make sure he couldn't grab her. She scrambled to standing, then grabbed the shovel again. She took aim, raised it over her head, and whacked down on his closest hand, which made a sickening crunch.

He shouted in pain, a loud, high cry that pierced the air. He tried to grab Dasha's leg with his good hand. She hurried around to his other side, giving his feet a wide berth. She took a deep breath and cracked the other hand, wincing at both the act and the obscenities he yelled. Finally, she knelt and brought both his hands, now limp, behind his back, working around Dasha's feet. She used an excessive amount of rope to make sure she tied him up good and tight.

She stood. Pete gave her the tiniest of smiles.

Chapter 33

The wide barn door slid open two minutes later. Cam glanced sharply up from where she knelt at Pete's side, both hands pressing his wounds. She hadn't heard any sirens. Richard moaned. Dasha growled. He had let go of Richard's neck but kept his front feet on Richard's back.

"Cam? What's going on?" Ellie rushed toward them.

Cam let out a breath. *Friend, not foe.*

Vince, a skinny teen with sandy hair poking out from a navy watch cap, followed Ellie in, closing the door behind him. Ellie's hands flew to her face when she saw them: Pete bleeding, Richard tied up, Dasha standing guard.

"We're okay," Cam said. "Mr. Broadhurst there tried to kill us. But Dasha came to the rescue."

Vince whipped a folded bandanna out of his rear pocket and knelt at Pete's injured side. "We just finished a first aid course. Let me help."

Pete nodded. Cam withdrew her hands from his wounds. Vince pressed the cloth against Pete's arm with both hands. Cam tore off her coat and slid it under Pete's head, grateful to have human help at last. She sat cross-legged behind him.

Stunned, she stared at her bloody hands for a moment before wiping them on her jeans. She stroked Pete's ashen face.

Vince said, "Ellie, come and relieve me. I want to get my coat off."

Ellie replaced Vince with the wound pressure. "Are you okay, Mr. Pappas?"

Pete nodded again but winced as he did. Vince removed his wool pea coat and laid it over Pete. He pulled off his glove and pressed his fingers into Pete's neck, watching the old-school clock on the wall. "Pulse is a little high but okay."

Richard reared his head and spat out a string of obscenities. "My hands. She broke my hands." He writhed, and Dasha growled at him, readying his open jaws above his neck.

Ellie stared at Cam. "You broke his hands?"

"I guess so. I whacked them pretty hard with a shovel. I had to tie him up, and he wasn't cooperating." Cam let out a shaky breath. Apparently, she had the capacity to be violent, after all.

"You rock, Cam," Vince said.

Ellie whistled in admiration. "You're so brave."

"I couldn't let him get away with more murders." This was one time when physical violence was justified.

"More murders? He killed Bev?" Ellie asked, eyes wide.

Cam nodded. "And maybe somebody else."

"Vince, tie up his legs, too," Pete croaked out. "Then sit on his back."

Cam pointed Vince to the rope. He tied Richard's feet with it. Vince stroked Dasha and convinced him to move to the side, then plopped onto Richard's back. Cam knew Vince had been lifting weights recently in an effort to get stronger, but he remained a bony young man. She wasn't sure exactly how effective he'd be if Richard, who looked like he weighed twice as much as Vince, really started to struggle. But she knew they could count on Dasha to help.

"Why aren't they here yet?" Cam gazed at her phone. "Should I call again?"

"No. Be here soon. Probably dealing with Rosemary." Pete closed his eyes.

"Mr. Pappas, you need to keep your eyes open," Ellie urged. "Tell us what happened."

"What did you say to Dasha? What was that command you gave him?" Cam asked.

Pete opened his eyes. "Means 'attack' in Greek. I trained him."

"It sure worked. You should have seen Dasha." Cam smiled. "He performed like he's been doing this all his life."

"Damn dog," Richard said.

Still alert, a foot away from their attacker, Dasha barked at him.

"Good boy, Dasha," Cam said. "But, Pete, why aren't you wearing your gun? You had it earlier today."

Pete sighed. "Have it locked in the car. Didn't think I'd need it. Wrong."

A chill ran through Cam. All of a sudden, she wasn't sure her legs could hold her up. She was glad to be sitting down. It had been so close. Richard had shot Rosemary. Was she dead? Richard had intended to kill both Pete and Cam, as well. And she'd smashed Richard's hands. She shuddered again, remembering the sickening crack of bones.

The welcome sound of a siren in the distance grew louder. She glanced at Ellie. The girl looked determined as she pressed on Pete's arm, not rattled at all by the situation. Cam wasn't surprised.

"What brought you and Vince over here?" Cam asked Ellie.

"I said I'd come and help you with the shares, but I needed to wait until Vince got off work. He was going to drive me and said he'd help out, too."

"I'm sure glad you didn't get here a few minutes earlier. I hope I never see another gun in my life."

Sirens blared close by and then shut off. The barn door slid open. Ruth Dodge rushed in, followed by another officer, both with guns drawn, and then came two EMTs, each carrying a bag of gear.

"Detective, Cam. Give me the one-minute summary," Ruth said, lowering her weapon after surveying the scene. The other officer strode to Richard. Vince scrambled to his feet when the officer gestured that he'd take over for him. The officer set one foot firmly in the middle of Richard's back and pointed his gun at Richard's head. The EMTs knelt on either side of Pete and got to work, with Ellie handing off the pressure to one of them. Cam got out of the way, too. One of the EMTs handed Cam's and Vince's coats to Cam and covered Pete with a blanket. He cut open Pete's coat sleeve and bandaged the wound, while the other EMT put an oxygen mask over Pete's mouth and nose.

Pete pulled the mask off. "Arrest Broadhurst," he said. "Threatened both of us. Told us he convinced Rosemary Contini to poison Bev Montgomery. And I believe he shot her at his farm."

Ruth's eyes widened. "Yes, sir. The Jackson arrest is invalidated?"

"It is. Sorry about that . . ." Pete's voice trailed off, and he closed his eyes again. He let the EMT replace the mask.

"Not a problem," Ruth said.

"Dasha and I managed to get Richard down," Cam told her. "Dasha bit his wrist, the one that was holding the gun, but the gun went off and got Pete in the arm. I hit Richard on the head with a shovel, and he went down. Then he came to, or maybe never was out, and he grabbed my ankle. I, um, whacked his hands pretty hard so I could tie them. Vince secured his feet."

"Where's the gun?" Ruth asked.

"I heard it hit metal." Cam looked around. "There. It landed under the tiller." She pointed. A glint of metal was nearly hidden under the tines of the heavy, formerly red machine.

"I didn't do anything. Flaherty there maimed me." Richard struggled, his head turned to look at Cam.

"Quiet, Broadhurst." The officer pressed his foot more firmly into Richard's back. He leaned over and brought the revolver into Richard's line of vision.

Detective Jaroncyk hurried into the barn with her left hand on her waist under her jacket. "Got here as soon as I could." Her eyes widened when she saw Pete. "Pappas, you all right?"

"He will be," Cam said. She repeated what had happened.

"Got it." The blond detective nodded.

Ruth turned away when the radio on her shoulder chattered a staticky message. She spoke into it and then walked over to Detective Jaroncyk. Dasha still stood in an alert stance next to Richard. Cam slipped on her coat and handed Vince's to him.

"Come here, Dasha. They've got it now," she said. She patted her thigh.

Dasha trotted over to her but kept right on going to Pete's side. Dasha whined. He pushed the EMT's hand aside with his head. He licked Pete's cheek. Pete brought his good arm up to stroke the dog.

Cam called Dasha again. "It's okay, buddy. He's going to be fine."

Dasha gave a little bark. He trotted to Cam's side, tongue out, panting. Moments after one of the EMTs wheeled a stretcher into the barn, he and his partner had bundled Pete onto it. A sob bubbled up in Cam at the sight of his white, strapped-in form, the mask still covering his mouth and nose. Pete's gaze went first to Dasha and then to Cam.

"I'll see you at the hospital," she called, her hand on Dasha's head. Both of them watched as the EMTs hurried Pete out of the barn.

Cam turned back to see Ruth and Ann Jaroncyk conferring. Ann nodded and pointed at Ruth.

Ruth moved to Richard's side. "Richard Broadhurst, you are under arrest for the murders of Beverly Montgomery and Rosemary Contini, and for the attempted murder of Peter Pappas and Cameron Flaherty," she said, then proceeded to read him his rights.

The other officer replaced the line around Richard's wrists with handcuffs and loosened the binding on his ankles until his feet were a shuffling distance apart.

"You should arrest Flaherty there." Richard grimaced. "She broke my hands."

Dasha looked at Richard and barked in loud, sharp bursts. Cam grabbed hold of his collar with one hand and stroked his head with the other until he quieted. "It's okay," she murmured. "It's okay."

Two more officers hurried in. They maneuvered Richard to his feet.

"You ought to put that dog down. It's dangerous," Richard snarled. As they led him out, he narrowed his eyes at Cam and spat in her direction. "Now what'll happen to all that fine farmland? Huh, Flaherty? Mine and Bev's, both. Ginger will cut down all the trees and build some crappy development. Is that what you wanted?"

Chapter 34

Cam found her way to emergency department bay 8C two hours later and peered around the green privacy curtain. Detective Jaroncyk had insisted on questioning her on the spot, despite Cam insisting she needed to get to the hospital.

"Anybody home?" Cam now whispered.

Pete lay on a bed with the head raised, a white blanket drawn up to his waist. His eyes were closed, and a blue sling held his forearm over a hospital johnny. She walked to his uninjured side. His hand rested on top of the blanket, with a clip on his index finger that attached him to an oxygen monitor. An IV taped to the back of his hand dripped fluid through a slim tube from a bag hanging at head level, but he didn't seem to be connected to any other machines. The air held the medicinal scent that Cam wished wasn't so familiar.

As she stroked his forehead, Pete opened his eyes. And smiled.

"Hey, good looking." His voice came out low and slow.

"Hey, yourself." She mustered a smile in return. "How's it going?"

"I'm alive. Been x-rayed, scanned, poked. Bullet passed

right through my arm. Nicked a blood vessel . . . it's why I bled as much as I did. Didn't get the bone, though, so all I have is two big, honking holes in me. I'll heal." He reached out his hand and found hers. He squeezed a little, then closed his eyes. "Tired," he said.

"Then rest." She kept hold of his hand and watched his chest rise and fall with his breaths. The fluid dripped silently out of the bag. Voices and a rolling cart hurried by outside the curtain. Beeps and buzzes sounded from other bays.

His eyes flew open. "You're still here. Good. How's Dash?"

"He's good. I left him with Ellie and Vince. I didn't want to leave him alone, and they said they'd stay until I got back."

"Thanks. Listen, I need to apologize."

"No, you don't."

"I do." He nodded. "Should have protected you. Should have kept my firearm on me."

"Don't be silly. We didn't know Richard was going to show up with a gun. You thought the murder was all tied up, with Frank's arrest."

Pete sighed. "Yeah. Big mistake."

"Anyway, your awesome Dasha rescued both of us. He deserves a medal. Or at least a nice piece of steak. I'll get some on the way home."

"You showed a lot of courage with that shovel, Cam. Bet that wasn't easy for you." He squeezed her hand again, the flat plastic of the clip pressing against the back of her hand. "Thanks. For everything."

Cam frowned. "Well, if I'd told you about Rosemary earlier—"

"Forget it. No second-guessing."

"So his shots must have killed her. Ruth arrested him for her murder, and for Bev's."

"I missed it. Shouldn't have."

"Hey, no second-guessing, remember?" Cam tried to sound upbeat through her sadness at Rosemary being gone. She'd been an odd mix of caustic and naive, but she'd seemed happy to be with Richard. Not a mutual feeling, apparently.

A woman in a white coat bustled in, carrying a tablet device. "Dr. Fujita," Cam said. "I'm Albert St. Pierre's—"

"I remember you. How is your uncle doing, Ms. Flaherty?"

"He's getting better every day. He was hallucinating for a while, but that's starting to pass."

"Did he remember how he came to fall?"

"Not yet." She wasn't sure he ever would at this point.

"And how's our gunshot wound?" Dr. Fujita moved to Pete's injured side and adjusted the sling slightly.

"Alive," Pete murmured. "But tired. So tired."

"Well, you are on a narcotic for the pain, and that makes you sleepy. You're heading into surgery now to fix up that blood vessel, and then we're going to admit you for the night." The doctor set her tablet on a tray and typed something. "But you should be able to go home tomorrow. Do you live with anyone? Have anybody who can take care of you?"

Pete glanced at Cam, who smiled and nodded. "I'm all set with that."

In her house an hour later, after thanking Ellie and Vince and sending them home, Cam cubed the steak she'd picked up on the way and placed it in Dasha's bowl. She was pretty sure the dog would appreciate it more than a medal. She had also stopped by Pete's condo and had picked up Dasha's kibble and his bed, since the dog would not be going home tonight. And she'd selected a set of clean clothes, including a front-buttoned cardigan, to take to Pete in the morning. Blood had stained what he'd been wearing, not to mention the fact that his coat and his shirt had been cut off his arm.

Cam held out one of the Pawsitively Organic Gourmet dog biscuits she'd found in the pet food section of the market. "Dasha, here, boy." Dasha trotted in from the other room and gulped down the biscuit in two bites, then hurried to his dish after she set it on the floor. Cam could swear he smiled before he started in on the meat. She watched him enjoy it. She still felt a little sick at having to crush Richard's hands, despite the necessity. Dasha showed no such remorse. From the opposite corner, Preston gave one of his tiny mews. The two animals seemed to have arrived at a cautious truce. Cam filled Preston's food bowl and stroked him a few times. She yawned. What a day it had been. Sleep threatened to take her even as she stood. But she had a couple of things to do before she rested, and the first of them was to join the animals in eating.

She found leftover stew in the fridge. Three minutes later she sat at her table with the microwaved stew and a glass of merlot. She ate and sipped for a couple of minutes, then reached for the house phone and dialed Albert, comforted by the zzz of the wheel as it returned after each number.

"Uncle Albert, you wouldn't believe what happened today."

"Oh, I know all about it. They arrested Jackson wrongly, as it turned out. That Broadhurst character killed our Rosemary, as well as Beverly. And you had quite the kerfuffle in your barn."

She pulled the receiver away from her ear for a moment and stared at it. She pulled it in. "How in the world do you already know all that? How could you?"

"My dearest Cameron. Do you remember the size of this town? News travels. Now, tell me every detail. And I also heard Broadhurst shot your detective Pappas. He's really going to be all right?"

Cam smiled to herself at the "your" and sipped the wine. Nothing escaped Uncle Albert. "He is." She filled him in on a few details of the encounter in the barn, since he knew most of it already.

"Broadhurst is a sick man," Albert said.

"Agreed."

"Pete didn't have his own firearm with him, I gather?"

"No. And Richard planned to make it look like a murder-suicide."

"You must have been so frightened, my dear."

"I was terrified. But Pete gave a special command in Greek to Dasha, and the dog attacked Richard." She glanced over at Dasha, feeling Richard's hand grabbing her ankle. Her desperation, her fear for Pete. Hearing the crunch of Richard's bones breaking. She took a deep breath.

"Glad to hear it. And I'm grateful that you weren't harmed, my dear," he said. "I know your views on violence. I'm here if you want to talk about what happened as time goes by."

Her throat thickened. "I know," she managed to murmur.

"Oh, I have news for you, too."

"What's that?" Cam didn't think she could take any more bad news.

"Why, I finally remembered how I fell. It was my consarn crutch getting all tangled up in my lap blanket. I simply tripped. Don't know why it took me so long to recall what happened, but there you have it. The nurse here told me my memory would come back, and sure enough, it did."

Cam let out a breath. "That's a relief. And it ties off a piece of the puzzle. I'm glad nobody assaulted you."

"I don't have any enemies. You know that." He chuckled.

"I didn't think I did, either." But being threatened three times in a year was getting ridiculous.

Chapter 35

Cam straightened in the hoop house the next morning. She'd filled almost an entire bushel basket with dark purple mizuna, deep green tatsoi, red komatsuna, and the frilly light green shungiku. The mix of shapes and colors of the cold-hardy Asian greens made an attractive salad that the customers seemed to crave in the winter shares. Greens were about the only newly harvested vegetables Cam could offer at this time of year. She stretched her back before hefting the basket and carrying it out of the structure.

"Come on, Dasha." He didn't seem to run off while she worked, so she'd let him accompany her without a leash. It was comforting having him nearby. He didn't make many demands and was simply a quiet companion. She was starting to understand what people saw in dogs, after all.

She paused. Every snow crystal sparkled in the mid-morning sun. Only a month after the winter solstice and already more light graced the days with the earth tilting back toward the sun. The air was still below freezing, but no wind rustled the bare branches of the tall maples and the evergreens that stood next to them, and it felt almost mild on her cheeks. She inhaled, smelling clean snow with a hint of pine and a touch of spice from the greens. Her own clear, bright mood stemmed from having the worries of the week behind her: Pete not seriously hurt and their relationship on track again, Albert recovering, a murderer in custody.

A beige Prius pulled into the drive and gave a little beep. Felicity climbed out with a wave. Dasha barked once but stayed at Cam's side.

"Need help?" Felicity called.

"Good morning," Cam called in return. She waited until the petite woman came near. "We need to wash these and bag these. I'd love some help."

Felicity bent down to stroke Dasha, then glanced up at Cam. "Gorgeous day, isn't it?" She shifted her large farm basket to her left hand and extended her right toward one handle of the bushel.

Cam let her take the handle. "It's lovely out. Isn't it nice to feel a little warmth and no wind?"

Felicity agreed while they strolled together toward the barn. "Heard you were attacked here last night. Pete is going to be all right? The news said he was shot."

"He is. I talked to him this morning. In fact, whenever the doctor clears him, I need to go pick him up. Which is why I'm glad you came early. Alexandra said she would come by to help, too."

"It all must have been terribly scary."

"No kidding. Richard Broadhurst turned out to be a desperate man. Dasha rescued us." Cam patted Dasha's head. "Such a good dog."

Cam slid the wide barn door open and waited until Felicity had come inside before shutting it behind her. She carried the bushel over to the washing station, glad she'd had the forethought to include it when the barn was rebuilt. The hoop house stayed warmer than outdoors, but if she had to stand in it to wash greens in frigid water, she wouldn't be able to offer midwinter salad. Customers wanted their greens plate ready, not dusted with soil. She ran water in the deep sink, then loaded the greens into a big cloth mesh bag and submerged them. An old washing machine sat plugged in next to the sink.

"We'll let them soak for a couple of minutes, and then I'll spin the water out of them before we bag." She'd learned the trick from chatting with another grower at the farmers' market. Spinning them like that turned out to be a brilliant way to get the water off the greens, water that, if left on, would rot them in a couple of days.

"You can help me make the rest of this look nicer than it does now, if you want." Cam gestured to the long table where she'd dumped all the share offerings without arranging them in any kind of order or creating an attractive display.

"Hey, I wanted to tell you something Dad told me yesterday," Felicity said, emptying a bag of potatoes into a wooden box. She began to sort through them for bad ones.

"Oh?"

"Remember he said the person he saw that day was an Indian?"

Cam nodded.

"Frank Jackson wears his hair in a ponytail. And I've seen him with a dangling earring that has a silver feather on it. I asked Dad if it was Frank he saw, and he said it was."

"He knows Frank?"

"Sure. Frank worked for Dad in his landscaping business one summer when he was out of work. But Dad probably lost his name, you know, because of his dementia."

"Well, we know Frank was in the building, visiting Bev that day, anyway. But he didn't kill her, after all, despite what Pete first thought." Cam hauled the bag of greens out of the sink and lowered it into the washing machine. She turned the dial to SPIN and started the machine.

"I sure hope there's no more detergent in that machine," Felicity said.

"I scrubbed it thoroughly and ran plain water through it a dozen times. Your greens and lettuces have been spun in this since last August." Cam laughed. "Did you ever taste detergent on your salad?"

The barn door slid open. Alexandra and DJ, holding gloved hands, sauntered in with a rush of fresh air.

"Great to see you both," Cam said.

Felicity waved at them.

"We read the news on *Wicked Local* about . . . ," DJ said, frowning.

"About Pete and me being attacked by Richard Broadhurst?" Was Cam going to have to repeat this for every customer? Probably. She sighed and explained that they were fine, that Dasha took Richard down, that Pete was shot in the arm, but he was going to be all right. She left out the part about breaking Richard's hands.

"I'm really glad," Alexandra said.

When DJ nodded his agreement, Cam was relieved they hadn't pressed for more details of the attack.

"Hey, me and DJ were talking. We're going to start a petition to keep Bev's farmland as open space. Maybe the town can buy it as conservation land or with a farming restriction. That way nobody can build on it."

"Interesting idea," Cam said, musing on the idealism of young adults, or of those younger than her, anyway. Who knew? Maybe it could happen. "I hope the town goes for it. I wonder what will happen to Richard's property now, though."

"We plan to include his in the proposal," DJ added. "They abut, and it just makes sense."

"It's true, he's likely going to have to sell it to pay off his debts." Cam nodded slowly. "Hard to manage an apple orchard from prison."

"So how can we help you here?" Alexandra opened her hands.

"How about seeing if the girls produced any eggs for us?" Cam pointed to the top of the egg fridge. "Cartons are up there."

"We're on it," DJ said with a smile, the dimple creasing his left cheek.

Cam's cell phone rang, playing the theme song to *Star Trek: The Next Generation.*

"You are a geek, aren't you?" Alexandra laughed, shaking her head.

Cam helped Pete into the truck an hour later. He wore the clean clothes she'd brought him, plus her down jacket, since his own winter coat was ruined. One sleeve flapped empty over his injured arm in the sling.

On the way back to the farm she told him what Felicity had said about her father describing Frank as an Indian.

"It makes sense," Cam said. "With that silver feather earring he's always wearing. And his long hair."

"I wondered about that," Pete said.

"Oh, and last night Albert told me he remembered what happened to him. His blanket got tangled in his crutch, and he fell." Cam glanced over at Pete. "So you were right about that."

He nodded, the faintest hint of a smile on his lips.

"I still wonder about that house cleaner I talked to," Cam said. "Maybe she was just scared of being reported for an infraction."

"Let me get you all set up in the house," Cam urged as she pulled into her driveway. She helped him out of the truck, then tucked her arm through his good one and turned toward the house. "I'll fix you a nice cup of hot tea. You can rest on the couch while I get these shares distributed. It'll be only an hour or two."

"No." His olive skin had started to regain some color but still looked faintly green to Cam. "I've had enough of hanging out alone. I'll keep you company."

"It's cold in the barn," she protested.

He held up his hand. "You have work to do and people around. I'll sit in a chair and watch. I'll be fine." He shrugged off her arm and trod carefully toward the barn.

She had no choice but to follow. Snow crunched in the driveway. Cam darted her head around to see Lucinda pulling up behind her truck. With a toot from her horn, she jumped out and hurried toward them.

"Detective, glad to see you alive," she said.

"Really?" he asked, pulling his mouth, as if trying not to smile.

"Really." Lucinda patted him on the back before they entered the barn.

A chorus of "Welcome back" was followed by scattered applause from the core group of locavores. Ruth had come by with her girls, Nettie and Natalie, as well. Ellie ran to Pete and gave him a kiss on the cheek. Cam smiled at seeing the color return to Pete's face. Vince stood there grinning, with his hands in his pockets.

Pete waved everybody down with his good hand. "No fuss, now. I'm going to be fine. Dash?" he called. "Where's our real hero?"

Dasha emerged from the office. He barked and trotted toward his human. Pete squatted and put his good arm around Dasha, then gazed up at the circle of people.

"This is the guy who deserves the applause," Pete said.

Alexandra started clapping, and soon everyone joined her.

A tiny "Yay, yay," came from little Nettie Dodge, followed by, "Mommy, why are we clapping?"

Pete beamed and stood. "It's for this great guy here."

Dasha sank onto his haunches and front legs. Then he turned his head sharply toward the rear of the barn and sprang to his feet, assuming an alert stance. The cat door flapped, followed by Preston streaking by. The door flapped again. Ruffles pushed his way through and chased after Preston on his dinosaur feet. Dasha barked. Preston leapt onto the top of the rototiller. Ruffles stopped short. He turned toward the group, extended his head a couple of times, and crowed as if he were onstage at the opera.

"So it's not a cat door. It's a rooster door." Cam shook her head in amazement. "How about rooster potpie for dinner?"

Recipes

Roasted Root Stew

Serves eight.

Use local ingredients whenever possible.

Ingredients:
  4 cups ½-inch cubed parsnips
  2 cups ½-inch cubed carrots
  2 tablespoons olive oil, plus 2 tablespoons for sautéing the
    onions
  8 cups ham stock
  4 medium gold-fleshed potatoes, cut into ½-inch cubes
  2 medium yellow onions, peeled and diced
  4 fat cloves garlic, peeled and minced
  ¾ head green cabbage, sliced thin

  6 cups baby kale or kale leaves, finely chopped
  2 cups herbed tomato sauce
  ½ pound ham, cut into ½-inch cubes
  ¼ cup basil pesto
  1 tablespoon minced fresh rosemary
  1 tablespoon minced fresh sage
  1 habanero chili pepper
  Salt and freshly ground black pepper, to taste

Directions:

Preheat the oven to 400°F.

In a large bowl toss the parsnips and the carrots with 2 tablespoons of the olive oil and then spread them out evenly on a rimmed baking sheet.

Roast the vegetables in the oven, turning every 10 minutes, until they are tender, about 30 minutes. Set aside.

Meanwhile, combine the ham stock and the potatoes in a large soup pot. Bring them to a boil over medium-high heat, and then reduce the heat and simmer until tender, about 20 minutes. Set aside.

In a separate large soup pot or in a large Dutch oven, sauté the onions in the remaining 2 tablespoons olive oil over medium heat until soft, about 8 minutes. Add the garlic and sauté until soft, about 4 minutes, being careful not to brown it.

Ladle all but 2 cups of the reserved ham stock and potatoes into the pot with the onions and garlic. Stir in the cabbage, kale, tomato sauce, ham, pesto, rosemary, and sage. Bring the mixture to a boil over medium heat.

Float the habanero chili pepper in the pot, and then reduce the heat and simmer until the cabbage and kale are tender, about 20 minutes.

Lightly mash the potatoes in the reserved ham stock and potatoes. Add the mashed potato mixture to the pot along with the reserved roasted parsnips and carrots.

Simmer the stew until the flavors mesh, about 5 minutes more. Add salt and pepper to taste.

Remove the habanero chili pepper with a slotted spoon. If you like a spicier flavor, press the habanero between two spoons over the pot, releasing the juices, and then discard what remains. Otherwise, simply discard the entire pepper.

Serve the stew hot with a hearty red wine and a salad of local greens.

Note: You can substitute chicken stock and cubed chicken for the ham stock and cubed ham, or substitute vegetable stock and 2 cups cooked dried beans for protein.

Apple-Almond Cake

Serves eight.

Ingredients:
2 medium local apples, peeled, cored, and thinly sliced (Cortland, Macoun, or Spartan varieties work well)
2 teaspoons ground cinnamon, plus ¼ teaspoon for the almonds
½ cup sliced almonds

1½ cups unbleached white flour
1 tablespoon baking powder
½ teaspoon salt (Note: NOT cyanide salt . . .)

½ cup local salted butter, softened
1⅓ cups light brown sugar
4 large local eggs
½ cup local milk (fat content of your preference)
Whipped cream for garnishing the cake

Directions:
Preheat the oven to 350°F. Butter and flour a 9-inch springform pan.

In a medium bowl toss the sliced apples with 2 teaspoons of the cinnamon and set aside.

In a small bowl, combine the sliced almonds and the remaining ¼ teaspoon cinnamon. Set aside.

In a separate medium bowl or large measuring cup, combine the flour, baking powder, and salt. Set aside.

In a large bowl, cream together the butter and brown sugar until light and fluffy, about 3 minutes.

Add the eggs, one at a time, and beat after each addition. Gradually fold in half the reserved flour mixture, then the milk, and then the remaining reserved flour mixture.

Pour half the batter in the prepared springform pan, layer the reserved apples evenly on top, and then pour the remaining batter over the apples. Sprinkle the cinnamon almonds evenly on top.

Bake for 40 to 45 minutes, or until the cake is golden and a toothpick inserted in the center comes out clean.

Serve warm with whipped cream dusted with cinnamon.

Winter Rummy Cider

Serves five.

Ingredients:
    1 quart local apple cider
    1 cinnamon stick
    3 whole cloves
    10 ounces local rum (can be spiced)
    5 ounces Cointreau

Directions:

Combine the apple cider, the cinnamon stick, and the cloves in a large saucepan. Heat the cider over medium heat until it just begins to boil, and then lower the heat and steep the cider just short of a simmer for 1 hour.

Ladle the cider into 5 mugs, filling each two-thirds full.

Add 2 ounces rum and 1 ounce Cointreau to each mug and stir well. Serve at once.